Now t

her pr

Desire he couldn't act on. *Ever.* He'd never felt anything like the overwhelming urge he felt to be near Amy. It didn't matter. To protect her and his clan, he had to resist.

The quandary wasn't a pleasurable feeling, but more like a vise grip or maybe quicksand. "I, uh, guess I'll see you later. Sometime. Call me if you need anything."

The space seemed to close in and he avoided her gaze. His heart beat so hard, he was sure she heard it. The more he woke up, the more he realized she was not some random woman who wanted to rent his cabin.

Awareness punched him in the gut.

She was *the* woman.

Mate.

Amy is mine.

Watch for the next books in the Shifter Wars series from Kerry Adrienne and Carina Press

Pursuing the Bear
Taming the Lion

WAKING *THE BEAR*

KERRY ADRIENNE

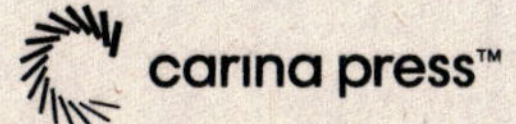

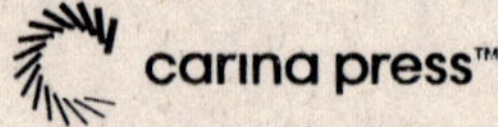

Recycling programs for this product may not exist in your area.

ISBN-13: 978-0-373-00426-3

Waking the Bear

This is the revised text of the work first published by Kerry Adrienne as a short novella in 2015.

This edition published by Carina Press, 2016

This edition published by arrangement with Harlequin Books S.A.

www.CarinaPress.com

Printed in U.S.A.

Dear Reader,

Thank you for giving *Waking the Bear* a spin. This story was originally a novella in an anthology, but it has become so much more. The world has grown on me, and although I'd written wolf shifters before, I've really enjoyed learning about and writing about bears. There's something about the mystery of a shifter that appeals to a deeper connection with nature, I think, and bears, wolves, lions, ravens—all can be interesting reflections of human nature.

Griff Martin has turned out to be one of my favorite heroes I've written. For me, he's just the right amount of alpha. He is sexy, smart and strong, but not arrogant—and he's never afraid to be wrong. Oh, and he always protects the ones he loves. For me, that is so important.

I hope you enjoy Griff's story as he tries to balance work and love, duty and honor, the past and the present. He doesn't have an easy journey, but it's his journey to make.

Thanks!

Kerry Adrienne

To my good friend Lia Davis.
Without her, there would be no bears.

WAKING
THE BEAR

ONE

"You've got to be fucking kidding me." Griff Martin tugged at his scruffy beard. "They pretty much came and shit all over our territory." He stared at the map his bear clan buddies had brought to his house, one hand splayed across the paper landscape that denoted Deep Creek bear territory.

The map was as big as the kitchen table, and showed the topography of the entire forest around the Deep Creek National Park, including the secret entrance to the ancestors' cave, the full park from boundary to boundary, and even a bit of the local areas that weren't part of the national forest Griff and his fellow rangers patrolled.

Almost every grid sector had a red mark or squiggly line, showing where Sen Pal mountain lion pride tracks had been found or other evidence of encroachment was seen.

Damn lions. Tension surged through him. *How dare they?*

"Yep, they sure did." Powell moved closer and squinted at the map. "Those rat-tailed bastards are sneaky as shit."

Griff frowned. Something wasn't right, and it wasn't just the marks on the map. He could feel it in the pit of his stomach. The timing didn't make sense. "Maybe they're trying to lure us. Get us to spread out and check all these locations. Then attack while we're dispersed."

"Maybe. Or maybe it's something more sinister." Powell scowled.

"I can't believe it." Griff shook his head. The gnawing feeling in his gut worsened to full-blown nausea with a side of anger. Protecting the bear clan was his top priority. "I was awake several times a week for the whole winter, and I drove all the passable roads and ran the trails. I never saw a single lion. Or any evidence, for that matter."

Dammit, how did I miss this? The tension that gripped him turned to frustration. He wasn't sure who he was angrier with, himself or the lions. The semi-hibernation of winter was a pain in the ass. He could blame being sleepy for his mistake, but it didn't matter.

He'd screwed up.

"They came all the way in to Tiny Fork." Derek spoke quietly and traced a line on the map. "I saw those footprints myself when I was out looking for wood last week." He shook his head. "I'll admit, I was shocked. I spotted a male running along Oak's Ridge a few weeks ago. They're getting braver, that's for sure."

"Or more stupid." Powell grunted. "Better hope I don't meet up with one. This pisses me off." He thumped his fist into his other palm.

Griff shook his head to clear the fuzziness from his hibernation hangover. Powell walked the line between bravery and stupidity himself. How he'd ever become a ranger was a mystery. "Well, there's no evidence of them getting anywhere near the cave."

The Sen Pal pride couldn't really think they had a chance at reclaiming the Cave of Whispers. After so many generations, the Deep Creek bears had everything under control and they weren't about to relinquish it. The bears protected the cave and the land from the nearby town of Oakwood to the town of Henredon on the far side, and through the national forest up to Buzzard's Peak. Griff wasn't about to lose the area to the lion shifters who'd killed his parents.

"No way they're coming near the cave without a fight. They know that." Powell jammed his fingertip onto the map. "Guards here. Here. And here."

"I'm going to recommend that Elijah station more sentries and have the rangers patrol more. We can't take any chances." Griff stared at the map. With more than a hundred bears to defend the park if necessary, they could protect it well as long as they were prepared. Unless the lions wanted an all-out war, nothing was going to change those logistics. Certainly not a few paw prints in the snow.

"Good." Derek nodded.

"They won't ever take the cave. Not while I'm alive." Griff stuck his hands in his pockets, his stomach pooling acid. He let out a low growl.

"Same." Powell paced.

Keeping the den safe had been Griff's top priority for a long time. One of his favorite memories of his mother was her taking him to the cave when he'd been very sick. She'd begged the cave spirits to choose her life instead of his. He didn't remember anything answering, but her reverence of the place was enough for him to want to protect it. Plus, both his parents—and many other bears—were buried in the cave, so it was important to the whole clan. "The question is, what's Elijah going to want to do right now? I'm sure he's not happy."

"When the den leader isn't happy, no one is." Derek pulled out a chair and straddled it. He'd gathered his long dark hair back into a messy knot but a shock of it fell over his face, concealing his eyes.

"Brother, first thing Elijah's going to tell you to do is get a haircut." Powell grinned and ran his hand through his own buzzed hair. "I already took care of my winter growth. Nice and smooth like a soldier. Ready to fight and then slip away in the night. If there's an attack coming, I'm ready."

"I don't think there's any doubt an attack is coming." Griff met Powell's glare. "The question is how soon. I don't trust them, and I won't let them harm the people I care about." His stomach burned with anxiety and anger.

Derek growled and straightened his messy hair. "Elijah's got more to worry about than my hair, Powell."

"Yeah, we'll see. Soldiers don't have long hair."

"You two stop. This is serious. Didn't you hear me? They want the cave back." Griff pursed his lips. His bear growled.

"They've always wanted the cave back." Derek shrugged.

Griff fisted his hands and calmed his bear. *Save the anger for the lions.* "Where's Elijah? I want to know his plan."

"He'll be here soon. Don't worry about the lions. He'll take care of them." Powell straightened. "If I have to, I'll take care of them. All of them. They'll wish the only deep creek they ever heard of was a watering hole they read about in a children's book."

Griff took a breath to bite back a sharper retort. "Anybody want some coffee while we're making a plan to save the world and get haircuts?"

"Yes, please." Derek picked up the map. "I want to study it closer to see if we can pick out a pattern to their tracks. We may be missing something obvious." He folded the map under his arm. "Who marked all these hits and trails, anyway? Took a lot of time."

"I did." Powell raised his hand and stretched. "Barely slept all winter. That's commitment."

"Of course." Derek rolled his eyes at Griff then motioned Powell to follow him to the living room. "Let's see if we can figure this out."

"Be there in a minute." Griff shuffled over to his kitchen sink to fill the coffee carafe with water. His kitchen in the provided ranger cabin was small but adequate, and of a much newer design than his old cabin. The park service even provided a dishwasher, which some of the older cabins didn't have.

As the water ran, he stared out over the forest and the steep incline of the mountains in the distance. Mist covered the low pines and the gray sky seemed to blur the lines between rock and cloud. The lions could be nearby and an attack might be imminent. His hand shook as he filled the carafe. Finding out the truth could mean life or death.

Griff's yard dropped off at a sharp angle into a valley littered with branches and leaves from last fall. Trees crisscrossed and limbs went every which way, making the slope appear like a briar patch. All camouflage for a lion or two who might be trying to spy on his ranger cabin. He didn't see any movement at all, not even a squirrel.

Maybe the bears weren't thinking clearly yet—it was pretty early in the season—but the lions' encroachment didn't necessarily mean they were coming after the cave, or wanted a full-scale war. Maybe they were gathering information while they knew the bears were mostly sleeping. Maybe everyone was overreacting.

That was a lot of maybes for a Monday morning in early spring.

He turned off the faucet and carried the carafe of water to the coffeemaker. The lions should've attacked while the bears slept. The advantage would have been theirs, if they could've located all the bears. After pouring the water into the coffeemaker, he grabbed the box of filters from the upper cabinet.

The situation didn't make sense. Too much randomness in the footprints, maybe. He pulled out a filter from the stack of white cones. Elijah would know. The old bear had a knowledge beyond what could be considered ordinary.

Griff's head throbbed, and every movement made it worse. All he wanted was a modest spring and summer park season with no injuries or crazy activities. He scooped in the coffee he'd ground fresh that morning. The bears would drink a full pot, no question. Maybe two. All of them needed caffeine to help stay awake after a long dreary winter.

Griff clicked the coffeemaker on and the familiar gurgle bubbled through. Derek and Powell were mumbling in the living room, still trying to interpret the Sen Pal patterns on the map. They'd have to involve the other bears soon, but Griff dreaded that. Some would react pretty strongly to knowing the lions had been in bear territory.

He reached for the ibuprofen bottle then a glass of water to get rid of his post-winter's nap headache. The rich aroma of fresh-ground beans rose from the steam and he breathed it deeply. He stifled another yawn and popped a couple tablets, chasing them with a gulp of water.

Waking up was hard to do, especially when he knew his bed was piled with plaid flannel sheets, a heavy down comforter and enough pillows to cover the living room floor if he wanted. No shame in liking his bedding soft.

He heard Powell raising his voice. Something about a "damn lion." Griff yawned. Elijah would temper the response and present a reasonable plan. He had to trust the den leader. It wasn't up to Powell to decide how they'd handle the lions.

Thank goodness.

Right now, Griff could sleep another week without even trying. He set out coffee cups. His anger had receded, replaced with true worry. He didn't want a war. People died in wars.

People he was close to.

He didn't want anything to happen to his best friends, Derek and Powell, or any other bears for that matter. He'd already lost his parents and younger sister. A lump lodged in his throat and he swallowed hard. Elijah had been a great surrogate parent, but Griff often thought about what it would be like to be raised in a nuclear family. He missed them all, but knowing the lions had murdered his sister—a child—

was something he'd never overcome. What would she have done with her life? He wondered if they'd still be as close. Her death drove him to protect the den more than any sense of duty ever could. He'd never get over the murder of his family.

Or forgive the murderers.

Where is Elijah?

A loud knock came at the front door, followed by a heavy slam. A blast of power swept through the kitchen like a rush of electricity, and Griff's heart sped—Elijah had arrived. He felt the clan leader's powerful presence as soon as he entered the house. Though Griff didn't fully believe in the mojo magical mystical stuff Elijah and most of the den did, something happened when Elijah showed up.

Everyone felt it.

"It's great to see you, Elijah," Griff called. He stepped into the living area and took a sharp intake of breath.

Even after knowing the old bear his whole life, the man still held an impressive presence, almost frightening. In human form, he stood closer to seven feet and probably weighed nearly three hundred pounds of mostly muscle. The graying of his beard and long hair made him even more fierce, and even as a person, he carried himself like a bear. One half of his face was covered with a terrible scar and a black eye patch, but it didn't affect his performance or leadership of the clan.

"You slept well, son?" Elijah trained his working eye on Griff then a smile flickered at the corners of his lips. "Did you dream of my grandchildren while the snows came down?"

Griff's face burned as Powell and even Derek snickered. Elijah knew he wasn't intending to have children. Hell, he wasn't planning on having a mate. The world was too dangerous and things he loved tended to get yanked away. He wasn't putting himself in that position, not after losing his family. Sure, the others could joke about it—and they could have mates and protect them. Griff would never be able to take the chance.

"I slept well." He looked at the floor to avoid making eye contact with anyone.

Powell laughed. "How many children? You do know how children are made don't you, Griff? Maybe you dreamt of Elijah's grandchildren being conceived. How many mothers did you mate?"

Elijah's growl set the windows rattling and for a second, Griff worried Elijah was about to shift into bear form. There'd be no stopping his anger if he did.

Griff turned away, wishing Powell wouldn't tease him in front of Elijah, especially about such sensitive matters. The bear was old. How old, none of them was sure, but it wasn't nice to poke fun at him. Powell took things too far, too often.

"I'll see my grandchildren," Elijah said. "My dreams in the cave have told me."

Griff took a deep breath. Maybe one day the Sen Pal would no longer be a threat and *maybe* he could consider a mate. It wasn't likely. Elijah would be devastated if Griff didn't have children. He considered him a full-blood son, so carrying on the line fell on Griff's shoulders.

A low growl formed in his chest and he let it rumble as a warning. Powell knew when to stop playing around, and the bear would shut up now that both Elijah and Griff had made it clear they weren't amused.

"Maybe you should take a look at the map." Griff waved toward the coffee table. "It shows all the Sen Pal ingresses onto our land while we slept."

Derek tossed a log on the waning fire and Powell stuck his hands in his pockets and then sat on the couch.

Elijah nodded and coughed. "I knew the lions were starting trouble." His voice was low. "I dreamed it. A massive war with many losses is coming. More than ever before, this war will nearly wipe out the shifters around Deep Creek. We have to try and stop it."

"If you look—" Powell nodded toward the map "—the lions explored all around us while we slept. Stayed out of the ranger paths and out of our Sentinel paths, too. We were studying the positions to see if we could figure anything out."

"Maybe they have a plan of attack or were just gathering intel." Griff raised his eyebrows in question.

Elijah shook his head then sauntered to the table to look at the map, moving slowly and steadily like a bear in a human-shaped skin. No mistaking his power, both over those in the room and over the Deep Creek bears in general. He owned a small grocery store in town, and the humans trusted him as much as the bears did, despite his frightening presence. They didn't even ask questions when he disappeared during winter, letting his trusted manager, a human, run the store for him.

The bears stilled, awaiting Elijah's appraisal of the situation. He studied the map a couple of minutes then his broad shoulders slumped a fraction. "The lions are up to something and it isn't something of the happy kind, for sure. For once, I had hopes my dreams were wrong, but I think they were accurate."

"So what do we do?" Derek asked. "We can't attack their compound. We'd be slaughtered."

"No, not attack, but we're gonna have to be ready to engage them when they attack us. The war we've been dreading is on the horizon and growing closer, and right now, I think a defensive position is the best option."

"Why now?" Griff asked.

Elijah turned to him. "Why not now?"

Griff closed his eyes, his head throbbing. *Why not now?* Elijah seemed to be able to cut through everything and see the truth. The lions would come, without rhyme or reason.

The bears had to be ready.

He opened his eyes and saw Elijah staring. A slight nod was all it took to show his deference to the wisdom his surrogate father held. The clan needed and trusted Elijah. Whatever he said, would be done.

"Everyone should be awake, sir." Derek stared out the large picture window into the forest. "I don't think we'll have trouble holding our own. We're strong and we've trained."

"We still have some winter fat, so we need to train more and harder. I don't want to lose anyone in this battle if we can help it. Gather the clan and get them back on training schedule A." Elijah folded the map. "We'll meet in the Cave of Whispers on the night of the full moon. Till then, make sure everyone is keeping alert and watching out for lions. Report anything unusual."

"Yes, sir," Powell and Derek answered in unison.

Griff motioned toward the kitchen. "Coffee's ready, if anybody wants some." He rubbed his throbbing head. As soon as everyone left, he would take a nap.

"Me." Derek ducked into the kitchen with Powell on his heels.

Griff started to follow but he felt Elijah's hand on his shoulder.

"One more thing for you, Griff. It's important." Elijah reached into his pocket and pulled out a folded piece of paper. "We found this when we were downloading data from one of the cameras."

Griff took the paper. "What is it?"

"Open it."

Griff unfolded the paper. A printout of a grainy picture from a wildlife camera filled the page in black and white. Dizziness made his head swim.

It couldn't be. Griff looked to Elijah. *It can't be!*

Elijah nodded, frowning.

"Evers." Acid pooled in Griff's stomach and he fought the urge to hurl. "But how? I thought he'd moved on. That lion is crazy."

"He must have been away and now he's back. Who knows? One thing's for sure." Elijah stared into Griff's gaze, his eyes filled with fire.

"What's that?" Griff crumpled the paper.

"He's going to try and avenge his parents' death."

"That wasn't my fault."

"I know, but he insists it was. He's not going to give up until you pay for it."

"I never should have taken his father to the cave."

"You tried, son." Elijah put his hand on Griff's shoulder.

The weight of it calmed Griff and he stood firm.

He wasn't afraid of Evers, but the lion was unstable. Unpredictable. He was a ghost from the past, one that he'd take care of if need be. "I should have let him die in the car. He wasn't healed in the lake and now Evers thinks I killed him."

"You need to go to the cave and talk to Shoshannah." Elijah squeezed his shoulder and warmth radiated from his fingertips. "She'll give you the guidance you need."

"You know I don't believe—"

"Doesn't matter what you believe. You're my son and I've asked you to go. You go."

Griff bowed his head. "I'll try to get out there sometime in the next week." He backed away from Elijah's grasp. The last thing he wanted was to spend any more time than he had to in the damp cave trying to talk to some ancestral spirit he didn't believe in. The cave lake might have healing mineral waters, and many bears were buried there, including his family, but that didn't mean the cave held a shifter spirit that handed out advice like fortune cookies.

Besides, he didn't have time to go now. Not with Evers back and on the warpath.

"No. You need to go before tomorrow, before Evers is seen again." Elijah's voice dropped a register. "Promise me you will. If you don't, you may not ever get the chance."

"Why not?" Griff paused.

"Doesn't matter. Just go."

He couldn't tell Elijah no. "Fine. I'll go. But she's never appeared to me or helped me at all. Not once.

I don't know why you think it will be any different now. Especially now."

"Maybe it isn't that she appears to you that's important. Maybe it's that you appear to her."

TWO

"FROM THE DESCRIPTION in the ad, I kinda expected something a little..." Amy looked around the living room. This was the living room, right? "...bigger, maybe? Yeah, it has tall ceilings and sort of an open floor plan, but..."

Could she live in such a small space? The Realtor had emailed her plenty of photos, but still images couldn't capture the size.

The cabin was quaint and tiny—nothing like her home back in Atlanta where she had a separate art studio and a spacious guest bedroom. It even had a spare full bath that she'd basically used as an overflow closet. Since she'd wanted to be out in the woods, the cabin certainly fit the bullet point. Close to the park, and also close to town. Adventure required letting go of a few luxuries, she supposed.

Okay, a lot of luxuries.

"I think you'll find the cabin has plenty of room for your needs for a temporary stay. You're the only tenant, right?" The real estate agent plumped up one of the couch cushions and a spray of fine dust rose into the air. She coughed. "It's not rented in winter while the landlord is unavailable to check on it regularly. I can make sure it gets cleaned before you move in."

"Just me. I can clean it myself." Amy pushed aside

the heavy curtains to peek out the wide living room window. "If I decide to rent it, of course."

The view across the valley stunned her grayed city vision. The bright greens of an awakening spring traced the edges of old growth, outlining the forest in conifers of varying shades of light. Just outside the window a large jasmine bush bloomed, the dewy white petals offset with the deep greenery of the leaves.

She relaxed her shoulders. So much green. The east-facing window would bring in the perfect morning sunshine for painting and the warm summer sunsets would bathe the whole world in hues of gold.

Painting here would be a dream come true. In fact, painting anywhere would be a dream come true, but the cabin in the mountains was the perfect place to reawaken the dreams she'd had since high school. She should have never let her practical side tell her that making money was more important than doing what she loved.

Being in advertising had seemed to be a worthwhile compromise at first—creativity and money, but it was a false creativity. Art school would have been a choice more true to her calling.

Never too late to follow your dreams, right?

She had to get away from the bustle of city life for a while or she was going to break. Maybe she already had broken and didn't realize it. She'd find out here. Away from the city. Away from Darren and his games and lies and abuse. Away from all the stress that had been slowly killing her.

Win, win.

"What do you think? It's relaxing up here, for sure." The Realtor walked over to join her.

Amy startled. She'd almost forgotten the Realtor was in the room. "It feels amazing. So peaceful." She looked out the window. "Thank you for showing it to me, Ms. Watkins."

"Please, call me Jill." The Realtor stared out the window. "I've always loved this view."

Amy nodded. "It's lovely."

Rolling mountains surrounded the little cabin like a rumpled bedspread after a dream-filled night. From the porch swing, she'd be able to see the expansive national park as it parted into a deep valley where a blue river flowed like a thin crumpled ribbon, barely visible in the distance.

This could be the fresh start she needed after finally getting away from Darren and being ousted from a job she hated but felt compelled to keep because it was the responsible thing to do. All in one week.

She sighed. *Yes.* For two months, she could be as impractical as she wanted. Paint to her heart's content. Not worry about bills and work and boyfriends. At the end of that time, she'd know what to do next.

She was sure of it.

The cabin was perfect. The location was right and her soul already told her this was where she belonged. Going from city chick to nature gal would be an interesting change, but it was one she looked forward to.

"I'll take it." *I think. Yes.* "Tell the owner I'll pay the two months' rent in full as soon as she draws up the contract. It'd be great if we could sign today so I don't have to find somewhere to stay the night tonight. I've already had a long drive today."

So I don't back out. Chicken out.

"The owner's a he." Jill smiled and clasped her stack of papers a little tighter.

"I'd rather not have to drive back into town if I don't have to. Not yet. If I can sign today, then I can worry about extra supplies tomorrow." *I need to do this. You don't know how badly I need to make this move on my own.*

"As it turns out, Mr. Martin is the park ranger for this area of the national forest. Since he moved into the government-provided house down the ridge, he rents out his old cabin during the spring and summer. So, you really couldn't have a better landlord, well, unless he was a cop." She rocked back on her heels, smiling.

"And?" Amy stared at Jill, who was clearly dying to gossip. She knew the signs. There had been plenty of those types at ADvert, and she'd not participated in their games. Might have been one of the reasons they let her go. She didn't play politics.

"He's a fine sight to look at, too." Jill stood on her tiptoes and reached up high. "'bout this tall. Big guy."

"I beg your pardon?"

Jill blushed. "Nothing. I just said the owner is a he and he's handsome. You'll be glad he is. A he, that is."

"Fine. He. She. Whatever. How soon can I sign the lease?" Amy pulled the curtains back into place and the room dimmed. So what if the landlord was a hot guy? That was the very last thing she needed. This was Amy time and no guy was going to push in on it and use it up. Two months was short already.

No harm in looking, though.

The agent shuffled papers in her notebook at the kitchen table. "The rental agreement is the same paperwork I emailed you last week. I printed it out because I knew once you saw the cabin, you'd want to rent it."

"Yes, of course." Amy scanned the room again. Before she could work on anything, she'd need to give the place a thorough cleaning. That meant a trip into Oakwood for supplies and food—she only had a cooler and a couple sandwiches with her, and some bottled water.

It'd be great if she could wait till tomorrow to drive back into town. She was so tired. She moved aside her thin scarf and rubbed at her tense neck muscles. A good night's sleep would work wonders. The cabin wasn't *that* dirty. Just some dust from not being used. Cleaning could wait a day. "How close are we to Oakwood? I drove here through Henredon, but Oakwood's closer, yes?"

"Yes. The national park, Deep Creek, sits between Oakwood and Henredon, but we're closer to Oakwood. Oakwood is fifteen minutes away, at most. Henredon is forty-five and in the other direction. Oakwood only has one hotel and I think Henredon has three or four."

"I don't think I could make it all the way back there tonight." She slipped the scarf from around her neck and set it on the table. "The cabin is still available? That's shocking. It's so nice."

"It's one of the nicest short-term rentals within fifty miles. Too bad he doesn't rent the place in the winter season. People would be all over it. Someone tried to start a camping park outside the national forest but we only get a few RVs in the summertime."

Amy ran her hand over the soft chenille spread draped over the couch's back. Yes, she wanted this cabin. She belonged in the place. "I'm sure they would. Let's make this legal. Has Mr. Martin signed the lease?"

The drive from Atlanta had taken two days, the last of which meandered through tiny roads in New York. Having a bed for more than one night, a bed she could call her own for a while, was pretty appealing. She picked up the paper and glanced over the terms. It was the same form she'd read before arriving and things looked to be in order.

"No. He wanted to meet the prospective tenant first. I'll call him right now."

"Great. Thanks."

Jill pulled out her phone and scrolled through numbers. "If we're lucky, we'll catch him at home. The ranger station is down the ridge near the park entrance. Would save everyone some trouble if he could come on now."

"Thanks! I'm going to check out the rest of the place." She set the paper on the table and squared it with the edges.

Her hands shook with excitement. Even the air felt alive here. Maybe it was getting out of the city or maybe it was the chance to finally do what she loved, she didn't know. She was as close to happy as she'd been in—she couldn't remember.

Here, she'd be able to get out into nature every day and paint and take photos, or stay home and relax, whichever she preferred. She could sit out on the porch and work, or go into one of the little towns and spend the day doing nothing. No one to tell her what to do, when to do it or if it was done well enough for their satisfaction.

She could even stay in bed reading all day if she wanted to.

Jill nodded and began tapping on her phone. Amy headed down the short, narrow hallway toward the only bedroom and bathroom. The wooden floors creaked as she walked and she noticed the paint was chipping from the bead board on the hall walls.

Quaint.

She peeked into the bathroom, finding an okay-sized room with an antique clawfoot tub and shower. The pine vanity was small, but the room held a bit of wire shelving and a small closet for linens. With a toilet tucked in the corner and a large beveled mirror over the vanity, no one could say the room was impractical. Certainly not the marbled spa with jetted tub she had in Atlanta, but it would do for two months.

The bedroom had to be the next room—the last one in the hall. She turned the crystal doorknob, pushed the door open and reached in to flick on the light. The room held a white king-size wrought-iron bed and a boxy mid-century dresser with a framed mirror above it.

What looked to be a small closet was tucked beside the dresser. Sufficient. Even charming. Larger than she expected. The room was the same size as the living room, if not a bit bigger. Why on earth would such a tiny cabin have a king-sized bed? A quilt in hues of blue and trimmed in florals covered the bed and several extra pillows lined the iron headboard. Sure looked comfortable.

She moved to the closet door and yanked it open. Two shelves and a rod for hanging. A few extra pillows crammed on the shelf up top. Adequate. She didn't have a lot of clothes and shoes with her anyway. This was a trip to get away from formality and structure. She'd relax. She didn't need a new pair of shoes for every day of relaxing. *Hopefully.*

The small window over the bed was framed with frilly white dusty curtains and a small oil lamp sat on a doily on the dresser.

Yes, this will work very well.

She sat on the spacious bed and ran her hand across the smooth quilt top, admiring the handiwork. A lot of time had gone into making the quilt—and it was old. The tiny rows of stitches, while almost parallel, weren't perfect. This quilt had been stitched with love, not in a factory.

A sigh escaped her and she listened to the quiet. She couldn't even hear Jill talking in the other room. Hopefully, she'd reached Mr. Martin.

She patted the bed. She wouldn't have a lot of laundry since the rent included linen delivery service. Good thing, as the place wasn't equipped for washing. The listing had mentioned a Laundromat in Oakwood, which was fine for as infrequently as she'd need to do laundry.

She lay back and closed her eyes, imagining herself living in the little place all alone. Away from the hustle and bustle of Atlanta for two months.

Away from Darren.

Her job at ADvert Inc. had been stressful and busy, and most of her coworkers were ladder-climbing jerks, not ashamed to step on someone to move up in the ranks. That, plus a failed relationship with a different kind of jerk made holing up all alone in a cabin pretty damn appealing. She wasn't running from her problems, at least not long term. The acid in her stomach rose to her throat.

She'd never been able to handle being alone, and that had gotten her into more than one bad relationship. Painting would fill her days. Not running away. Running to what she needed to do to regain her sense of self. Finally choosing to do what she wanted instead of what everyone else expected.

With her generous severance pay, she had enough money to live for several months, so a two-month vacation had seemed like the perfect transition to the next phase of her life—maybe she'd do something completely different when she got back.

Finding herself. She had to be in there somewhere and she was intent on improving her life.

Definitely without Darren or any Darren substitute. It would be a long time before she went looking for a relationship again. Besides, he'd made her feel like she was the bottom of the barrel. Part of her knew that wasn't true, but another part kind of believed it. No one would want her. Not now. Not that it mattered. Too much of her own stuff to tend to have to worry about dealing with a man.

Truly a fresh start.

The options seemed endless and overwhelming, and none stood out as the right choice. She sat up and brushed her hair back. She couldn't continue to doubt herself. This was the time to take risks. Be brave.

"Ms. Francis?" Jill pushed the bedroom door open. "I caught him at home. He hopped in his Jeep and headed over. Said he'd had meetings this morning, so what was one more. You'll see what I'm talking about now." She winked.

Great. "Thanks. I hope he isn't upset we asked him to drop things and come over."

"No, no," Jill whispered. "I think he was asleep." She glanced down the hall then peeked back into the room. "So, he's here already. You ready to talk to him?" She leaned closer. "And see him?"

"Yes." Amy took a deep breath. Time to make a commitment. "I'll be right there."

Jill nodded and left, a tiny maelstrom of dust swirling in her wake. With the door open, Amy could hear her talking to someone in the living room but couldn't make out what they were saying.

She looked around the bedroom, noting the lack of pictures hanging on the walls, the prim white lace curtains, and the handmade quilt. Soon as she signed, there'd be no backing out. The cabin would be hers for two months. Every time she thought about it, acid filled her stomach. Or maybe it was excitement.

Let's go with excitement. New things. I can do this.

She stood and smoothed the worn quilt. Already, the little cabin felt familiar—like it was supposed to be hers. If that wasn't a promising sign, what was? All that was left was signing on the dotted line and giving the Realtor a check, and meeting Mr. Martin.

Let's do this!

When Amy stepped into the living room, the first thing she noticed was the backside of Mr. Martin—or rather, his broad back. She stopped in her tracks to stare. She knew she shouldn't, but it wasn't every day she had such a view. No harm in looking.

He was tall—maybe six four—and his presence filled the room with an unmistakable masculinity that took her breath away. Dressed in a blue flannel button-up shirt and jeans, he looked nothing like a park ranger. At least not any park ranger she'd ever seen. She looked at his feet. Cowboy boots. She swallowed hard. This wasn't the West, but damn those boots looked fine. The way his blue jeans hugged his backside was a sight she thought only existed in advertisements.

He was the real thing, and standing right in front of her.

Even though Jill had said he was handsome, when she said ranger Amy had expected some Smokey the Bear type uniform on a balding, middle-aged man with a paunch, not a sexy cowboy come to life with shoulders as wide as a doorframe.

"Hello." She licked her lips and cleared her throat, aware that a blush crept up her chest and neck. She instinctively put her hands up to cover her neck.

"Griff, this is Amy Francis, your new tenant." Jill rushed over to Amy and took her by the elbow to lead her to the small kitchenette table. "I've already done the background check and credit check, and she's prepared to pay two months up front. Just gotta sign the papers."

As Amy passed the ranger he peered down at her, his hazel eyes locking on to her, examining. Warm, and soul-deep, they stared. Not judging or comparing, he truly seemed to be studying her without any pretense. She gazed back, her mouth partly open, her heart rate accelerating from being so close she could smell his woodsy scent. He wore a full beard, the kind of scraggly brown mess of wiry hair usually reserved for reality TV. His hair matched, curling to his shoulders in a tangle of waves.

Something about his eyes warmed her to her core.

"Nice to meet you, Ms. Francis," his deep voice almost growled. He set her scarf on the table.

What had he been doing with her scarf? She'd left it on the table. She grabbed it then wrapped it around her neck, hoping to conceal her flush. "Nice to meet you, too."

She was instantly at ease with him, despite his gruff appearance and her body's reaction to his maleness. He had that Grizzly Adams kind of comfort in his posture. Big, but safe. Trustworthy. At ease with himself and his environment. The kind of guy that made you feel like everything was going to be okay.

Not the kind of guy she was used to being around.

"Glad you find my cabin to your satisfaction." He continued to stare, but it wasn't threatening, it was curious.

"It's a lovely place, and the view is amazing, but you know that. Exactly what I was looking for, though. So thank you for agreeing to rent it to me." She could tell she was babbling but her mouth wouldn't stop. Something about the sexy ranger made her slap happy. She squeezed her scarf, trying to keep quiet and slow her thoughts down. *Amy time. Amy time. Not looking for a man. Shouldn't even be looking at a man, especially not a man like this. Whew, is it hot in here?* She fanned herself.

"I have some questions." He eyed her for a few seconds before continuing, his gaze cutting into her. "This is my family's cabin and it's very special to me. I don't rent to just anyone that shows up. Even someone Jill has picked and background checked." He nodded toward Jill. "Even though I've known her a long time."

"Her background check was clear." Jill nodded.

"I hope you'll consider me." Amy shuffled her feet. Her heart thudded and her palms dampened. She hadn't considered that he might not rent to her. If he didn't, she'd have to stay in a hotel till she found another place, and that wouldn't be easy.

He ran his fingertips across the chairback and paused before speaking. "This cabin is a special place to me."

She followed his fingers, watching them slide across the smooth wood. "I can see how it would be." Her mouth went dry. His long fingers and large hands exuded the same power his height did. No wonder Jill seemed to have a crush on him. Who wouldn't? She cleared her throat. "What questions do you have? I'm prepaying."

"I've got the contract," Jill interjected. "Ready to go."

"No, it's not that." He ran his fingers through his beard. "I need to know how you'll use the cabin."

"Oh, I wouldn't damage anything. I'm an artist and I draw and paint landscapes and florals. Mostly watercolor, and almost always outdoors. That's why I thought about coming to the mountains of New York. It's so beautiful here." Damn, she was still babbling. What was it about the big man that both put her off guard and comforted her at the same time? Her body hummed with excitement being in his presence and she'd left her cool in the cabin bedroom. She had to get control. She was in New York to get away from people, not meet new ones. Especially not sexy new ones.

He had facial hair and she had a rule. No facial hair. That was simple enough, right? No facial hair meant zero facial hair. Well, except eyebrows. She'd dated a guy in college who shaved off his eyebrows as part of his Goth sensibilities. Best guy ever at quoting Whitman. No facial hair except eyebrows had been a rule since that guy was out of her life.

"I see. Well, I'm glad to hear you aren't painting with harsh chemicals." He yawned and rubbed his eyes. He gripped the back of the kitchen chair and scooted it across the wooden floor to its place under the table. "Sorry. I'm having a hard time staying awake."

"Sorry." Her face heated again. "I'm trying to tell you how lovely I think this area is, especially compared to the city."

"The mountains are picturesque, especially in springtime. I think you'll be an ideal tenant, long as you can follow the rules."

His gaze lingered, and she crossed her arms over her chest. "Th-thank you," she stammered at his close inspection. "I can follow the rules." *The landlord won't be too bad to look at, either. Not a bonus I was expecting. Looking is okay.*

"One thing you need to know. Take it to heart, please. The mountains are very dangerous. Especially if you don't know what you're doing or where you're going. You don't want to go traipsing around these trails by yourself. You could get lost pretty easily and it could be days before someone finds you. There are things—"

"I don't think you need to worry about Ms. Francis," Jill spoke up. "She'll be fine." She fiddled with her notebook, flipping pages quickly. "She's from Atlanta."

Griff reared up to his full height and stared at the Realtor. "This is not Atlanta."

Amy bit her lip. So close, he seemed larger than was possible for a man, and he gave off the strongest vibe of power she'd ever felt from a person. Even stronger than the VPs at the ad agency. Griff *commanded* the room without even speaking. In a positive way. A trustworthy way.

"The mountains *can* be dangerous," he continued. "With the spring thaw we've had and the rainy season starting, you never know when a safe, dry place can become a hazard without warning. Flash floods, rockslides, dangerous animals…" He spoke low, gritting his teeth and fisting his hands. "There *are* dangerous animals out there. Animals that will tear her apart. So don't assume she'll be safe. I know these forests and mountains."

"I'm sorry, Griff." Jill dipped her head in clear submission. "What I meant is that I'm sure Ms. Francis will be careful. She's smart. That's all."

"Of course I'll be careful. I can take care of myself. I've handled a lot of difficult situations. I won't do anything stupid." Amy pulled out a chair and sat. "Now let's get these papers signed so I can bring my things in. I'm exhausted."

He paused a moment then… *Did he just sniff the air?*

He stared at her. "No one implied that you couldn't take care of yourself."

"I'll be okay."

He definitely sniffed, then he folded his arms across his chest. "I'm saying that the dangers here are different and potentially more serious than the dangers in the city. Here, things can be deadly and your body may not be found for days. When it *is* found, there may not be enough left to identify."

"I'll be okay." She gave him her eighty-five cent smile, but he looked away, avoiding eye contact. Men rarely dismissed her at eighty-five. Even Darren.

"Maybe."

"Are you having second thoughts about renting to me?" She couldn't decide if he was worried about her or what. She wasn't scared, and he wasn't going to scare her away from the first place she'd felt comfortable in months. No, she was renting this cabin and painting for the next two months. He could get over it. She didn't plan to find herself at the bottom of any rockslides anytime soon.

"He said he thought you'd be a great tenant." Jill raised her voice.

"A couple more questions. No pets? Dogs, cats, other?" He yanked out the chair across from her and sat down. "No parties, no drugs…" He yawned again, then tugged at his beard.

"No, just me." Amy reached for the papers the Realtor held out. "Plus my paint set and camera. What you see is what you get."

He nodded slowly, lost in thought as his gaze raked over her.

Amy fidgeted in her chair. He certainly stared a lot. Did he think she looked odd? She'd brushed her hair. She crossed her hands on her lap. "Oh, occasionally I might have a beer, if that's okay."

"Yup." He jerked his gaze away and looked out the window and tapped his fingers on the table. "Of course. Why would I care if you had a beer?"

"I don't know. I'm just trying to understand your rules." It was her turn to feel powerful over the big guy.

He turned to look her in the eye for a second and she swallowed hard. She gave him a ninety-cent smile and the look in his eyes softened.

The moment was gone as quickly as it came and he was back to all business.

"Fine on all the other, then." He rubbed his hands together then began rolling up his sleeves. "Let's do this."

Seems the man couldn't be still for a moment. He revealed his forearms bit by bit as the blue fabric of the shirt inched up his arm. He was kinda hairy but she guessed that was normal for men raised in the mountains.

"You mentioned paying two months' rent?" Jill leaned in and pointed to the lease. "In full?"

"Yes. Makes me commit." Amy signed her name on the line labeled *tenant*.

"You have problems committing, Miss Francis?" The smile that slid across Griff's face was as obvious as his nose. He wasn't hiding a thing with his teasing jab.

Jill inhaled sharply.

Amy looked down. No way was the sexy ranger flirting with her. She must be interpreting it wrong. "Sometimes, Mr. Martin, but that wouldn't be appropriate conversation for people who just met, would it? Unless you want to lead?" She surprised herself with her brazenness. Being on her own was agreeing with her already.

"No." He leaned back in his chair.

"Fine. Check okay?" She flashed a full-on one-hundred percenter, complete with a couple of bats of her eyes. Why the hell was she flirting with the landlord? This was Amy time, dammit!

"Long as it's a valid one, right, Griff?" Jill laughed and stepped closer to Griff. "Make it payable to me."

Amy had flirted with the landlord more than once. Jill was probably embarrassed by the tone of the conversation. "I have it prepared."

She signed the check. When she set the pen down, Griff closed his larger hand over hers and squeezed. Warm and strong, just as she'd imagined. She looked into his eyes, a hazel green—as green as the dark pines that lined the road on her way up—and blinked. He leaned in.

"Stay near the cabin or in town. Plenty of things to paint close by." His voice vibrated her insides and sent a shiver up her back. "Please. Don't go wandering in the forest on your own, okay? People go missing out there, and though it's my job to search for them, I don't always find them in time. Or ever."

He pulled his hand away and a chill passed over her.

Mesmerized by his gaze, she nodded, even though she had no intention of following his order. She knew her mouth hung open and it took every bit of will to snap it shut.

THREE

GRIFF'S HEART RACED and his bear paced inside him. He had to get out of the cabin before his body betrayed his newfound feelings. Amy was his. She was meant for him, of that he was certain.

Still, she was off-limits.

"I hope you'll enjoy the cabin." Griff set the pen down. *Business relationship only.* "There's a creek not too far away, and lots of pretty spots to take on nature without going deep in the woods." He set his jaw. "Close by."

"Yeah, I saw lots of places in the photos. I'm looking forward to painting here."

Renting the cabin to Amy was a bad idea, he could feel it in every bone in his body—like standing on the brink of a cliff without a safety harness and jumping up and down seeing if the wind would blow you over the edge.

"If you need me, here's my number." He handed her his business card from his wallet, his fingers brushing against hers and sending an electric shock up his arm. He shuddered and yanked his hand away as soon as she took the card.

Dammit. Bad idea. Bad. Idea.

He stuck his wallet back in his pocket. He should've told Jill to pull the cabin from her listings for the year, especially with the Sen Pal encroachment, but it hadn't even crossed his mind with all the other things he had to catch up on since fully waking up. His patrols weren't much more than a quick ride around the park and a bit of trail running, but combine that with semi-hibernation, and there wasn't a lot of time for other things.

Now he had another person to protect. Someone he felt like he'd known his entire life. One who made him feel something unlike anything he'd ever felt. It was a new kind of scared, coupled with excitement and joy.

Bad news, all around.

He tugged at his beard. He shouldn't be renting to a lone woman. A city woman at that. He could tell that from first sight. He could also tell she wasn't the kind of woman to listen. *Stubborn.* He wasn't sure if that annoyed him or excited him, but she seemed completely oblivious to any dangers she might face in the wilderness outside the cabin's doorstep.

His wilderness.

"Griffton?" Amy raised her eyebrows.

He tried not to take in her fragrance too deeply. "Everyone calls me Griff." He smiled but didn't make eye contact. "Let me know if you need anything. My cell's on the card. I can be here quickly." *Naps are shorter with each day. By summer, they'll be completely optional.*

She returned his smile. "Park ranger. Saving lost and wandering people from mountain dangers. Like lions and bears. And the lone tiger, I'm sure."

"You're making fun." He scowled. *City woman.* He shook his head. "I'll protect you from lions and bears. No promise on the tigers."

She laughed and the floor fell from under his feet.

So lovely. He had to get out of the stifling cabin and away from her intoxicating presence.

He needed to think.

"I find it hard to believe I could be in so much danger in the forest. I mean, I'm afraid of snakes and spiders, but I'll watch for them. I doubt I'll run in to any bears or lions." Amy slid her fingers through her long blond hair and raked it over her shoulder, and Griff couldn't help but stare as the tresses slid over her hand like molten gold. "Or rogue tigers."

"I hope you're right." He looked into her eyes again, searching. Every time, she met his gaze. She wasn't scared of him. She didn't know she should be. He needed to keep it that way, no matter what his psyche was telling him.

He wasn't ready to accept what he knew was true.

The timing couldn't have been worse for her to come into his life, yet here she was, practically delivered to his doorstep and tied up with a pretty bow. The urge to be near her was overwhelming, but he had to keep his distance or he was going to make things a lot worse.

Every bit of his essence urged him to put his hand on her shoulder, run his hands through her hair, and pull her to him. They'd fit together seamlessly. Her soft curves to his hard muscles.

A perfect match.

He sighed.

Jill cleared her throat. "Well, I'm going to get going." She grabbed the contract and Amy's check off the table then collected the pens and stuffed everything into her notebook. "Glad everything worked out." She headed for the door then turned. "Ms. Francis, be sure you do stay close to the cabin. I'd hate for you to get lost, and Griff's right about how easy that is to do around here. Happens all the time."

"I get the message. What's in the woods around here that no one's telling me? Dinosaurs?"

Jill and Griff exchanged glances.

"No, no dinosaurs that I'm aware of. But…other animals…" Her voice trailed off and she looked out the window. Then she snapped back. "I've got another client waiting on me to meet them at a house in Oakwood, so I need to run. Thanks. See ya, Griff." Jill headed out the door, pulling it shut behind her with a loud *click*.

Now that he was alone with Amy, the need to be in her presence overwhelmed Griff with fierce desire. Desire he couldn't act on. *Ever.* He'd never felt anything like the overwhelming urge he felt to be near Amy. It didn't matter. To protect her and his clan, he had to resist.

The quandary wasn't a pleasurable feeling, but more like a vise grip or maybe quicksand. "I, uh, guess I'll see you later. Sometime. Call me if you need anything."

The space seemed to close in and he avoided her gaze. His heart beat so hard, he was sure she heard it. The more he woke up, the more he realized she was not some random woman who wanted to rent his cabin.

Awareness punched him in the gut.

She was *the* woman.

Mate.

Amy is mine.

Shit.

He had neither the time nor the inclination to pursue that path of thought to its natural conclusion. Not now. Not while the Sen Pal roamed Deep Creek. He needed out, now. "Bye." His head spun with the weight of his realization as he dashed toward the door. "I've gotta go."

"Bye." Amy hurried to hold the door for him. "I'll take care of your place, I promise. Thanks again."

"You're welcome."

Griff stomped out to his Jeep, which he'd parked right behind Amy's clunker. Suitcases lined her backseat and bags filled the passenger side. *Surprised she made it all the way here in that piece of junk. Looks like it's been on the road way past its lifespan.* He shook his head. Hopefully, it was safe, at least, and in repair. Breaking down while driving through the mountains would be bad. A flash of worry crossed his mind but he pushed it away.

Why had he rented the cabin to Amy, when he knew it was a bad idea? He had to blame his decision on not being completely awake, because if he were in his right mind, he'd never have rented to her, or anyone else. Especially after he saw the photo of Evers on the prowl. Evers was a game changer.

Dammit!

When Jill had called and woken him from his nap, he'd been too groggy to think straight. Once he met Amy, it was too late to back out.

He was on some kind of bear autopilot.

He pulled his keys out of his pocket. Now the cabin was rented for two months. To his mate. A human mate, to boot.

Elijah was going to have fun with this one, despite the inherent danger, and there'd be no keeping the news from him. Hell, the old bear probably smelled it in the air already or had hummingbirds spying on Griff's supposed mating habits.

He shook his head. He felt the attraction with every atom of his being. A low burn that started somewhere deep in his gut and spread throughout his body to the end of every hair and into every cell, lighting his essence with a fire that couldn't be quenched.

Mine.

He kicked at the gravel in the driveway. *This is bad.* The Sen Pal mountain lion pack was coming, and they would do whatever it took to get what they wanted. They hadn't operated or moved in during the snowy winter, but now that the spring thaw was underway, they could move at any time.

It didn't matter who or what stood in their way.

It didn't matter who got hurt.

It didn't matter that Griff had a mate.

They'd kill anyone in the way.

The brushes with them in the past had proven that they didn't give a shit about anything or anyone who wasn't part of their plan. He growled and clenched his fists. Too many bears and humans had paid the price for the lions' attitude, including his sister, Charlotte. He clutched his keys and leaned against his Jeep, then stared up into the cloud-streaked evening sky, colored red and orange by the setting sun.

Charlotte.

She was only seven.

Griff was nine, and he remembered the night like a Technicolor horror movie. He hadn't saved his sister, and he'd never forgiven himself for not trying. His parents were already dead when he woke up, but he could've done *something* to save Charlotte.

But he didn't.

The Sen Pal showed no mercy, and the only reason he'd lived was because he'd smeared the blood from the gash in his thigh up over his neck and face and played dead. The lions had been in too much of a rush to check on him thoroughly or they would've realized he was alive.

He closed his eyes.

Charlotte's screams still echoed in his dreams and on those long lonely nights when he patrolled the forest.

His heart clenched with sorrow and he took a ragged breath before scanning the cabin.

Now the lions were coming back and they wouldn't stop until they got what they wanted and destroyed everything he held dear.

With the lions making a play for the national forest land nearby, Amy could easily be a pawn in a battle she couldn't know anything about.

The lions wouldn't hesitate to use her and Evers definitely wouldn't hesitate to hurt her.

Or kill her—especially if he knew she was Griff's mate.

"Dammit!" He ran his fingers through the coarse strands of his beard.

He stared up into the tall pines that bordered the property, their tops neatly outlined in the spring sunset like a paper silhouette.

Things were about to get more complicated than any of the bears had bargained for.

A bird whistled in the distance, somewhere in

the tree canopy, and its mate responded with a trill. Springtime in the forest. Time for mates and mating calls as dusk settled over the land.

Ugh.

He climbed into the Jeep and pulled the door closed. He smacked the steering wheel.

Elijah was right. It was time to pay a visit to Shoshannah. Maybe she would finally give him the words of wisdom she seemed to give all the other bears. Didn't matter that he really didn't believe. The process was more like meditation and finding your own true feelings—not an ancient shifter spirit. At least that was how he had come to terms with it. Regardless, he'd promised he would go, so best not piss off Elijah.

Besides, the run through the fresh air in the woods would help him unwind and maybe sort out his newfound feelings.

He kept the radio off on the drive to the cave, the only sound in the compartment the tires on the road and the overload of thoughts in his mind. He slowed the Jeep to a crawl as he shut his eyes just for a moment. Exhaustion sculpted his every move and his brain fuzzed. He'd tried to do too much today. He yawned. Why had he told Elijah he'd go to the cave? It was already closing in on evening. The visit could wait until tomorrow. Right now, he needed sleep.

He pulled off the road and rested his forehead on the padded steering wheel, the vibrations of the motor lulling him further into lullaby land. *No.* He had to wake up. Every time he closed his eyes, Amy filled his mind. Intelligent, well spoken and kind, she was exactly his type.

Only he didn't get to have a type.

A lump swelled in his throat. His parents dead in their bed. His little sister's screams as the lion dragged her away. Him playing dead with a leg injury. He rubbed his thigh. *Coward.* He should have gone after the lions. Maybe he could have saved Charlotte. It was his fault she died.

No, he couldn't fall in love with Amy, even if she was his mate. Until every Sen Pal was gone, he would remain alone.

Lonely.

He leaned back and flicked on the radio, then turned it a bit louder than he usually kept it, hoping to dull his mind's scream.

He clicked the radio off. Even in human form, his ears were sensitive. He couldn't sleep. Not yet.

After he rolled down the driver's window, he pulled the Jeep out onto the deserted road and headed toward the cave, intent on finishing the errand then getting home to a hot shower and bed. He might not even get up tomorrow.

The road slung back and forth and the damp smell of rotting leaves and forest detritus filled the Jeep. Griff breathed it in, his bear pacing and begging to run in the cool spring air. His heartbeat quickened and his alertness returned. As a bear, he was powerful. Strong. Brave.

"Hold on, boy. You'll get your chance." His bear hadn't had nearly enough time out in the forest since he woke. Now that his mating senses has awakened, his bear pawed to be released.

The cave wasn't accessible by road; he'd have to park and run the last mile on foot. Bear feet. The damp air on his fur and the mud on his claws would feed his soul.

The thought of Amy and her high-pitched wind-chime tinkling of a laugh slid through his memory again and he got the same tingling in his gut as he had at the cabin. He shook his head to clear his mind.

Who'd have ever guessed his mate would be human? Or that he really did have a mate?

Elijah would. Griff growled. As much as he loved the old bear, it was really annoying that he was always right. He'd hinted about the prospect before, but Griff had ignored him, along with all other talk about mates and cubs.

He pulled onto the road's shoulder, the tires crackling in the rocky grass. No one really came through the park at night once the gates were locked, and he had his own keycard to get in and out, so it would be safe to leave the Jeep. This early in the season, the park still closed at dusk.

More importantly, no one was around to see him strip naked before he shifted. He hopped out of the car and looked around out of habit. Humans couldn't know about shifters. Most humans, anyway. He panned the forest.

Silent.

A crisp breeze hit his face and he shivered. Fur would feel warm and toasty. He slipped off his shoes and socks and placed them on the Jeep's floorboard. A horned owl screeched in the distance, followed by the lone howl of a wolf. Not a shifter. Griff could tell by the tone.

He unbuttoned his blue flannel shirt, folded it and set it in the seat. The waxing moon, about halfway risen, cast a bluish glow across the underbrush and boulders jutting from the hillside. No lions in sight.

No animals visible at all. No humans.

It was as if the forest was his and his alone. His bear roared for release.

He undid his jeans and slid them and his underwear off at the same time, then folded them and set them on the shirt. He thought about leaving the Jeep unlocked, but decided against it. After he clicked the lock, he slid the keys under the front bumper for safekeeping.

Goose bumps littered his body and he shook. *So cold.* He closed his eyes and called his bear. He was near, waiting at the edge of consciousness and pacing. Ready to be set free. Demanding it.

He was going to run!

A hot spot in the pit of Griff's stomach expanded and grew till it covered his whole abdomen, and streaks of white pain leeched through the heat as his body changed form. Griff was never fully aware of how the change happened, only the linear feeling of man ending and bear beginning. Not so much pain as a deep ache that wound through his very soul till it reached his essence.

That's where his bear resided. Where it hid when it wasn't in charge. But this time the bear met him closer to the surface and he welcomed him, relaxing into the pulls and tugs of skin and bone as he morphed.

He reached for his face and found his snout, and teeth that were long and sharp. He rose up on hind legs and let out a growl as he sniffed the air.

The bear was in the forest.

He ran toward the cave in a half-gallop, half-loping motion, through brush and over downed limbs that would've taken him many times longer as a human to scale. The cave wasn't far. He could smell the lake inside and his bear knew exactly where to find the entrance.

As he went deeper into the forest the sounds of the night, much louder to him in bear form, created a symphony known only to animals. Insect wings buzzed against air and night-hunting birds and bats tracked motion and sound. Hares scurried from bush to meadow to nibble fresh buds and dewy leaves. Many rabbits tended litters of furry kittens, trying to protect the gangly little creatures from predators and teach them the ways of the wild.

He was no longer alone.

Griff smiled a bear smile, his tiredness fading as he became part of nature again. No longer an onlooker, he was part of the whole. Where he belonged.

The Sen Pal were part of the whole, too, but they were a blight that needed to be taken out.

He scowled at his failure. How could he have missed seeing any signs of lions in Deep Creek?

Every hair on his body stood and saliva filled his mouth. He smelled him. A lion, nearby and running. He couldn't tell if it was Evers, but right now that didn't matter. A lion was in Deep Creek.

He debated chasing it, but stayed on task. Maybe one of the sentries would catch it.

Kill it.

Then, as quickly as the scent had come, it was gone again and the woods filled with evening birdsong.

Griff climbed over a fallen pine tree, the trunk as thick as a truck tire and the coarse bark scratched away by a newly awoken bear, leaving the pale white center exposed to the elements. The rough bark scratched at the pads on his feet.

One thing was for sure, things would be different this spring. The lions had a plan.

Evers was back. Griff growled and ran faster.

Elijah was the last bear to try to reason with Evers, and he had lost an eye and part of his face in the resulting fight.

Evers had likely reclaimed his spot as Sen Pal Enforcer. The lion held a grudge between his teeth like a piece of meat. No one was going to take it from him until he'd torn it to shreds and spread it throughout the forest.

Griff picked up his pace as he loped between the trees, the ground damp and cold underfoot. He sniffed the air again for danger but only sensed peace. He'd be at the cave soon and his duty to Elijah would be fulfilled, whether Shoshannah appeared or not.

He passed the first cave sentry station and nodded to the bear patrolling. The bear grunted back.

No lion scent.

Almost there. The land plateaued a bit right before the mountain rose steeply near the cave entrance. Several large elm trees grew in a misty grove that must have been at least two hundred fifty years old. He looked up as he ran through them. He could barely make out the moon from this angle; the trees were so dense and the mist veiled the night air.

He nodded to the last Sentinel and nosed to the boulder that partially concealed the cave's entrance.

He sniffed the opening of the cave and scraped away a slab of mud from the ground with his claw. The Cave of Whispers was kept under close guard, and it appeared its secrecy was intact. Sure, the lions used to know where it was, and maybe they still did, but they hadn't been able to get close to it in a long time.

He stooped as he entered the cave, hating how the first room was so small and cramped and claustrophobic when he was in bear form. Condensation dripped from the ceiling and a cold drop landed on his snout. He shook it away and waited on his eyes to adjust to the darkness. The shadowy room looked smaller in the dark, and felt like it pressed in on him as he breathed.

As soon as he could make out the lines of the rocky walls and the path along the floor, he moved into the next room where the cave opened into a larger room. He shook to clear the mud from his fur and padded to the nearest wall where the lanterns hung.

He'd have to shift. He grimaced. He could move much faster in bear form, but he needed his thumbs to turn the light on.

His bear huffed and he roared and he shifted to human, his body changing and moving to its other form in protest. A growl, deep in his belly, never fully formed, as his snout shortened and his human vocal cords replaced the bear's.

Soon, I promise.

A twinge of pain shot through his legs as they changed. His claws shortened and formed into fingernails and toenails. He was so small in human form. So fragile. The last changes moved through him and he relaxed in acceptance. *Bear will have to wait.* Several seconds later, he stood naked in the damp darkness.

"Damn, it's cold." He shivered and reached for one of the lanterns hanging on the wall. The cave held just enough light to see the glint of metal but not much more, even to his shifter eyesight. To a normal human, the place would appear almost completely dark.

He clicked a lantern on, its rusty knob grinding. He held the light up so he could cast a bright beam across the vast room. Stalactites, colored in red and green mineral sediment, dripped from the ceiling like a million glistening icicles. The cave walls shone in the damp air.

His hands shook. He wasn't going to be able to stay in human form much longer or he'd freeze to death. He headed for the next room in the cave, a smaller one, and last before the massive room that held the healing lake.

The anteroom was the room where the bears held most of their clan meetings. Chairs and couches lined the walls and a few tables littered the area. He spotted a pile of stacked blankets in the corner. Elijah made sure the bears were always prepared.

"Ah, thank the gods for blankets!" He raced to the pile and pulled off the top blanket, a green wool square plenty large enough to wrap himself in. He shook out the folds and wrapped it around his shoulders.

He yawned as his exhaustion set back in. "If I don't get some sleep soon, I'm not going to be any help to anyone." *If I don't stop talking to myself aloud, people will think I'm all sorts of crazy.* He tugged the blanket tighter, the wool itchy against his bare skin. It would be so easy to make a pallet and lie down for a short nap, even with the scratchy blanket.

He was that tired.

No, he'd wait till he got home. His bed was much softer.

He carried the lantern into the next part of the cave,

the largest in the explored area of the cave system. The light swung as he walked, casting stripes of yellow onto the walls. The vast room had a vaulted ceiling that domed at least forty feet over a lake.

"Hello..." He called more to hear his own voice than that of the ancestral shifter.

His echo pinged off the walls and lake.

Fed by an underground stream, the large lake exited the mountain through a waterfall and rivulet on the north face. The water was said to have been treasured by shifters for millennia, and many legends were told of its healing power.

All Griff knew was that it was freezing cold and he wasn't going in the lake unless someone pushed him.

The fish that swam in the clear deep waters were white as ghosts and had no eyes, like most cave fish. Elijah said that some of the fish were hundreds of years old and could hear and understand human language. In their lifetimes, they'd seen both lion and bear guarding the lake.

He shivered. Lantern high, he let the beam play across the dark water, sending sparkles of light bouncing across the surface. In the far edge of his vision lay the tunnel that led to the ancestral burial ground. He hadn't visited his family in many years, and he wouldn't be tonight. He pulled the blanket closer.

Let's get this over with.

Getting to the larger island out in the lake would be easy. He'd done it several dozen times. *Where are the boats?* The bears had a few small boats tucked away near the shore at a rocky outcropping, and Griff scanned the half light, trying to find them.

There.

He'd take the boat out to one of the islands in the middle of the lake. Meditate and wait. He placed a set of paddles into the closest boat. Plenty of room for one. He dragged the boat to the rock the bears used as a launch point.

He didn't know how long he'd have to wait for Shoshannah's advice, or if she'd even appear, but he knew the procedure as he'd tried it at least a hundred times. He'd give it a shot for Elijah's sake, but then he was going home to rest.

Griff climbed into the cold boat, its wooden bottom creaking as he centered himself. He pulled the blanket over his knees with one hand and set the lantern down with the other.

Chills raced along his skin. What he wouldn't give to have his fur coat on. But then he wouldn't be able to row. He pushed the oars against the rock and shoved the boat off into the cold water. The splash echoed in the cavern.

The lantern illuminated the dome of the cave in a faint arc, and glistened off the water. He rowed. The echo of moving water sounded off the cave walls and reverberated through the space, the only sound in the space other than his breathing.

As he rowed, he stared into the darkness.

He rowed faster until he reached the little island. His arms burned from exertion. He carried his lantern and blanket to a large rock on the shore and sat, bundling himself in the blanket and waiting. If anything was going to happen, this was the place.

I should've grabbed another blanket.

His teeth chattered.

He sat for an hour waiting for Shoshannah to appear, but she didn't. No visions, no words. No guidance of any kind. Not even a pattern in the mist now rising off the lake. He tugged the blanket close. The cave grew colder by the moment, and he struggled to stay awake.

The slow drip of water from somewhere behind him helped him tick off the minutes. He debated shifting back into a bear to warm himself, but feared that Shoshannah would appear and he wouldn't be able to speak to her.

I'll wait a bit longer.

He closed his eyes and an image of Amy materialized. Her golden hair, her sweet face and the half-smile when she teased. His pulse quickened as he realized he couldn't wait to see her again, even though he knew it was a bad idea.

He couldn't give in and claim her as his own. *I want to see her.* Mating would mean condemning her to death by the Sen Pal. All he could do was protect her and try to keep the lions from learning his secret.

He heard sounds. Faint at first, then louder. A whisper of a melody, growing stronger as it floated over the water in the wispy fog. A song of mates and slaughtered bears and fire and death.

So much death.

Violence.

And love.

His heart thumped as he reached for the source of the music. There were no words—only notes—and they moved through the air and into his head. The meaning came across clearly, as if the song had unsung lyrics.

Trouble was coming to Deep Creek.

Trouble unlike the bears had seen in a very long time.

Griff startled awake, chills racing along his arms and legs.

He'd have to protect both the clan and Amy, and it wasn't going to be easy. But he would.

To do his duty and keep his loved ones alive, he had to.

FOUR

AMY WRAPPED HER wet hair and twisted the towel on top of her head. She grabbed her other towel and pulled it across her shoulders. The shower ran and she towel dried as quickly as she could. Steam filled the bathroom, condensation covering the mirror over the sink.

She had to get the water turned off. The knob had felt loose the last time she took a shower, but this time it had made a clicking sound when she turned it on. Now, it was broken.

The water was continuing to run.

She tried the knob again, but it twisted freely with no resistance. She tugged at it but it wouldn't release, and the water continued to pour out of the showerhead. She jammed her hand onto the button and the water diverted from the shower to the bathtub faucet. At least the water wasn't coming down on top of her now.

It wouldn't turn off. The knob was broken.

Ugh.

After she hung her towel, she slipped on her fuzzy pink robe and tied it at the waist. No way around it, she was going to have to text Griff. He'd said to let him know if she had any issues. She'd only been in the cabin a couple days and she'd already broken something. He was going to think she wasn't taking care of his place.

Double ugh.

She was pretty sure he wasn't expecting a problem so soon, but she didn't have a choice. She had to contact him. He'd probably call a plumber if one was available for emergencies in the small town. It was late and plumbers would charge extra.

She headed to the bedroom to retrieve her phone. Eleven p.m. He might be asleep. She hesitated. The water couldn't run all night. She grabbed his business card from the nightstand and texted. His reply came almost instantly.

Be right there.

She sent him a thank you and tossed her phone onto the bed. He must not have been asleep. Waking up Darren to help her with something would, more often than not, have caused more problems than she started with.

"One more try." She headed for the bathroom, cinching her belt tighter. The water ran at full blast, and she turned the knobs again. No luck. She tried pushing on them as she turned, but the hot water knob wasn't getting any traction to turn off.

Realizing she'd better get dressed before Griff showed up, she went back into the bedroom. She was pulling off the robe when she heard the knock at the door.

Shit.

She pulled the robe back up over her shoulders, tied it, and tugged the towel off her head. Talk about awkward. She finger combed her hair as she made her way to the door.

"I'm coming," she called.

She opened the door.

"Well, hello." Griff's eyes went large for a moment as he briefly looked her up and down.

Amy took a step back, thankful her blush was hidden by the flush of heat from the shower and the pinkness of her robe. "You're...quick."

"And you're...pink."

She looked down at the robe, but everything essential was covered. "Sorry. No time to change. Come on in."

"I told you I'd be here fast if you had a problem." He followed her in and shut the door. "I was home."

His voice, low and deep, whispered seduction. That had to be only in her head. He wouldn't want her, even if she was in the market. She was damaged. Darren had made that clear from early on. No one else would want her. Besides, Griff probably had girls throwing themselves at him. Jill was certainly enamored with him.

Stop those ridiculous thoughts. Darren is the past.

He carried a small toolbox and the muscles in his forearm flexed as he gripped the handle. With his snug jeans and black T-shirt, his toned physique wasn't hidden a bit.

Her breath caught in her throat. Damn, he was gorgeous. "T-thank you."

He nodded toward the bathroom. "Let's check out the bath before the place is flooded. The water won't turn off?"

"No, and I've tried everything." Amy headed toward the bathroom with Griff on her heels.

She paused in front of the bathroom door and Griff

put his hand on her shoulder. Tingles raced across her body from his point of contact. A twinge of loneliness struck her in the gut and she closed her eyes to savor the warmth of his touch. It wouldn't be so bad to pretend he was her boyfriend.

No harm.

"Excuse me." He squeezed her shoulder. "I need to get in the bathroom if I'm going to take a look at the problem."

The blush returned. "Yeah, of course." She stepped aside so he could pass. The black T-shirt set off his broad shoulders and muscled arms to perfection. He didn't look like a gym rat, but he definitely did some type of workout to maintain his physique.

The water ran full blast into the tub, and though the mirror was covered in condensation, no more steam rose from the tub. She'd run all the hot water out. Griff set his toolbox down then kneeled and tried the knobs.

Nothing. The water continued to pour out of the faucet.

"I'm going to need your help." He opened his toolbox. "We need to take off the handle so I can use a wrench to turn the water off with the stem. I need you to hold the knob in place while I take out the set screw."

"Okay." Amy joined him by the tub, and crouched on the floor. She wished she'd at least put on panties. Being naked under the robe and so close to Griff was weird, in an exciting way. She wasn't sure if her dampness was from the humidity in the room, or something else.

He took out a small screwdriver with a pointed tip. "Hold that knob as tightly as you can."

Amy grasped it, every nerve in her body on alert at Griff's proximity. No denying it. If she were in the market, he'd be at the top of the menu. He reached over her arm, brushing against her as he worked on the screw.

She shuddered. It took every ounce of her resolve not to lean into him.

"Grasp it tighter," he instructed. "It will only take a minute to get the knob off."

Heat shot through her. Had he really said that? She gulped. "I'm trying."

He turned to her and winked. "Almost done." He leaned closer, his thigh against hers as he worked the screw.

She concentrated on the feel of him. Even through her fuzzy robe she could tell his legs were muscled, too. Knowing only a bit of fabric separated them from skin to skin contact heated her even more. Maybe a no-strings-attached night would be exactly what she needed. He probably flirted with everyone, but he wouldn't want to actually follow through with her.

A few stray drops splashed her face, cooling the burn that seemed to be permanent with Griff around. She wanted to pull the robe tighter, as it had separated to reveal her legs, but held the knob and waited as he turned the screwdriver.

Dreams of bedding the landlord would stay just that—dreams. Darren had made it more than clear that she wasn't a catch to anyone but the dregs, and Griff was far above that category. His kindness only added to his sensuality.

After one more rotation, the screw dropped into his

waiting hand. "There we go. It should come off easily now. Give it a pull."

Amy tugged at the knob, but it wouldn't budge, only rotate. Before she could speak, Griff's larger hand covered hers, twisting the knob and pulling it free.

Her stomach turned flips. The whole incident was like a setup in a romcom movie. A bad, bad one. She couldn't entertain the thought of a relationship with him. What about a no-strings sex angle? The more she thought about it, the better it sounded.

If only.

She set the knob on the ground as he rummaged in his toolbox. She watched the way his forearms flexed as he moved the tools around. He pulled out a large wrench.

"Back up, please." He held the wrench up. "I need more room for this tool."

Amy scooted back. Bent over the tub as he was, she got a plain view of his very nice ass. She traced it with her gaze. More than once. No question he would be at the top of the menu. Á la carte or full course, it didn't matter. It was all Prix Fixe to her.

Griff pushed down on the wrench, grunting as he forced the faucet stem to close and cut off the water. He sat back on his heels, staring at the pipe as if watching for watergeddon.

No water.

"You did it!"

He smiled, his hazel eyes wide and welcoming. "No, *we* did it."

She pushed her wet hair behind her ears. "Sorry to call you out so late."

"I was awake. Besides, this couldn't wait."

"I tried to fix it myself."

"It was a two-person job." He put the wrench back in the toolbox. "I'll have to get a plumber out here tomorrow to fix this properly. The stem is stripped. That's why the water wouldn't turn off."

"Thank you." Amy stood.

He clasped the box closed and picked it up. "It's my job." He stood beside her now, and if he'd been any closer, they'd be touching.

"I do appreciate you coming out so late."

"I told you to call me if you need anything. I meant *anything*." His gaze lingered on hers, and his mouth parted as if he wanted to say something else. He licked his lips and stepped toward her.

She looked down, fighting the urge to step out of his way. Was he flirting with her? More importantly, was she enjoying it?

Oh, hell yes.

Having a boyfriend was not an option. Rebound relationships were not her style. She bit her lip. He'd never said anything about a relationship.

"Amy?" His voice was a low growl. "Look at me."

She met his gaze again, her heart in her throat. "Do you have a girlfriend?" She blurted the question.

His eyes took on a wild look, like a frightened animal, and he stepped back.

"No." He moved past her out of the bathroom. He was halfway to the door by the time she caught up with him.

"I'm sorry," she called. "I don't even know why I asked."

He stopped at the door and turned. "It's my problem, not yours."

"I don't understand." She straightened her robe. The situation couldn't have been any more awkward. Like the hot water running cold, so had her and Griff's interaction.

He paused. "I don't, either. It's late and I need to get home."

She nodded, head bowed. "Thanks again."

"I'll send a plumber tomorrow."

"Okay."

He started off the porch then turned to face her. "And no. I don't have a girlfriend."

With that, he was gone. Amy closed the door against the dark night, leaning her back against the hard wood. She needed to learn to filter what she said, not just open her mouth and let whatever she was thinking spill out. She'd screwed up, for sure.

GRIFF CLIMBED INTO the Jeep, his heart thudding and his palms damp. *She asked if I have a girlfriend.* He pushed the toolbox over and buckled his seat belt.

She has no idea.

It would be funny if it weren't so ironic. Amy wasn't going to be easy to deal with. His *mate*. Being so close to her was going to cause problems. His bear growled its protest, the yearning evident.

"I know, I know." If it were up to his bear, he'd have already killed Evers, attacked the Sen Pal on his own and claimed Amy. Probably all in one night. Only Griff's humanity had given him pause. So much was at stake and a wrong move could mean many lives lost, including his mate's.

His humanity made him wait for the right time to go after Evers.

Amy was a different matter. She would be a challenge. Being near her was intoxicating. He wanted to protect her, make her happy, shield her from the world and bed her—all at once. The whole mate thing was confusing.

Turning the water off had been easy. Figuring out what Amy wanted was more difficult. If he didn't know better, he'd have thought she was flirting. He sensed that she also wasn't wanting to date. She wanted alone time, she'd said as much.

Just as well.

He couldn't ponder a fictional relationship. He started the Jeep. She'd asked about him having a girlfriend, and for a split second, he thought about telling her the truth. No girlfriends. No entanglements. Not as long as the lions roamed Deep Creek. Not after what they'd done to his family. If she pushed, he'd have to tell her.

He'd caved. He needed her to complete him. How that would happen was another matter. That part of him had already grown stronger, and would continue to grow.

He backed out of the drive and headed home. He drove slow, the forest around him dark and deep. No sign of any animals around. The woods were nearly silent tonight.

Sleeping.

Amy, dressed only in a pink fuzzy robe that matched her rosy cheeks. Next to him. Touching him. He knew she wasn't wearing anything beneath the robe. Claiming her would've been so easy if he'd let his bear loose. All she'd have to do is say yes, and maybe give him a smile and blush like she did when they were working on the faucet. Yeah, that would do it.

The headlights cast a path out in front of him. If only his path to Amy was so clear.

If she'd reached for him, he might not have been able to hold himself back. That scared him. His bear pushed him to do things his human might not be brave enough to do. But his bear was also very angry with Evers.

Griff's head ached with the dichotomy of his wants and needs.

He couldn't tell Amy anytime soon, and maybe not ever. Perhaps once the bears had defeated the lions once and for all. Until the time came, if it ever did, he would watch over her, protect her. Whether she liked it or not. They'd be friends—for now. Nothing more. He could do that. No entanglements until the danger had passed, and who knew how long that would be?

No one had told him how strong the attraction to one's mate would be. It was going to be hard to be near her and stay just friends. He screwed his nose up and his bear paced inside. Occasionally, his bear growled and whined, wanting him to take her in his arms. At other times, his bear growled in anger at the thought of her being out alone, unknowingly doing unsafe things.

He sighed. Living in Deep Creek had never been easy, but right now, things were more dangerous and complicated than he'd ever seen them since his family had been murdered. He rubbed his thigh where the scar remained.

Far away, he heard Charlotte singing, her little-girl voice high-pitched and innocent like fresh spring blooms before a storm. Then, the screams.

Tears flooded his eyes and he slowed as he pulled into his driveway.

He parked and climbed out of the truck, leaving his toolbox in the cab in case he had to go back to the cabin. He wiped his eyes and looked up.

The stars fanned out over his head from mountain peak to mountain peak and he spotted Ursa Major, the Great Bear, dipping into the night sky. Ursa Minor always represented Charlotte to him and tonight, the haze obscured the tiny constellation. He let out a long breath. The stars always reminded him that taking care of the bears of Deep Creek had to remain his top priority. Until the Sen Pal were gone, one way or another.

No matter what.

FIVE

"IT'S TIME WE move in on the bears." Evers paced the room filled with other men in the pride, plus the lone lioness warrior, Lara. He didn't know when Max had started letting women fight, but clearly the old man was getting soft. He edged around her and she hissed as he passed by.

Bitch.

"Sit down, Evers. You'll get your chance to talk to my father when he gets here." Mason, one of the twin heirs to the pride's leadership, raised his voice. His black hair fell in a clump over his eyes like a tough guy, but Evers wasn't fooled. He wasn't afraid of the twins.

Anger coiled inside Evers's chest, constricting his breath. Marco and Mason, the twins, had long been his friends. They'd tousled and played as cubs and learned to fight as young men. Things had changed since he'd been gone. The other lions were acting as docile as housecats.

He paused then spoke louder. "They're still sleepy from winter and we'd get the jump on them before they even knew what was happening if we attacked now."

He'd never liked being cooped up in the compound where the lions lived, but Max insisted the pride live within the confines of the little area just outside Henredon. He'd said it was safer if they stayed together, and easier since they'd all be close in case the bears attacked. But Evers had been gone awhile and he'd been plenty safe out in the human world.

He preferred roaming free, but he came back for one reason alone.

To kill Griff Martin.

Stuck in the compound felt like being in a zoo, only no one was coming to see them or tossing them juicy steaks.

He clutched the back of a chair, savoring his knuckles turning white under his ferocious grip. He thrived on his anger and the physical pain it caused, and it made him feel more powerful, especially in the room full of lions in sheep's clothing.

The rec room the pride used for meetings was even more stifling than the compound, especially when most of the decision makers were in attendance. Too many people in too small a space. Like today.

He stood to his full height. "I'm tired of waiting."

He couldn't let the others know his true agenda. Once Griff was out of the way, he might help regain the cave, depending on his mood and how many bears he might get the chance to kill, but then he was heading out of the area and making his home elsewhere. He scanned the group. "I'm ready to fight for what's ours."

All the lions kept their heads down except Lara, who met his gaze with a scowl, but Evers knew none would truly challenge him except the twins.

Maximillian, the pride leader, was another matter. Evers did respect him some, though as Max had aged, he'd lost some of his hard edge.

Evers held his nose high and sniffed the fear wafting through the air. Fear he'd caused. He stifled a grin. No denying it, he enjoyed the power he still held in the pride. The men knew to respect him, and the women didn't count.

"Sit down and shut up, Evers." Lara let out a low growl and crossed her arms. "You don't make the decisions. Max does."

Evers moved to stand in front of her and leaned close. "Don't try to tell me what to do. I'll crush you."

Lara rose, her hands fisted, and Evers stepped back. "You're even more of an asshole than you were before you left." She moved toward him. "Why don't you go back to whichever garbage pail you were scavenging from? We don't need you. Or want you."

"You need me. You're just too stupid to realize it." Evers sneered. "War is coming."

"We'll be ready, despite you. I'm training a group of lionesses to fight, and we'll be helping when we go after the bears. Whether you like it or not."

"Your place is here in the compound, having babies." Evers ran his hand through his short hair. Disgust rolled through him. He was going to have to talk to Max, as he'd clearly lost his mind.

Lara shrieked, and the slap that followed echoed across the room. Evers reeled, his face stinging, his pride stinging even more. The other lions jumped to their feet and Mason rushed over and pushed between Evers and Lara, jostling Evers backward.

"Enough!" Mason's voice carried in the room, booming off the walls.

"Come on, Evers." Marco pushed him. "When are you going to learn to keep your mouth shut?"

Evers steadied himself and wiped at his cheek, the

low-level anger he'd had boiling up exponentially. His face burned where Lara slapped him. If Marco weren't standing there, he'd punch her.

"You'll pay for that." Evers spit on the floor then glared at Lara.

"Bring it." Lara sat down. "I'm not afraid of you. There's more where that came from, and next time it won't be just a slap."

"You'd better be afraid of me," Evers muttered and turned away. The pride was out of control.

The lions scattered and returned to their seats, whispering and staring.

"Evers, calm down before I get up and beat your ass myself." Marco leaned back in his leather recliner. He already had the regal posture, his shoulders squared and his spine straight. He looked ready to rule, if Max tapped him. "Until my father speaks, we wait."

Most of the lions in the upper echelon had already arrived to talk about what to do about the bears and Max was late as usual. Evers huffed. The old lion had gotten even worse about being tardy.

As pride Enforcer, Evers knew the best plan for war. After all, enforcement was his job. He didn't need the old man to tell him it was time to attack the bears and take the cave.

It *was* time.

Time for a new generation to shine in Deep Creek. A generation of lions. He didn't care if he was around to be part of it, but he wanted the bears crushed.

Especially Griff. He set his mouth in a hard line and swallowed down the acid that crept up his throat.

Preston, a young lion, crossed his arms and leaned against the wall, his golden hair falling past his shoulders in loose waves. "I agree with Evers. We should've attacked while the bears were sleeping."

"Finally. Someone rational." Evers put his hands on his hips.

Preston continued, "Could've taken them out while they lived off their own fat. They are so groggy and slow in winter. Simple. Maybe no glory in a sneak attack, but it would've worked. We'd already be in control of the cave."

Mason took a swig of his Buck's Beer and set the green bottle down hard. Everyone looked toward him. "That wouldn't have worked." He glared at Preston. "We'd never have found them all because they're so spread out. Even living in Oakwood and Henredon. Not like they have a compound like we do. The ones we didn't find would have come after us like hornets out of a nest and there are a lot more of them than us. We've got to play this smart if we want to win decisively."

Evers ground his teeth. Marco and Mason annoyed him these days. Sometimes they were too passive, especially Mason. Marco was fairly stern.

As heirs to the leadership of the pride, they had both grown into weak versions of their father. All talk and no action. Instead of leading with power and strength, they wanted to hold meetings and discuss what to do.

Bullshit. Time to put up or shut up.

"By all accounts, there are twice as many bears as lions." Marco doodled on his notepad. "That's a big problem."

"We don't know that for sure." Evers closed his eyes and counted. *One, two, three...oh, the stupidity.*

"We don't know it's not true, either." Marco set the notebook down. "Until we know all the facts, and until my father says so, we don't attack."

"Total bullshit." Evers glanced around the room at the lions. They all looked fit and muscular. Battle-ready. No reason to wait, none at all. "Preston agrees with me."

The young lion looked down at his hands.

"No accounting for ignorance." Lara tapped her fingers on the chair's armrest.

Evers growled. "Why is this female here?"

The rest of the lions in the room once again refused to meet his glare. Didn't matter. He preferred to work on his own anyway. Didn't need sloppy minions to do his work. If it weren't for Maximillian, he'd not think twice about heading out on his own to take care of the bears. He might do it anyway. Out of respect for what the old man had done for him, he'd wait to hear out his plan.

Griff. Park ranger and bear bastard.

Saliva filled his mouth. Yeah. He'd take care of that bear. As soon as possible.

"Lara is an excellent warrior. We're going to need her." Marco kicked the recliner back and put his arms behind his head. "It's not going to be long before it's time to go after the bears, Evers. We'll take what's rightfully ours."

A general group of "yeah" and "you bet we will" and "go lions" went out amongst the lions. Evers shook his head and rolled his eyes. He'd left the pride strong and tough and had come back to a pompom squad.

Most of the lions seemed to prefer hanging out and playing eight ball at the clubhouse or, as he'd heard, in the summer, sunning themselves by the pool Max had put in. No one wanted to actually fight for what the bears took from them. Max had even built a bowling alley and the lions had teams. *Ugh.*

The pride had no pride.

Evers grabbed a can of soda from the fridge and popped the top. *I'm surrounded by idiots.* He gulped the drink. Max would be ready to attack soon, he was sure of it.

They'd already waited long enough, and the cave belonged under the lions' care, not the bears'. Not that Evers believed any of the funky superstitions about it, but the land had been lion territory and Max knew that. He'd wanted access to the cave for a long, long time. If some fairy lived there that granted wishes or told the future, then even better.

All Evers knew is that his parents were buried there. Griff had taken him there to kill him. That was reason enough to take the cave from the bears.

The door opened and Max entered, along with a crowd of young lions following him. Evers watched the group enter, noting the almost-cubs fawning over their leader like he was a rock star. He shook his head.

Max stopped and looked around the room, giving a quick nod toward his sons, Marco and Mason.

Large and muscular, with a head of thick pale white hair that framed his face standing out at least six inches in all directions, Max held a presence in the room that wasn't matched by anyone. His gaze, centered around gleaming blue eyes set in sun-tanned skin, pierced anyone who dared meet it. He stood at least half a foot taller than everyone in the room. No question he was the alpha, leader of the pride. Marco and Mason rose to meet their father and the other lions all stood, heads down, to acknowledge his entry.

Evers took another gulp of the soda. *Finally.*

Max hugged each of the twins, giving them a sharp pat on the back before moving into the room, nodding and greeting everyone. The boys' mother had died in childbirth, and since then they had been raised and spoiled by the whole pride.

After his own parents had been killed when he was a teen, Evers had naturally filled in as a third son for Max, since his parents had been Max's best friends.

He'd always been envious that Marco and Mason had a father. A real one. His own was dead and buried.

And it was Griff's fault.

Evers's parents' car had run off a muddy road in heavy rain and flipped multiple times down an embankment. According to what he'd heard from Max, they'd been driving through the national park, having spent the day hiking and picnicking near one of the scenic waterfalls near the gorge. The same park that Griff was now ranger for.

A teenaged Griff had come upon the scene of the accident. Supposedly, he had been out collecting mushrooms to dehydrate for use in cooking, but it was all too convenient that he'd been in the same area of the accident. Somehow, he'd either caused the accident or finished off Evers's parents, not that it mattered now. After all, he was a bear, and the bears were sworn enemies. Max hadn't told him directly that it was Griff's fault, but it wasn't hard to figure out.

The police hadn't arrived for forty-five minutes and the ambulance took over an hour to wend its way through the park to the accident scene. Evers held his hand to his throbbing head and bit back the bile taste in his mouth. He pulled out his roll of antacid from his pocket and popped three, chewing the chalky mint tablets like he was tearing into meat.

At the very least, Griff had allowed his parents to die. Otherwise, they would still be alive. Max had kept him from investigating the crime for a long time, first because Evers was too young, then by directing him to other tasks, but finally Evers had enough and decided it was time to find out the truth. When he'd pulled the police report in Oakwood last winter, he'd seen little mention of Griff—and no mention that he'd tried to save Evers's mom and dad. Only that the bodies were dragged off by animals.

Griff had not only killed his parents; he lied about it.

It was at that point Evers decided that revenge, once and for all, was the answer. No more speculation or excuses.

The bastard was going to pay for his parents' deaths. A bear wouldn't save a lion, much less go out of his way to do it.

Evers clenched his fists.

"Evers." Max hugged him then moved past. "It's wonderful to see you again. You weren't around much this winter."

Evers jerked out of his train of thought. "I had a lot on my mind. It's good to be home."

Evers breathed in the scent of power that Max gave off. What he wouldn't give to have that power.

The room quieted as Max plopped down and spread himself in the large chair in the corner. He pushed his hair behind his ears, revealing a large diamond stud in his left lobe, and cleared his throat. "Happy to see you all, my family."

The lions answered their greeting in chorus. Evers rolled his eyes.

Max leaned forward. "Let's talk about killing bears."

"I'm all for that." Evers nodded. He'd thought about hunting down Griff during his semi-hibernation, but even if he could've gotten to him inside his cabin, what joy would it be to kill him while he slept? He wanted Griff to be looking him in the eye when he took his life. And completely awake and aware of why he was dying.

It was the least he could do for his parents. He could smell revenge now. Close. Sweet.

"I'd like to hear the latest reports." Max leaned back in his chair. "What did we learn this winter? Anything that will help us regain the Cave of Whispers or give us an advantage when we attack? I'm very proud of all of you that went in—no one got caught."

The lions mumbled but no one spoke up. Even Marco and Mason were quiet.

"We should attack now." Evers approached Max. "We've waited too long. The bears are growing stronger every day and if we don't do it soon, we won't have a chance. We're already outnumbered."

Max steepled his fingers and drew in a slow breath. "I take it from the lack of information that we learned nothing that can help us."

"I was able to travel around the park without being spotted." Evers crossed his arms. "I didn't go near the cave but I ran most of the trails and roads with no issues. I think the bears are too relaxed. We could take them before they wake up any more."

"We need to make sure the time is right," Marco said. "We're only going to get one chance. I think we need to make sure that one chance is in our favor. We did a lot of reconnaissance, but found nothing new, really."

"Guards keeping a tight perimeter," Mason added. "More guards than before."

"Yes, that's true," Marco said. "We noted several more guards near the cave. Still, we can plan for them. With the element of surprise on our side, I think we'll do well when we're ready."

Max rubbed his chin. "What's our biggest obstacle?"

"We don't have a count of how many bears there are. Maybe twice as many as there are of us. Maybe more, maybe less."

"We need to find that out. Marco and Mason, find out." Max propped on an elbow.

"Yes, sir," the twins said.

"I can make sure there's one less bear to worry about." Evers stepped closer. "With your permission."

Max shifted his gaze to Evers. "This can't be about revenge, do you hear me, Evers?"

Evers slitted his eyes and nodded. "I want to take out all the bears, same as you do."

Griff is first.

"I'll assign someone else to take care of Griff Martin. Your need for revenge cannot cause a weakness in our attack. I won't allow it." Max leaned forward in the chair. "I need to make sure you're not making any careless mistakes."

"But—" Evers felt the flush of anger rise up from his gut. Max didn't understand. This was something he had to do. Needed to do.

"Most of his family is already dead," Max said. "I don't know how he survived, but you don't have to worry. He *will* die this time. I'll make sure of it."

"It's time to let go of your vengeful feelings. We'll take care of Griff." Marco smiled. "He won't live to see his children."

Evers clamped his teeth together and nodded. No point in arguing. Max might be old, but he wasn't weak and he wasn't stupid. Insubordination would get Evers into more trouble than he could deal with, and that would keep him from any chance at getting back at Griff. Better to feign allegiance.

"Once we go in, that is." Max let a low growl rumble across the room. "Which isn't going to be now. I haven't heard one reason we should attack now and until we know how many bears there are, we won't be attacking."

"I agree." Marco crossed his arms.

"It won't take long to find out and finish preparations," Mason said. "I, for one, want to see this war over with as soon as possible. I've been drawing up a plan of attack, but I'll need some more time to polish it before I present it to you."

"Very well." Max scratched at his chin. "Prudence it is. In the meantime, let's talk about what we can do to gain every possible advantage. Sounds like we're going to need them."

Evers fisted his hands and tried to still himself. He closed his eyes. *Calm down.* He couldn't let Max see his rage or the old lion wouldn't let him near the bears. He probably smelled the anger anyway. *Fine.*

Max wasn't ready to fight? Evers would handle Griff on his own. He preferred one on one anyway.

The war could wait until another day but a certain bear wasn't going to live to see it.

SIX

AMY SAT IN an empty vinyl-clad booth in Oakwood's only café—the Lazy Moon. Faint strains of country music lilted through the air. She took a deep breath, and exhaled it slowly like she'd learned in yoga class.

Years of tension had begun to ease, and her shoulders no longer ached with knotted muscles.

Being at the cabin had produced a response she didn't expect. She was a bit lonely. She hadn't seen or talked to anyone in person since her last trip into town, right after she'd arrived a week ago.

No, it was when Griff had come over to help with the water. The night he dashed out after she'd asked him if he had a girlfriend. That had been embarrassing.

She closed her eyes and replayed the image of him bending over the tub to reach the faucet, then his weird reaction to her question. She shook her head. It didn't make sense—first he was almost flirting, then he ran off like she'd asked him his heart's desire. Maybe she had. Something was going on with him, for sure, and it had to do with relationships.

It was just as well that he wasn't coming by to chat. The last thing she needed was to have a crush on someone who was unavailable or carried too much baggage. She had enough of her own issues to sort through. As sexy as Griff was, he was a bit bossy about her not going into the woods and staying close to the cabin. Same as Darren started out. She didn't need that kind of man in her life again.

The smell of hot food wafted through the air and her stomach growled. She opened her eyes and looked for the waitress. No one in sight.

Yeah, it was best that Griff remain at a distance. She checked her phone for messages. Nothing but the text from her mom earlier, asking how she was doing and updating her on her dad's fishing injury.

A little loneliness never hurt anyone. Solitude was needed for soul-searching.

The music shifted to a more upbeat country song and she tapped her foot to the rhythm. Country had never been her style, but trying new things was good for her.

She yawned. *So tired.* She'd picked up most of her supplies and groceries in trips to town in the last week, and was eager to get back to the cabin. Hunger had pushed her to grab a lunch and the café looked so quaint, she had to try it. The exterior appeared a bit hippie with its crescent moon logo and colorful façade, but inside, she felt like she'd stepped back even further in time.

Maybe to the 1950s.

She flipped over the laminated one-page menu then set it on the table. Mostly American staples like burgers and sandwiches and fried dill pickles. With the retro décor—photos of old Hollywood icons lining the walls and a jukebox in the corner—what had she expected? She smiled.

"Perfect," she mumbled. The aroma of fried food

drifted on the air and her stomach rumbled its agreement again.

"May I take your order?" A middle-aged waitress, the only waitress Amy had seen in the café, popped over to the table, pad and pen in hand. Her hair, perfectly coiffed into a miniature beehive, went well with her pale pink uniform and dark purple apron.

The café décor matched: pink and purple booths and tabletops filled the space and set off the black-and-white photography well. If the food was half as decent as the décor was adorable, she'd found a place she would frequent while she rented the cabin.

"Sure, I'd like a cheeseburger, medium well, ketchup only. Definitely no onions. Oh, and fries and a soda. Thank you." Amy handed the menu over.

"Got it." The waitress looked up from scribbling on her pad. "Anything else?"

"No, not yet." She looked up at the waitress. "Are you the only restaurant in town? I didn't see any others."

"New here?" The waitress chewed the end of her pen. "Just passing through?"

"Only been here just over a week." Amy nodded. "But I'll be in the area for a couple months." She smiled her warmest smile, making sure to make eye contact. "Taking a long vacation."

"Man trouble?" The waitress chuckled.

A blush of heat crept up Amy's neck and cheeks. "Is it that obvious?"

The waitress crossed her arms and smiled. "Honey, it's always man trouble. One way or another. Men are always trouble."

Amy laughed. "I think you're right. I also left behind a job I hate."

"Oh, I'm sorry life's been dealing you bad cards."

"I'm okay, but thank you. I need some time to figure out what I really want."

"Glad you have something to do, 'cause around here, there isn't much excitement."

"Exactly what I need." Amy warmed. She liked the waitress's straightforward talk. Though she was different than the people Amy normally ran into, she could see herself becoming friends with her.

"I can't help you with the life thing, but I can tell you that Oakwood has an Italian restaurant down the block. Mario's. It's only open on weekends for dinner, though. Gets pretty busy, but they'll stay and cook as long as there's someone hungry. Besides that, nothing. You'd have to drive to Henredon. It's a bit bigger town and has a few more restaurants. They even have a fast food burger joint, if that's something you like."

"Thanks, I'll check out Mario's sometime." Amy pushed her hair behind her ears. "I'm sure I'll get into Henredon some, too, while I'm here." The waitress seemed nice and Amy smiled. Maybe she'd gotten more lonely than she realized. Best if she planned coming into town twice a week from now on.

"Where're you staying? In town?" The waitress tucked the pad back into her apron and set the menu on the table behind her. "If you don't mind me asking. We don't have but one hotel, and it's not really a long-term location. In fact, they only have a few rooms."

"Oh, no, I'm not at the hotel. I'm staying at Griff Martin's place." Heat rushed to Amy's cheeks when she saw the waitress's eyes go wide. "His old cabin. Alone! I mean… I'm not staying *with* him."

The waitress grinned, showing a mouthful of grayish teeth. "It's okay. You don't need to explain. That Griff is a catch, and it's about time he settled down with someone. When you say man problems, well, he's a man I'd love to have a problem with."

Did everyone who knew Griff have a crush on him?

"Oh no, you've got it all wrong." Amy shook her head, her palms sweaty. The waitress thought she and Griff… "I'm renting his old cabin for a few months." Even worse, it felt kinda awesome to have the waitress talk about her and Griff like they were an item.

"It's okay, sweetie." The waitress winked. "Really, it is. Nobody is judging. Not in this town."

The bells on the glass door jingled and they both turned to look. Standing in the doorway, silhouetted against the sunshine, towered Griff. He looked even bigger than Amy remembered, his shoulders broad over trim hips and long legs.

"Speak of the devil," the waitress whispered. She raised her voice, "Hey, Griff, your girlie's over here. We were just talking about you."

Amy crouched in her seat. This was about to get awkward.

The waitress waved and motioned Griff over. "Come on over and sit with her. I'm sure you want to, being that she's staying at your place and all."

Amy cringed. What if he thought she'd told the waitress they were staying together? Surely he wouldn't.

"Thank you, maybe I will." Griff appeared beside the table. "If Amy will have me."

His voice vibrated her insides, in a pleasant way. Amy stared. Where a beard forest had once grown was now a mountain range of chiseled jawline, smooth as the surface of a still lake. The shaggy hair on Griff's head remained, but it framed an angular face with possibly the most delicate lips she'd ever seen on a man.

Firm, kissable lips.

Her cheeks heated. *These thoughts are not permitted.* Especially not about her landlord, and especially not during her "me time." She was not on the hunt for a man. She was in search of her own needs. *Some of which can be fulfilled by a man...* She brushed her thoughts away.

"So?" Griff put his hands on the table and leaned forward. "Mind if I join you?"

"N-not at all." She sat up straight. "I mean, of course not. Sit. It's nice to see you."

The waitress nodded at Amy and smiled with an *I knew it* look plastered on her face. Exactly what she needed in her new hometown—to be the center of gossip. Even friendly gossip.

Griff slid into the booth seat across from her, which couldn't have been easy, given his height. His head almost reached the top of the tall wooden seat, and his knees bumped hers. "Sorry." He reached under the table and patted her knee. "I'll take my usual, Tina."

"You got it. I'll be back with drinks." She took off for the kitchen, sashaying across the tile floor like she had hot, breaking news.

No doubt, gossip about Griff's new girl. Amy held her face in her hands. Her knee tingled where he'd bumped into her then patted it. She didn't need this attention. She'd come to Oakwood for anonymity. She certainly didn't need any kind of boyfriend attention, even the gossip variety. Hopefully it wouldn't be much of an issue since she didn't know anyone.

"Small town. Everyone knows everyone's business." Griff rubbed his chin. "Don't let it get to you. This isn't Atlanta."

"Ugh." Amy put her hands in her lap and tried not to stare at him. Guess she wasn't safe from discussion. "I know. It's just a little embarrassing." She peeked at his clean-shaven face. What would be the harm in one night with him? She'd pondered it several times since the night the water wouldn't turn off—fantasizing about him opening her robe, his hands slipping inside… She blushed again, embarrassed at her own brazenness—even if it was only in her mind.

"Not used to being the center of attention?" He grinned and a hint of dimples showed on his cheeks.

She shook her head. Of course she wasn't. How could he ask such a thing. Who would answer yes?

"Well, I'm afraid you'll have to get used to a bit of extra attention, at least for a while. You're like the shiny new bauble on the Christmas tree. Everyone is going to want to take a look at the pretty new thing in town." He stared, his eyes dilating. "And I don't blame them."

This time she couldn't duck her head fast enough to avoid the blush rushing up her chest and neck and onto her cheeks. They burned. "I just want to paint. Not be gawked at."

"Oh, they'll get tired of talking about you quickly enough." He flexed his fingers. "As long as you don't give them something special to talk about. You're not planning on doing anything wild or strange, are you?

Like dancing naked in the moonlight or casting spells in the town square?"

"Of course I'm not." She sat back. Surely he was joking. People in Oakwood weren't really going to talk about her. She couldn't be the only new person in town. In Atlanta, you had anonymity from city block to city block. "I'll save the moonlit dancing to a night when I have a partner."

"Is that an offer?"

Amy's mouth fell open, then she closed it. All she could manage was shaking her head no.

He winked. "Then you've got nothing to worry about. They'll be bored with you in no time."

"Good." She looked past him at the door. She could make it there in ten seconds. No, she needed to eat before she left. She was too hungry to leave without eating and it wouldn't kill her to enjoy a meal with her landlord. That wasn't weird or a date or anything. His flirting, as bold as it was, made her warm and fuzzy inside. Who was she kidding? It made her hot as hell. She squirmed on the seat.

"How's the cabin? Any more issues with the shower?"

"No, it's great. Guy came right out and installed a new stem. No problems at all."

"I got the plumbing bill. I'm glad to know he did an excellent job."

"He did. He replaced the working parts and it's good as new."

Griff sat up straight. "I'm sure the cabin isn't up to your city standards. I know it's rustic."

"Oh, it's great. I love it. So peaceful." She smiled, happy for the change in subject.

"I'm glad."

"I've pretty much unpacked. Most of my supplies, even. I feel at home, and that's something I didn't expect. At least not so soon." *That, and the loneliness.*

"I'm really glad you love it." He steepled his fingers. "The place is special to me."

"It's going to be special to me, too. I can feel it."

"How are you sleeping?"

"I'm sleeping well." Odd question. Amy unrolled her silverware and fiddled with the paper napkin, her hands shaking. "Maybe it's the mountain air."

"Yeah. Fresh and cool. Just don't—"

"I know, don't go traipsing around the forest. You told me that at least ten times already. Lions and bears and evil clowns or something like that stalking around."

"Something like that." Griff grinned, his eyes twinkling as he met her gaze. "Call me stubborn."

"I'm sure everyone calls you that." She looked up and met his gaze.

"Only those who know me well." His smile faded, but his eyes gave away his teasing.

"I've only known you a week, and I'm pretty sure you're one of the most stubborn people I've ever met." She paused. Did she really just say that to him? Out loud?

Because she could have added a lot more things that he was. Like one of the most handsome men she'd ever met. One of the most comforting men. In some odd way, she felt pretty safe around this man she'd only known a little more than a week. Now, she might have offended him.

He ran his hands over his smooth face. If he was

offended, he didn't show it. "Guilty. Stubborn, as charged."

"I do wish you would stop with the orders to not go outside though. I came here to avoid being bossed around." She looked toward the café's kitchen to avoid staring at Griff's smooth skin. Did it feel as firm as it looked? How would his face feel pressed against… She shook her head. *Not going there.* It was definitely an improvement over the bearded wonder he'd been last time she saw him.

"I didn't mean to be bossy." Griff leaned back in the booth. "Call me overprotective."

"That's what my ex said." She slid her phone to the side of the table. "Before he *really* became overprotective."

"You mean…?"

She nodded and her eyes misted with tears. She had no intention of bringing up Darren. Griff wasn't Darren and it wasn't fair to compare the two. She knew that. Still, she couldn't help but bristle every time Griff gave her the order to stay out of the forest.

He fisted his hands. "No man should ever be that way toward a woman. I didn't mean to be so overbearing."

"It's not you. It's my own issues." She dabbed the tears away with her napkin. "I need to learn to be me again."

"Dammit. Amy, I'm sorry. I get overprotective of people I…people…friends. I didn't mean to hurt you."

She looked up at him, his face scrunched in pain. Darren had never shown remorse even in his thousand apologies. "I know. It's okay."

"I'll try to do better."

She smiled. She believed him. "Thank you. I don't mean to be so weepy. I'm tired."

"No apology necessary."

She took a ragged breath. "Okay, change of subject. Can I ask you something?"

He tensed, his shoulders rising. He probably thought she wanted to know about his girlfriend or lack of.

"Yeah, go ahead." He stared over her and out the front window. "I'll try to answer."

"Why did you leave the cabin? I mean, why don't you still live there, since you own it and it's right at the forest and park boundary?"

"It's complicated." He sighed.

She always managed to ask the wrong questions. It was a wonder that he didn't get upset. Darren would have. "I'm curious. I know you have the ranger cabin. Is it bigger or something?"

"I didn't have to take the ranger cabin, but I wanted to." He massaged his temples. "My family was murdered at my cabin. A long time ago. It's difficult to imagine the four of us there, but it's what we had at the time, and I was grateful for a home."

"Oh no!" Amy's stomach dropped and icy shivers ran up her back. "Why didn't you tell me?"

He paused, the muscles in his face tensing and releasing in a symphony of pain. The hurt from the past was evident, from the straight line of his mouth to the scrunched eyebrows. Losing your whole family, and by murder—shit didn't get much worse than that. No wonder he seemed a bit aloof. "I should've. If you want out of the lease, I understand." He looked up to meet her gaze. "I should've told you."

"No, it's okay." She shook her head. Her stomach flip-flopped at the news. His family murdered. She was surprised he even kept the cabin. "I want to stay. I get a positive vibe there—I have from the moment I walked in. I don't want to move." She wanted to ask more, but didn't want to hurt him. "I'm so sorry about your family."

"It's okay, really. It happened a long time ago. I'm glad you're still happy with the place." Griff chewed his lower lip. "I keep the cabin because it was our family's home and I have fond memories of us all piled up there. It's all I have left of them besides what I remember."

Griff's revelation explained a lot. She wondered who'd raised him, but now didn't seem the appropriate time to ask.

"My sister and I used to pick armloads of wildflowers and pile them on the porch swing. We'd sit out there all afternoon making flower garlands to hang in the house. Mom would bring our sandwiches out there and we'd picnic either under the elderberry tree or even down by the creek."

"You lost your sister, too?" The sting of tears burned her eyes. "My gosh, that's terrible. What was her name?"

Griff wiped at his nose. "Charlotte. She was only seven. I was nine at the time."

"What happened?"

He shook his head. "I can't talk about it."

She placed her hand over his forearm, feeling the muscles tense under her fingers. She squeezed, hoping to provide a little comfort. "I can't imagine what you've been through."

He pulled away and sat up straight. "It was a bad time in my life. It was a long time ago. I've moved on."

"I understand." Amy leaned back in the booth. The earlier chills she had were replaced with a deep sorrow in the pit of her stomach, like a hole that couldn't be filled. No matter what he said, Griff was still affected by the loss of his family. Anyone would be. But he carried his loss close and held on to it tight. "I'm trying to move on from some bad things in my life, too. That's why I'm so far from home. Trying to get perspective."

He looked up, his face red. "What are you trying to escape?"

She ducked her head, letting her hair fall forward to cover her face a bit. "Sucky job, bad relationship, boring life. You name it, I'm trying to find a way to fix it."

"Your ex-boyfriend?" He almost growled the word.

She peeked at him. "Yeah."

He visibly relaxed and she fought the urge to smile. It was gallant that he puffed up at the mention of Darren.

"I'm glad he's out of the picture. What about your job?"

"I'm done there. Definitely." She looked around for the waitress and their drinks. Her mouth had gone completely dry.

"I see." Griff scooted back on the bench. After a long pause, he continued. "Been painting?"

"Not yet. It's only been a week. I've been unpacking and unwinding." Amy let out a nervous laugh. He seemed like he felt okay, but the talk of his family had bothered him. She wasn't used to such intensity in a man. It was an alluring quality.

Very sexy, too.

"Wasn't sure when you'd start dipping your brushes in." He grinned, though the strain still showed in the tense lines of his face. "Don't worry about me going all emo on you. I can tell you're tiptoeing around the conversation now. It's been a long time since my family died. I've come to terms with it, really."

"Okay," she whispered. Sure he had. That's why his whole demeanor changed at the mention of them. Still, that softness beneath his sometimes-growly exterior was a hint at his heart.

He was a teddy bear, no question about it. One she'd love to snuggle and comfort.

"Change of topic." Griff raised his voice and cleared his throat. "This is important."

"Okay." She perked up at his tone and her hands dampened.

"Tell me about your art. What makes you want to paint?"

Her shoulders slumped and she looked at her hands. *Not sure what you expected.* "Well, I'm definitely not Picasso. I'm a little slower getting started than some might be." Why did Griff make her uneasy and comfortable at the same time? Maybe it was his size, or the way he commanded any room he entered, coupled with his genuine smile and baritone voice. Or maybe she was horny and her body knew a night with him would provide relief.

She shook her head. *Stop thinking such thoughts!*

"What is it?" He smiled, clearly aware of her unease. He moved his leg so that his knee slid across hers. "Excuse me. My legs are long."

"Oh." She flushed. "Don't worry about it." *You can wrap those legs around me anytime.*

Tina swooped in and set their drinks on the table. "Soda for Amy and ice water for Griff. Share a straw or need two?"

"Two, please." Now the waitress was playing matchmaker. This was real life, not a Disney movie.

"Can't blame me for trying." Tina tossed two straws on the table. "Food'll be up soon." She winked at Griff and disappeared as quickly as she'd arrived.

Amy opened the straw and stabbed at the ice in her soda. Anything to get the sexy vision of Griff out of her head. Seeing his soft side added to the attraction she already felt. Maybe if she thought of him ticketing innocent park visitors. She giggled.

"Yes?"

"Nothing." She shook her head. "I think I've already mentioned that I like to paint landscapes. Flowers, birds, animals. Things in nature."

"Yes. But why? I mean, why not people, or cars, or buildings?"

She thought a moment. "I've always wanted to be an artist, but I went into advertising to pay the bills. Painting nature was my escape from the mundane. Maybe because it's peaceful. Different from my normal life."

"You mean different from the city?" He put the straw in his water, spearing the lemon and pushing it to the bottom of the glass.

"Yeah, I guess that's part of it." She pushed her hair behind her ears. "But it's more than that. To me, nature represents freedom. A freedom I don't have.

It's like a magical gem, just out of reach. Shiny and glowing and beautiful, but not something I can grasp."

"That's why you came to the mountains."

"Yes. I wanted to get closer to nature. Not by camping or anything like that. I wouldn't know how to put up a tent and let's face it, I really like to shower."

Griff raised his eyebrows.

Heat ran up her cheeks. "You know what I mean. I'm not that much of a naturalist. I like modern conveniences."

He smiled and swirled his straw in the ice.

"There's something about nature that pulls me. I'd joke and say it was the call of the wild, but that sounds sort of crazy."

"Not at all." His voice lowered. "It makes perfect sense."

She met his gaze and her insides melted. His hazel eyes were the color of leaves at the peak of summer heat. The call of the wild definitely included one sexy park ranger. She ran her sweaty palms over her jeans.

"That's essentially why I like to paint. Though I've rambled about it. I want to capture that wildness, that part of me that's missing. I try to do it through art."

"Maybe you need to get closer to the local wildlife." He raised an eyebrow. "In a safe way, of course."

"Maybe bunnies and squirrels. I don't know what I'd do if I came upon a bear in the woods."

Griff harrumphed. "You can see bunnies and squirrels from the cabin porch. I don't think you need to be messing with bears."

Amy laughed. "Yeah, but I'm not doing all my painting on the porch."

He mumbled something unintelligible. "Please be

careful. I mean, you're from the city, not the forest. You really don't know what to expect."

"Well, I'll let you know if I have any trouble, how's that? Besides, you told me you'd stop being bossy."

"Sorry." He stared out into the restaurant.

"I may be from the city, but I can handle myself in the woods, Griff."

At his name, he looked at her. "I'm sure you can handle all the things you might face in the city, and probably a lot of things you would run into in the forest." He paused, his jaw muscle working on some tension, then continued. "But not everything. That's what I worry about."

"No one can handle everything." She spoke softly as she watched his pupils dilate like dark pools.

"That's true," he whispered. He placed his hand over hers. "No one can handle everything."

The tingle from his touch raced up her arm and she closed her eyes to savor the sensation. One moment she was annoyed with his overprotectiveness and the next, she was basking in the heat of his voice and the electricity of his touch. She kept her tone low and looked at him. "I'll be okay. I'm not some poor damsel in distress. I don't need to be taken care of."

"I know. Just be careful." He nibbled at his lower lip. "I don't want you to get hurt."

"I'll be careful. I promise." She peered out the front window of the café. Not a car in sight. The town's population must be the size of her neighborhood in Atlanta. Tiny. And people moved much slower.

"I'd love to see your paintings when you're done, by the way. I've often wished I had a talent like that.

Some kind of art." Griff leaned back, his hand slipping off hers. "I mean, if you show them to people."

She looked at him. He didn't realize how hard that would be, but part of her jumped up and down inside at the prospect.

"I don't know." She adjusted in her seat. "I'll think about it."

"I didn't mean to make you uncomfortable." He licked his lips and studied her. "In fact, that's the last thing I want to do. Maybe you need to get to know me better. Friends, of course."

She looked down at the table. "I'm not uncomfortable. Of course we'll be friends." Her heart raced. He had no idea how he made her feel. If he did, she'd be embarrassed out of her mind.

He lowered his voice to a low whisper. "I look forward to seeing what you paint while you're here."

She swirled the ice in her soda, watching the cubes spin and trying to ignore the lust he stirred in her. "Not today. Besides, I haven't painted any yet. Right now I've got to get home and put the food up—"

"The food will be okay while we eat." From the tone of his voice, she suspected he didn't take his eyes off her.

"Yeah, okay." Amy scanned the café, refusing to meet his gaze. It held maybe ten tables and booths—probably enough for half the town to eat at once—but only one other booth was occupied. Such a difference from metro Atlanta where you could go your whole life without seeing the same person in a restaurant twice.

Whether that was a good thing or not remained to be seen. One really great thing about the small town…

the park ranger was one sexy guy with a heart of gold. She hadn't found that in the big city.

"I mean it. I still want to see your artwork." His tone changed to teasing. "Do you do any nudes? Self-portraits?"

She whipped her gaze to look at him, feeling the color drain from her face. "You sure are persistent."

He smiled. "Always."

SEVEN

GRIFF TOOK A bite of his burger, savoring the juices that rolled over his tongue. Nothing like hot food to make him happy, and the burger was his first since waking up.

He'd snacked on chips and power bars between naps and drives into the park to check things and had finally woken up enough to head into town for real food. His first real meals after hibernation always tasted like the best food in the world. Sharing a meal with his mate was the right topping to it all.

Mate. He still couldn't believe it. And she was human. Beautiful, too. He shook his head. How he'd ended up so lucky, he had no clue. He wasn't exactly sure how to handle keeping his bear from acting out around her.

He set his burger down. No mistake, he could smell her even over the aroma of the delicious food. All female and meant for him. If he wasn't careful, he was going to end up ignoring his duty to the den. As much as Elijah wanted grandkids, this wasn't the time to even consider being with a mate.

What the hell was he thinking? Clearly, she was messing with his mind. His buddies who had mates had said it was like this when they met theirs, but he hadn't believed all the hype. They'd become all discombobulated, especially when their mates had rejected them. The way his feelings intertwined in his head, he understood what the guys meant now.

The bears needed him to be focused and ready to do his part in the upcoming war with the Sen Pal, not be following behind his beloved like a lovesick cub. He couldn't bear the thought of losing someone else he loved. His heart couldn't take it.

His mate called to him.

The golden-haired beauty had woven some kind of spell over his psyche without even trying. She hadn't meant to—that much was clear. She wanted to be alone and had allowed him to join her out of courtesy, not lust. Probably not even out of much like, either. Being human, she wouldn't sense that they were mates, would she? He'd have to ask Elijah. One thing was for sure, she made him feel things he hadn't felt since his family was alive.

The need to protect her overwhelmed him at times, like a waterfall over his better judgment. He'd think of ways to keep her safe, even at the risk of the den.

He sipped his water and pretended not to watch her, though he stole glances as they ate in silence. Then, she looked up at the same time and his heart felt like it swelled to ten times the size. If someone were animating the scene, he'd have rainbow sparkles floating around his head.

Amy was a slave to her manners. Though she was a city-dweller, she was Southern through and through. He knew the type. Polite to the core. She had no idea she was his mate but she wouldn't have refused anyone who asked her nicely if they could join her for lunch. That was just who she was. It's also what would make her a target for the lions, if they ever found out she was his mate.

If he'd told her the truth, she'd shoot out of there faster than a rifle bullet out of a barrel.

She couldn't know. For one thing, she'd never believe him. He spent so much time with the bears preparing for the war, she'd be alone and unguarded. The den couldn't afford such a high layer of security for one person, either.

This mate thing is confusing.

He chewed on a fry and took another peek. Amy shoved her burger into her mouth and chewed without a care. He liked that. Why she was timid about showing her artwork, he couldn't understand.

"Do you like the burger?" he asked.

She glanced up and their gazes met briefly before she blinked her soft brown eyes and looked away. "Yes, it's very tasty."

He watched her confidence drain by the moment as he looked her up and down. He forgot. Humans didn't like to be physically analyzed. He cleared his throat and stared at his plate.

He shifted in his seat and brushed up against her leg. Heat shot straight to his groin, followed by ice. "Sorry!" he almost yelled.

She smiled and dabbed her mouth with her napkin in an effort to cover it. "It's okay."

Did being near a mate make someone act stupid? Apparently, it did.

"The fries here are excellent." He almost laughed at himself. She probably thought that was as lame as he did. He didn't know what else to say. If he said, "You're my mate and I'm taking you to my cabin to claim you," she'd call the cops. But he wanted her. He didn't want to have to wait until the lions were gone.

"They are." She shoved another one in her mouth.

He imagined her mouth closing over other things. He shook away the thought quickly.

Soon, the rest of the bears would converge at the den, and he needed to be ready to help them plan the lions' defeat. Would he be able to keep his mate at a distance until things were safe? Maybe he should enlist Elijah's help.

Unless he planned to kidnap Amy, he could forget her being a willing captive until the war was over. She'd never agree; she was too independent. He could try to get her to go back home, but Evers could follow her, so she really wouldn't be safe until the lions were gone. He also didn't like the way she'd said "ex-boyfriend." The guy sounded like a controlling asshole, maybe even an abusive one. No, she needed to be in Oakwood at least, so he could make sure she was safe.

Where he could protect her from both Evers and the ex.

Dammit. He didn't know what to do.

"What's that on your burger?" She pointed, scowling. "An egg?"

"Yep. I love fried eggs on burgers." He took another bite.

"If you say so. Must be a regional thing."

He nodded. Being so close to her was causing his body to respond in ways that messed with his mind.

Maybe just one date would help ease the tension. She smelled so good. Who was he kidding? He wouldn't stop until he claimed her.

Mate. Mine.

"Can I get you anything?" Tina reappeared and refilled Griff's water glass.

"No, I'm okay." Amy wiped her mouth with her napkin. "May I have my check, please?"

Before he could stop himself, Griff said, "Put it on my tab." He saw Amy go tense and he shot her a look. "It's the least I can do for my new tenant. You can pick up my tab another time, how's that?"

Tina smiled a wicked smile and scuttled off to the kitchen.

"I guess that's okay." She looked down.

"Sorry, I didn't mean to be overbearing—" He squirmed. He needed to back off or she wasn't going to have anything to do with him. She was going to think he was like her ex. Which he wasn't.

"It's okay. Thank you."

He smiled. "Happy to treat my tenant to lunch. I hope we can do it again soon."

"Sure. We both need to eat."

I'm hungry for you.

AMY HOPPED IN her car and shut the door, wincing as it screeched on its way closed. She put her head on the padded steering wheel and closed her eyes. This was not happening. Griff Martin was trouble. Scratch that, he was sex in blue jeans. Now that he'd shaved his beard off, she could see more of the kindness in his face. And more of the handsome.

Hard to believe he could be more sexy.

Amy time. Amy time.

She sat back and stared out the window. After what had happened with Darren, the thought she was even looking at a man as something beyond a human to talk to was shocking. Griff appeared to be all the right things—and all the things Darren wasn't. It had taken a while for Darren to show his true colors. Why shouldn't she think Griff was hiding his? Maybe that was the way men played the game. But with the loss of his whole family, maybe he just didn't want to be involved with anyone.

Griff didn't seem like that type, though. She wouldn't be in town long enough to find out. Two months was long enough for a fling, nothing more.

"Too bad, Amy." She wagged her finger at her reflection in the cracked rearview mirror. "You don't even know what you want to do with your life. You will paint and think." If Griff wanted no-strings sex, she'd be all for it. That was it. No relationship. She laughed. As if that would ever be an option. His flirting had to be part of his personality. Everyone she met had a crush on him. He was nice. He couldn't help but flirt. He wouldn't want to be with her when he could have anyone he wanted.

She stuck the key in the ignition and started the car, then pulled the seat belt over and clicked it into place. No more thinking about Griff and his tight jeans and scrumptious lips. *Done.* She put the car in gear. He'd filled her dreams the last few nights; there was no reason he needed to fill her waking moments, too.

She'd head back to the cabin and clean him right out of her thoughts. Maybe even sketch a while after she put up her groceries. Flowers or something. Or rocks. Sketch something inanimate and…natural.

As she started to pull out, a loud *thwack* sounded on the trunk. Her heart leapt to her throat, and she slammed on the brakes, even though she'd not even left the parking space. She shoved the car into park.

What the heck?

A knock at her window, and she turned to see Griff smiling through the dirty glass and motioning her to roll her window down.

Adrenaline rushing through her veins, her heart sped. More than a little flustered, her hands shook with the shock. She pushed the button, and the glass lowered with a jerk and a squeal. "Oh my gosh! Did I hit you?"

She couldn't seem to ditch the guy—everywhere she turned, he was there. That was a bad thing. A very, very bad thing. Especially if she just hit him with her car.

Right?

"I'm okay. I thumped the car to get your attention before you drove off." He stuck his hand in his pocket. "You forgot this at the café." He held up her wallet. "Thought you might need it before I see you again."

She didn't know whether to strangle or kiss him and since neither were really options, she smiled and took the wallet from him. "Thank you. That was sweet of you to catch me before I left."

"No big deal."

"I wouldn't have noticed I was missing it till who knows when." Driving all the way back to town for it would have been a pain, yet she would've had to do it.

He bent down so that he could see eye to eye. "No problem. I'd already decided that if I didn't catch you, I'd stop by the cabin on my way home. Figured I could leave it on the porch if you weren't there."

"Well, I'm glad you caught me." If she could be

invisible, she'd fan herself. Griff's musky cologne wafted through the window. Woodsy and strong, like him. She set the wallet on the seat beside her. "I wouldn't want you to have to go out of your way."

"It's no problem."

She tucked her hair behind her ear then adjusted her earring. "Thanks again. In Atlanta—"

"You wouldn't have gotten it back."

"Probably not." She sighed. "Unless the person who found it really went out of their way to find me. It'd be gone. So many people there."

"Oakwood is more my size town for many reasons." He looked out over the street then turned to her. "Speaking of…"

"What is it?" Her heart thumped. Something about this man set her feelings all topsy-turvy.

"There was one more thing I wanted to ask you." He put his hands on his hips. "Just crossed my mind when we were talking about how small the town is."

"Yeah?" She checked to make sure the car was still in park.

"Townspeople like to gather at the bar across the street, the Oaken Barrel, on Friday nights for pool and darts and beer. A little dancing. Why don't you come join us this week? Join me?"

Sounded like the closest thing she'd see to Atlanta weekends, on a much smaller scale. She did like to play pool. But it meant spending more time with her sexy landlord. "I don't know…"

"It's fun. A perfect way to wind down." His voice held a tone she hadn't heard in him before. Almost plaintive. "Getting out occasionally has got to be good for you. You can't stay cooped up in the cabin all the time."

He was right. The loneliness she'd felt earlier was completely gone. It was sure to return if she didn't see people for a week at a time.

"Well..." She looked down the street.

"Come on, it'll be fun."

"I know, but I'm not sure a date is appropriate."

"A date?" He grinned a huge smile, so wide his dimples showed.

"I mean..."

"Who said 'date'?" He leaned toward her.

"Well, it sounded like you meant a date."

"It's two people getting together for a beer. We can call it a date if you want."

She blushed. Darn, why did he have to be so adorable? What should she say to that? "I don't know."

"I can introduce you to some of the people you'll see around here. I'll buy you a beer. You don't have to dance or anything, just hang out a couple hours with everyone. You know, some of them might have some suggestions of places to paint. It can be a friendly date, not-a-date date."

She covered her concerns with a smile. She needed a break from people, sure, but what was the harm in getting out once every few days? Griff was the harm. Being near him made her insides do things they hadn't done in a long time. It wasn't like she'd be alone with Griff—there'd be plenty of people at the bar. He was right, some of them might have some leads to some areas around to paint. She put her hands up in an *I give up* gesture. Nothing wrong with a little fantasy. "Okay, sure. A friendly date. What time? I'll be there."

"Pick you up around seven?" He grasped the edge of the car door. "That way, you don't have to worry about parking or driving home late."

She imagined his strong hands around her waist as they danced. Slow. In the dark. "Hmm?" Would they dance? No way. What the hell was she thinking? She was not going to dance with her sexy landlord.

"I said, I can pick you up at seven." He yawned. "Excuse me. I'm happy to drive."

She shook her head. "Oh, no, that's okay—I can drive myself. I prefer it, actually."

"We're both going the same way, and I have to pass right by the cabin on the way here."

"I'd feel more comfortable if I drove."

"Okay."

She stared at him a moment. "I'll see you Friday night at the Oaken Barrel at seven."

"I'll be there."

He was smiling as she took off.

The town's short buildings buzzed by like a line graph, and she was soon on the winding state highway toward the cabin. The mountains rose around her, greening up from their winter nap, with snowy patches on shadowy rock faces. An occasional bird flew from the underbrush and up into the clear sky where the air was pure and thin. Spring had most certainly come to Oakwood.

She was not seeing Griff till Friday. That gave her three full days to start painting or at least sketching some new projects. Already, over a week out of her two months in the mountains had flown by, and she wasn't going to look back when the time was over and be upset that she wasted it on a man.

Not even a man like Griff Martin.

Especially a man like Griff.

EIGHT

EVERS STARED INTO the dark thicket of woods, with the winding trails and tree branches crisscrossing like a forbidden briar patch around a fairy-tale castle. Only there was no castle and the only fairy tale was a dark one about a knight losing his parents to a dragon who took bear form. He spit on the ground.

An evil bear who now patrolled the very same woods he now scanned.

A bear who was soon going to be slayed.

He could almost taste Griff's blood on his tongue.

Was now the right time? Should he go against Max's orders and hunt Griff down before the lions attacked the bears? He shook his head. *I'm not sure what to do.*

Anger bubbled in his gut and he clenched his fists. Somewhere underneath the anger, grief ran deep. He'd buried it well and rarely did it creep through the mire of hatred and revenge to surface enough that he was upset. He missed his parents. They were the only people he'd ever loved. It was a rare day that he even allowed himself to think about them, much less miss them.

What was the point? They were gone.

Taken.

They'd been so happy. Evers remembered them talking about the future and about how he'd be the first in the family to go to college. The first to get away from the pride and have the chance to go further in life, even away from the pride and Deep Creek if he wanted. His father had been so proud. Evers grimaced. He'd not considered college since the day they died. Revenge had tainted his thoughts and those dreams had died.

If he could get Max's approval to take out Griff now, the job would be so much easier. Deep down, he really didn't want to disappoint the old lion. He'd been decent to Evers after the death of his parents.

Evers had disappointed him already. How many more times would Max tolerate or forgive before he exiled Evers? This could be his last chance.

Hands on hips, he paced, his boots clicking against the hard ground. Not a sound came from the trees or underbrush and the air was still and gloomy with the weight of anticipation. The humidity was high for spring, and Evers wiped sweat from his forehead.

Where are the twins?

Maybe everything and everyone was lying low and waiting on his next move. He was his pride's Enforcer, after all. A powerful position, and one that he'd earned through hard work and deeds.

Maybe he should wait to see what the plan was to attack. Maybe he could stand a few more weeks before killing Griff, if that's what Max thought was best.

No. The bear had lived long enough. Time to pay for his crimes.

What would come next? Evers scowled. The very grass waited to grow underneath his feet and at his command. He straightened and set his jaw tight.

Griff doesn't stand a chance.

He wanted to go after the bear right then. Every shifter cell in his body, lion and man, wanted Griff dead before the summer sun rose over the mountains again.

There they are. He heard their footsteps and turned to see the twins approaching. Dressed alike in black leather jackets and dark jeans, their black hair brushed their shoulders. Most people couldn't tell them apart, but Evers could. Mason had fallen from a tree when they were kids, breaking his nose and leaving it at a slight perpetual slant to the left.

"Evers, you can't go after Griff yet." Marco walked along the edge of the trail, little puffs of dust billowing in his wake.

"Max will be furious." Mason snapped a twig between his fingers. "You could ruin everything he's planning."

Evers scowled. The twins wouldn't stop him, but they'd try to talk him out of going after Griff, that was for sure. They had his best interest in mind—second to what they thought was best for the pride, of course. That was okay.

They had their priorities, he had his.

"Don't be stupid." Marco stepped closer. "You can't do this on your own."

"Really?" Evers laughed. He took a step back from Marco. The lion's presence took up a lot more space than his shadow.

"It's dangerous." Marco stuck his hands in his pockets.

"What are you going to do to stop me?" The lion twins hadn't lost their family. They didn't understand.

"You'll probably die if you try to take the bear by

yourself. Lions don't hunt alone. Not with the number of bears out there. You know that." Marco scowled. "Wait for us to help."

Marco looked more regal every day. More powerful. He was a bigger lion than Evers, and super smart. Evers really didn't want to go against him, but he'd have to take his chances since the twins weren't going to budge from their position. "This has nothing to do with either of you. Or Max. This is my issue."

Mason blew out a breath. "We've got more work to do before we're ready to go after the bears. I attack to win."

"We won't lose." Evers kicked the dirt. "We're too strong and too smart. The bears, not so much."

"Yet they control the Cave of Whispers," Marco said. "You have no way of knowing for sure that we'll win, and your plan feels like a suicide mission. We need a foolproof strategy, and that takes time. One that gives us the best chance and risks the fewest people."

The twins were telling him the same thing. Big surprise. They were always in sync with what their father said. It made sense, he guessed. Marco was the more outspoken of the two. Probably the smartest, too. He'd be the likely successor to Max.

Evers knew what was best, and he couldn't discount the gut feeling that said go after Griff now.

People didn't always agree with him and he was used to being second-guessed, but it never stopped him. "I'm ready to attack. I think the pride is ready. We gathered a lot of information over the winter."

"You're ready to take out Griff. We all know that. We understand why." Marco scratched his head. "You've waited this long. What's it hurt to wait a little longer while we prepare the whole pride for an offensive attack?"

Evers snarled. "I've waited long enough."

"I don't think we'd be surprising them with an attack now." Mason stared into the woods. "They're ready for us."

Evers watched the sun, its rays reaching out toward the lion compound as it set. In another hour, it'd be dark. Max would be at dinner, waiting for his two sons and his adopted son to join him.

Marco nodded. "A little patience, Evers. We'll all have our revenge and will get the cave back, too."

"I don't really care about the cave. My father was murdered there." Evers leaned against a pine tree, feeling its vibration through his back and smelling the sap running warm in its trunk. His lion panted. *Run. Kill.* Escape the pride compound and go far, fast. Maybe he couldn't take the entirety of Deep Creek by himself but he could take out Griff.

"The cave is an important part of our heritage," Mason said. "My father cares about it, and he cares about Shoshannah, too."

Marco nodded. "Once we regain control, we'll be able to use the power of the ancients to help us keep the cave forever."

"Like the bears do now?" Evers picked at a leaf. "I don't see them using some mystical creature to control Deep Creek. If they were, wouldn't they have used all that power to wipe us out by now?"

"They aren't the rightful owners." Mason rubbed his chin. "We are."

"Says you." Evers shook his head. The whole Cave

of Whispers bullshit was a bunch of nonsense. "We don't know what lives inside that cave, if anything."

"The location is strategic," Mason said. "That's reason enough."

"Regardless, you shouldn't go against my father," Marco said. "He's been good to you. Treated you like another son. Yet you disrespect him for your own selfish desires. I'm disappointed in you."

No, he shouldn't go against Max. He knew that. Still, that lingering voice in his head kept repeating that Griff had killed his parents. That voice was going to win.

"I'm not trying to disrespect Max." Evers pushed down the rage that boiled inside. His quarrel wasn't with Marco or Mason or even Max, and he couldn't let them get to him or drag him into another argument. His issue was one hundred percent with Griff. He was going to take care of that, even without the twins' approval. "Some things, a lion has to do on his own."

A loud clanging rang out from the center of the compound and they all turned in the direction of the noise.

"Time to eat." Marco patted his stomach. "I think I smelled stew when I walked by the kitchen earlier. Are you coming, Evers? We can continue this conversation over food."

Mason stuck his hands in his jeans pockets. "Let's go. You'll feel better after you eat. No more vigilante mission plans. We run together. Hunt together. Like always."

The twins waited and Evers closed his eyes a moment. He remembered Max pushing him on the tire swing, encouraging him to go higher. Evers had been afraid and Marco and Mason had laughed—until Max had given them a look that shut them down. Evers really didn't want to hurt the old lion.

He owed his own father's memory. Max had to understand that.

"Go on without me." Evers crossed his arms, aware his voice trembled as he spoke. "I'm not hungry. I'm going to stay out here and think. I need to be alone."

"Promise us you won't go after Griff." Marco touched Evers's shoulder. "I don't want you getting into trouble, or worse."

Evers looked into the forest. Somewhere out there, Griff patrolled. As a ranger for the area, he'd be out at least once a day now, driving the roads and checking the forest for any dangers. Alone.

A prime target.

"I can't make that promise." He didn't look at the twins. "I'm sorry." This job was his, and his alone.

The sun glared red over the tops of the houses as it set, casting a warm glow over the roofs, and a lone bird called for its mate from somewhere nearby in the trees. Evers shivered in the cooling air as a breeze puffed by. His lion paced, pushing harder to be set free.

To find his prey.

The dinner bell clanged again, this time in longer bursts.

"I wish you'd wait, but I know you'll do what you want. Be careful if you decide to go it alone. Holler if you need us." Marco headed toward the rec center then stopped and turned. "Don't forget that a lot of us have grudges with the bears. You aren't the only one wanting revenge."

"I know. Right now, I need some time to think."

"Thinking is helpful." Marco patted Evers on the back. "Whatever you decide, know that I'm with you in spirit. I know how much you're hurting. I can't go against my father and travel this path with you, brother."

"I understand. This is my path alone." He really didn't want the twins upset with him. As annoying as they could be at times, they were the closest thing he had to family. "I'm going for a run to think."

"Be careful," Marco said.

"I will." Evers took a cleansing breath. His lion paced faster. *Soon.*

Marco turned to Mason. "Let's give him his space."

"Yeah. Let's get dinner." Mason jogged over to Marco. "See you soon, Evers."

The twins headed toward the compound, power in their swagger.

Evers watched the two of them walk away. *I'm the one with the most to lose. I lost it already. They can't understand.*

Inside, his lion moaned in pain. Coming back to Deep Creek ripped away the bandages he'd applied to the wounds and exposed raw nerve endings. The deaths felt like yesterday, not years ago, and the only salve would be taking care of the bear who'd caused the pain.

A singular focus.

Now, to think.

Plan.

Attack.

His lion roared.

Evers's eyes rolled back into his head as the skin pulled and stretched to impossible lengths to cover the new facial structure that was much larger than his human form. His skull expanded, fractured and lengthened as muscle spread over it and skin pulled taut. The crack of bones and deep ache of rapid growth made him dizzy, and he tried to breathe to calm himself as he transformed.

Nausea overtook him and he vomited, even as his body lengthened to accommodate his new shape.

He'd never get used to how shifting felt, yet he'd never give up the ability, either. The pain wasn't unbearable, but it was such an odd sensation to feel everything but his very essence change form. His bones grew and new ones stacked to form a whip of a tail. Strong legs became even stronger crouching legs, and his arms shifted to thick front legs with padded paws and razor claws.

After vomiting again, he pawed at the ground to cover the mess. He ached. From his massive head to the tip of his tail, he ached.

He roared the pain away, then panted as the last of his body stretched and morphed to lion. He was twice his human size and three times his former muscle. Human emotions lessened when he was lion, so that meant he could think more clearly and objectively.

His parents? *Dead.*

Cause? *A bear.*

Recourse? *Death.*

Things were clear now.

The orange glow of the sun looked like it contained a thousand shades of fire and ash and the blue sky cracked and crystallized overhead. He stretched. He could spot an insect at fifty feet and identify it.

Being a lion was amazing.

He held out a tawny paw and listened before taking a step farther into the dark woods. A drop of water, somewhere, fell from perhaps a leaf, or branch, into a small puddle. The scent of wet mud and clayed soil filled his nostrils and he breathed them in. Squirrel excrement. Decaying leaves. Ruffled lichenous bark.

Nature awaited.

Run.

A rabbit, *close*, the rapid beating of its tiny heart and the twitching of its nose hitting his ears. His whiskers shuddered. A flutter of feathers as a plump bird took flight in the distance.

Dinner.

He ran into the stand of trees, the damp earth soft and cool under his paws. Skin slid over muscle as he moved, warmth seeping into every part of his body. He panted to cool himself.

He was lion.

Run.

He would go after Griff. Might not be today, but he wouldn't stop till the bear had suffered.

Die.

NINE

ALMOST TWO DAYS without spotting another human soul. Wonderful. Exactly what she needed. Amy scanned the room, hands on her hips. *Much better.* The cabin was clean—probably cleaner than it had been in years—and all her things were in place for her two-month stay.

Feels like home.

She'd piled her tubes of paint and drawing supplies on the kitchen table to sort through. Her easel stood assembled by the living room window, a blank canvas awaiting her touch. She'd already done some sketching and was almost ready to tackle a painting.

Almost.

Though she'd been relaxing, the creativity hadn't flowed as freely as she'd hoped it would. She was working hard to push thoughts of ADvert and Darren out of her mind at the worst moments.

Then there was Griff. He was sneaking into not only her dreams but her fantasies, too. She couldn't get the thought of him, arms wrapped around her and mouth over hers, out of her mind.

Then there was the shower dream. At first, she'd dismissed it as a stress dream from the water not turning off. It had become clear quickly that the dream was more about turning things on. Griff, shirtless and wet with his wicked smile and commanding hazel stare…

Amy coughed.

She was doing it again. Fantasizing about the landlord. At this rate, she'd never get a painting done while she was in the mountains. She adjusted the blank canvas on the easel shelf.

Good thing Griff had left a box of simple tools for tenants, or she would've had to go back into town to find the correct sized wrench to assemble the easel. Of course, the toolbox didn't have the big tool she needed to fix the shower, but he'd brought that with him.

Her smaller, portable easel was still collapsed in its case. A bucket full of brushes sat on the counter and a stack of sketchbooks sat on the table beside the tubes of paint. She'd packed plenty of supplies.

She tugged her T-shirt down over her jeans. Time to get out of the house for a while. Fresh air was waiting outside the door and now that the cabin was in order, she was ready to explore.

"All work and no play makes Amy unhappy. We can't have that." She grabbed her sketchbook and a couple of pencils. The sunshine glinted through the newly cleaned windows, warming the cabin and casting a golden glow across the wooden floors. Tiny remains of dust swirled and sparkled as they floated in the sunlit air and the cabin smelled fresh and clean, with a slight hint of coffee.

Perfect.

She'd head out to explore the area nearest the cabin, down toward the creek. The woods were close and she figured she wouldn't get lost on a short walk. Maybe she'd see some baby animals along the way, and the new growth of the season. The trees had bright green leaves and buds and even a few butterflies had appeared.

Spring.

Her favorite season to get outdoors and capture nature in the raw, whether by pencil or paint, spring screamed to be captured in art. A photo was a reasonable reference point, but it never quite captured the essence of the season of birth and regrowth.

A great time of year to settle in and figure out how to approach the rest of her life, too. Darren and ADvert were behind her. Atlanta might be, too. What lay ahead? Being in the mountains felt like home. That was weird since she'd never been here in her life.

She couldn't stay in Oakwood.

The lease was only two months. The cabin was a vacation cabin and the rent would surely go up as late summer hikers and fall leaf peepers escaped to the mountains. The place might have already been rented out.

Then there was Griff.

She stopped in her tracks. He was a wrench in all her plans. The dark mark on her schedule. The unknown. Right now she didn't have to let him ruin a perfectly awesome day of sketching and exploring, did she?

None of the decisions had to be made today.

Well, only one.

She smiled.

She'd need to pick where she was going to spend the spring day. Among the daffodils to the west of the cabin? Up the hill to the piney ridgeline and open meadow? Or to the rocky creek that ran near the cabin?

Certainly was an easy choice.

Away from the cabin, away from daydreams and fantasies about Griff.

A girl and nature.

The light breezes of fresh air always uplifted her mood, even in the city. The mountain air should be even more amazing and invigorating.

Sketchbook in hand, she slipped through the front door and out onto the porch, locking the door behind her and pocketing the key. Lining the rocky walkway were a hundred daffodils, their yellow blooms swinging heavy on deep green stems as they swayed in the light breeze, their fruity aroma scenting the air. She could swear she smelled green.

I love spring!

She stepped off the porch onto the gravel walk where tufts of errant grass popped through like sprigs of bright green in a sea of gray. A few violet blooms peeked from the cracks between the rock border. She hadn't explored the land around the cabin yet, and Griff's warning echoed faintly like a heavy overcoat. A wet, heavy overcoat she didn't want or need.

She wasn't going to let his overprotectiveness get to her—she was going to enjoy the wonderland outside the cabin without worry. Sure, she'd be careful. She knew he gave her great advice.

She wasn't going to be distracted by his butt, either. Not even a little bit. This was a day to sketch nature, nothing else.

A puff of wind blew by and she stuffed her sketchbook under her arm and tucked the pencils into her pocket. The breeze gusted, whipping her hair around her face, and she pushed the locks behind her ears. *Brrr.*

Maybe she should go and grab her jacket and a cap.

No. She needed to get going if she was going to enjoy the afternoon sunshine. A bit of wind wasn't going to stop her. It wasn't cold when the breeze was still and once she got busy sketching, she wouldn't even notice.

She pivoted to take in the area around the cabin. She remembered the creek in the real estate listings. Close to the cabin.

That way.

She headed the direction of the water, eager to see the clear stream splashing through a natural creek bed. The photo in the listing had shown a little stream with an accessible bank surrounded by large rocks. If that was true, there'd be plenty of spaces for her to sit. Down the hill from the cabin, and not very far into the forest, it looked like a path led straight to the creek.

Should be easy to find.

She headed toward the hill at the side of the cabin. She wasn't going to spend the day thinking about Griff and their date on Friday.

Not a date. Never was, never will be.

He could make me happy.

She pushed the thought away. Yeah, he could absolutely make her happy. Anything more than that was too painful to even consider. Though he'd been nice to her, he hadn't made any moves on her besides a bit of flirting. No reason to think he was even considering her as a potential girlfriend.

A summer fling? Possibility. Wishful thinking, most likely, but a wish she'd certainly ask a genie to grant if she had the chance.

In less than two months from now, she was gone. She needed to keep that in mind in all her wishful thinking and daydreaming.

Reality bit hard.

She stepped through the tall grass at the edge of the yard.

Being free of Darren felt awesome. He wanted to know where she was going, and who with, and for how long, and not like Griff did. Griff seemed genuinely concerned with her safety, whereas Darren wanted to control her.

She could see the difference when she analyzed it from afar. Eventually, Darren got to the point of controlling—or trying to—everything she did. She'd been in over her head before she realized his protectiveness had turned to crazy. He'd controlled most of her work, too, telling her that her advertising campaigns were horrible, then pitching the same ones himself.

The night he'd thrown a cup at her, missing and shattering the dish all over the floor, had been the last straw. Something had clicked at that point and she no longer wanted anything to do with him, or even with ADvert. They controlled her in other, more subversive ways, and Darren and work were too intertwined to separate, like some kind of conjoined emotional twins that fed off her unhappiness. Being laid off was the best thing that could've happened after getting rid of Darren.

Thankfully he hadn't bothered her since he'd found another person to control. Plenty of women were willing to take shit just to have a place to live. Too bad her friend Kelly had thought Darren was so awesome that she'd chosen him over Amy.

Amy rubbed her nose. She'd tried to warn Kelly that Darren was a creep, but she wouldn't listen. Hopefully she'd figure it out sooner rather than later.

If she had any regrets over the situation, Amy wished she could've convinced Kelly to stay away from Darren. Kelly thought Amy was acting out of jealousy.

Amy closed her eyes and turned her face toward the sun, pretending she was a flower bud. When she opened, everyone would be amazed at how strong and different she was.

After a few moments of feeling the sun's warmth on her face, she opened her eyes and headed toward the stream. Getting away to focus on her art and her heart for a change was the right thing to do, and the little cabin already felt more like home than her apartment. She never should've settled for an advertising job. She should've pursued her art, taking a waitress job or whatever was necessary to pay the bills without stripping her creativity.

Darren and Atlanta seemed so far away, like foggy memories or smudged postcards from the past. That was a great thing.

She felt like she could take on the world—or at least her little corner of it. How was that possible after only a few days?

She made her way down the narrow, dank path leading into the woods, carefully sidestepping the mud puddles and downed branches. The smell of moist earth and rotting wood filled her nostrils, and somewhere above, a bird shrieked. Amy searched the tree for it but couldn't pick it out amongst the budding limbs. Tiny white blooms filled one tree and bees swarmed it, buzzing from flower to flower in search of a micro-drop of nectar.

Amy paused. The bees worked swiftly and moved

to another flower, their knees covered in dusty pollen. Farther away, another bird chirped and she turned to try to spot it, but the leafy canopy camouflaged any movement. The spring mating calls had started, and soon the woods would be filled with baby birds and animals, if they weren't already.

Maybe she'd get lucky and see a fawn, or some baby rabbits. Hopefully next time she'd have her camera with her and could grab a few shots. Painting animals had never been her forte, but she was willing to give it a go, especially if it was from a living scene she could recreate.

She stepped over a fallen tree branch at the stream's bank. The water was only about six feet across and it bubbled and gurgled as it passed. It ran a couple feet deep in the very middle and was freezing cold with the occasional chunk of ice floating downstream. Filled with runoff from the melting snow higher in the mountains, it would be too frigid to walk through this time of year, and she didn't see a bridge anywhere nearby.

She picked up a stick and poked at the leaves floating through the water, twirling as they passed. The stream was nothing like the rivulets of water that ran into the storm drains that carried refuse out of the city after a big rain.

She dropped the stick and grasped her sketchbook more tightly and then climbed up onto a large, rounded boulder beside the stream, its surface smoothed by flowing water millennia ago. Warmth radiated from the rock, and Amy sat and listened to the water rush by.

No people. No deadlines. No Darren.

She yawned. She could get used to the near-silence

and peace of the place. Only the running of water as the little stream passed by. She stretched out her legs and lay back on the warm rock to look at the sky doming vibrant blue above her, not a cloud in sight.

The forest lay at the periphery of her vision, circling the blue sky like an outline, but the view above the water was unobstructed and bright blue with a haze of yellow sunshine.

The warmth radiated into her back and hips and she set the sketchbook beside her and closed her eyes. She hadn't been alone in nature, truly alone, in a very long time. Crickets chirped, or maybe it was frogs. She didn't know the difference from the sound. The water splashed against the rocks as it flowed by. The buzz of a dragonfly flitting by filled the air for a moment and she opened her eyes to watch it zip around then away.

Tension seeped from her body like the rock held magical powers to drain all the stress and negativity away from her very soul. A tightness she hadn't realized she even had began to release, slow and steady, almost painful in its blissfulness.

She closed her eyes again. What would she do after this vacation? She didn't want to go back into the big business of advertising. Too much stress for too little gain. Maybe work at a smaller company? She liked designing ads and doing print work, but the hours and competition at ADvert had been too much.

Did she even want to stay in Atlanta?

Maybe the beach, with its rounded waves and bright sunshine and golden sand. Or maybe the mountains? Or near a lake that spanned as far as she could see. The options were endless and, if she was honest with herself, pretty overwhelming.

A branch snapped and Amy sat up quickly. *That sounded like something stepped on a stick.* She looked around.

Nothing.

Maybe a limb fell, or a squirrel scampered by. She held her head at the sudden dizziness that filled her vision.

She watched the water run by in the creek, and followed a large leaf as it made its way down and over the tiny waterfall created by a large rock in the middle of the water.

Must've been nothing. Guess I should get busy.

After opening her sketchbook and making a few gesture lines of the ridge of pines, the hair stood along the back of her neck. She felt like she was being watched. She glanced up from her drawing. *Creepy.*

Someone was watching her.

Dangerous.

Who or what stared at her, she didn't know, but she felt it. Her heart raced and her palms dampened. Griff shouldn't have told her about the creatures in the forest so many times. Now, she had a complex.

She whipped her head around, trying to spot whatever it was that watched her. A low growl sounded nearby, almost lost in the trickling water.

Adrenaline shot through her like a streak of cold lightning, and her arms filled with goose bumps.

After closing the sketchbook and palming the pencil, she slid down the rock to the ground. Her hands shook and she leaned against the rock for cover. Dread coiled in her stomach, and she searched for the source of the sound.

She didn't want to run toward whatever beast was

making the noise, and she didn't know which direction it came from. She wasn't sure she could outrun anything.

Then she heard it. A huffing, semi-snarl.

She gasped and her heart rate blasted higher. It was all she could do to stifle a scream.

Across the stream, a mountain lion crouched and drank, its pink tongue lapping up the cold water.

She stopped.

Lean and graceful, the lion's curves were beautiful and its golden fur glistened in the sunlight. Beautiful but dangerous. She'd never known a mountain lion could get to be so big. Large as the African lions she'd seen at the Atlanta zoo, only it didn't have a mane. A mountain lion, for sure.

A deadly picture.

The lion raised its head from the water and faced her, and Amy swore she saw it smile, with glimpses of teeth. Its golden eyes, flecked with what looked like metallic glitter, seared into her, and she backed away, willing her feet to run, but instead, she stumbled backward. She dropped her sketchbooks and dashed to the fallen tree.

She fell, landing on her backside in the dirt and scratching her hands on the rocks. She brushed off her hands, never taking her sight off the lion. The big cat paced, huffing.

The lion likely could jump over the stream. *Probably...no, definitely.* She'd seen house cats leap nearly that far and this was one big cat. Paralyzed from a cocktail of fear and adrenaline, Amy stared, her mouth gone dry and her tongue sticking to the roof of her mouth. Her heart thudded and she tried again to move, but her legs wouldn't obey.

The cat snarled and hissed, its whiskers twitching as it paced. When it crouched, Amy closed her eyes and covered her head. She should've listened to Griff and stayed close to the cabin.

I'm going to die and it's going to be painful.

She could've sworn she smelled the lion's breath, hot on her neck, but that wasn't possible from the distance. Her whole body shook, her legs ice and unable to move. If she looked at the lion again, it'd shred her face to ribbons.

Griff was right. She wasn't even far from the cabin. No amount of yelling was going to get him—or anyone else—there in time to save her.

She peeked and saw that the lion was trying to cross the stream with one paw on a rock partly in the water. No way it'd make it across at that point. She saw a fallen tree branch with a broken limb she could wield if the creature succeeded.

The most deafening roar sounded, followed by a splash that sent a shower of water onto the boulder where she had sat. Splashes sounded and she looked.

Holy shit!

Wrestling with the mountain lion was a large brown bear. The bear was the largest bear she'd ever seen, in zoos or on TV. Like a grizzly or something. If it'd been white, it would've been a giant polar bear. It towered over the lion, lips raised in a deadly snarl.

There aren't grizzlies in New York. Right?

What the hell was this creature?

Her heart worked overtime and she remained locked in place, unable to move. The bear stood on its hind legs and growled again as it pawed at a fresh gash on its face. The brown fur on its cheek was overrun with dark and wet red.

Blood.

The lion crouched and hissed, its ears flattened against its head and its eyes drawn into angry slits. It had attacked the bear and now assumed a defensive posture. It tried to circle, but the bear wasn't taking the bait. The bear growled and pawed at the air like it was trying to scare the lion away. She grabbed a large stick and held it like a club, then ran toward the path. If she had to fight her way out of this, she would.

Somehow.

The lion roared and the sound echoed through the forest like a call to arms.

The urge to throw up hit the back of her throat, but as quickly as it came, it was gone. Her legs shook and her heart hammered. Her breaths came short and shallow. Either animal could turn on her and kill her with little effort. She wouldn't be able to outrun or fight either one of them.

Her only chance was to run while they occupied each other's attention but her hands shook so hard she could barely hold the stick, much less move. Fear like she'd never felt froze her in place, and another wave of nausea rolled over her. She tried to take in a breath to help settle her fear, but her lungs strained with effort and her stomach clenched.

No way this was happening.

A bear and a mountain lion fighting not ten feet away from her was not real.

Certainly not the relaxation she had come to the mountains for.

She regained control of her legs, and didn't wait to see which animal made the next move. She ran toward the cabin, hoping neither animal cared enough to chase her.

TEN

Griff patted at his face with his paw, careful to avoid the tender parts with his claws. The wound stung as the air hit raw flesh. The lion had run off through the woods at top speed. It hadn't stayed to fight to the death.

Dammit! Coward!

The lion had gotten in a quick swipe that hit its target and now Griff was injured. He moved so damned fast, like a martial artist or something. In a moment, the lion was gone, running off into the forest underbrush.

I must've surprised him. It was the only explanation that made any sense.

The damned lion seemed so familiar. Griff had scented him before.

Oh my gods.

Evers.

Why didn't I realize it immediately? Griff sniffed the air but didn't smell any more lions. That was odd, a lone lion this far into Deep Creek territory; even a rogue like Evers usually wouldn't be allowed. Not if he were operating under Maximillian's orders.

Usually where there was one lion, there were several, and yet nothing now. No lions nearby.

He traipsed through the stream, his claws clicking

against the stones on the creek bed, the water cooling his foot pads.

So Elijah was right, as usual. He'd have to call him and tell him he'd run into Evers.

Evers had recognized Griff. He'd fought like someone bent on revenge, even though they hadn't seen each other since they were teenagers. The scent was there.

Clearly the rage was still there, too.

They had a lot of unfinished business, Griff knew that. He was more than ready to finish it, but not in front of Amy. She'd run off, hopefully to the cabin. He climbed up the stream bank and shook the water out of his fur. He'd seen her leave so he knew she'd gotten away.

He sat for a moment. Evers blamed him for his parents' death, and Griff would like nothing more than to be able to explain what happened that day.

He knew the awful pain of losing parents. Even though the lions were their sworn enemies, he wanted Evers to know his mother was dead when he got to the car and his dad had died shortly afterward. Elijah had tried to tell Evers but he wouldn't listen.

Evers's father had lost too much blood. He couldn't be saved, even though he'd shifted. It had taken every ounce of strength Griff had to carry the lion to the cave Sentinels. They'd taken the body into the cave then, coming out later and saying it had been too late to save him.

Griff had nightmares for months after what he saw that day. The blood, the lion so limp in his arms. The hollow look in the Sentinels' eyes as he brought Evers's dead mother to the cave, too.

This movie had played a zillion times in Griff's head.

He'd deal with Evers. One way or another, they'd have their showdown. For now, he needed to get to Amy and make sure she was okay.

But not in his bear suit.

He relaxed, letting his large bear body morph into man. The warm spring sun shone on him, drying him as he shifted. Claws, fur, ears—all dissolved and shrank and were replaced by his human form. His arms and legs grew shorter and muscles withered. Changing to human was never as painful as morphing to bear.

He grimaced at the harsh stinging on his cheek and he hoped it wasn't bad enough to need stitches. Wounds sure hurt more in human form, and Evers had gotten in a swift swipe with his razor-sharp claws before retreating.

Thankfully shifters healed quickly.

He headed to the rock where he'd dropped his clothing, not far from where Amy had been sketching.

One thing Griff knew for sure: Evers would be back.

Another thing he was certain of: he needed to find Amy and make sure she was okay.

He'd been clear that she wasn't safe wandering around the forest and yet there she was, trotting down the path like a lamb to slaughter.

Dammit!

Stubborn female—oblivious to the dangers outside and not listening to her mate.

He stomped over to his clothing. Not that he planned to mate her. That didn't mean she should ignore his warnings and go out in the woods alone. He couldn't tell her that these woods weren't like normal woods. This forest held beasts that would rend a human to pieces and not think twice about it.

He pulled on his underwear and pants, then his T-shirt. Amy could've died. The thought sickened him. He yanked up his pants and zipped them.

Even if he wasn't going to mate her, she was still his intended and he was also her landlord. If Evers ever found out their relationship, even though Amy didn't know they were mates, she'd be *Lion Public Enemy Number One.*

Griff slipped his shoes on. He glanced around at the underbrush and into the forest and scented the air again. No sign of Evers.

Tracks into the woods where he ran away, and the slash on Griff's cheek, were the only things that remained. The water splashed and gurgled in the creek like nothing had happened. Amy's sketchbook lay on the ground, sprawled open on the dirt. He picked it up and dusted it off.

He pulled his phone from his jeans pocket.

Any service?

Wow, he must be close enough to the valley tower because he had four bars. He looked around again to make sure he was alone then he speed-dialed Elijah.

"Hello?" Elijah answered.

"I saw him."

"Where?" Elijah's voice grew strong. "Did he hurt you?"

"I'm okay." Griff continued to scan the area. Nothing. "Down at the stream below my family cabin. He got in a swipe to my cheek then ran off. Just a scratch."

Elijah grumbled on the other end of the line.

"I wanted to give you a quick update, but now I've got to go check on my mate. She was at the stream when I saw him."

"What?" The line went quiet.

Shit.

"Mate? Who…?" Elijah now spoke fast and loud.

Great. He hadn't meant to come out with that. Now Elijah had both Evers and Amy to worry about.

"Gotta run. Will talk to you soon. Bye." Griff clicked off the phone then silenced the ringer.

He grinned. Elijah would be beside himself trying to figure out who his mate was. He'd fill him in later. Right now, he needed to find Amy.

He touched his cheek and winced. *This hurts like hell.*

Griff had to come up with a plan to keep Amy safe. One she would willingly participate in or not know about at all. Evers wouldn't have followed her to the cabin this time, since Griff was nearby. He'd put things together. Evers would figure out she was at least someone Griff knew.

He wasn't a stupid lion, just an irrational one.

Griff grimaced as the stinging pain in his face pulsed. Blood dribbled onto his shirt, a few drops at a time.

"Dammit!" He held his arm to the cut to stave the bleeding. He needed to clean and bandage the wound quickly. Amy might think he was a freak if he showed up on her doorstep bleeding, but then again, it was an excuse to go by the cabin to check on her. There was a first aid kit there.

Fuck it. I'm going.

He steadied himself against a tree trunk, leaning

back and waiting on things to settle. He hadn't lost too much blood. This was purely an emotional rush, a crash from the adrenaline high. Too many conflicting emotions, and he was in turmoil.

Amy was fine and he'd fuss at her for being out in the woods all alone. He didn't want to worry her. With her sketchbook under his arm, he climbed the hill toward the cabin. When he got to the yard, he saw her ratty car was still parked outside.

"Good," he mumbled. He wiped at his cheek again. It throbbed even more after the exertion of climbing the hill to the cabin, but he took long breaths. His shifter magic was already beginning the healing process.

He stepped onto the porch and knocked, then wiped his feet on the doormat. A tiny strand of fear coiled in his stomach and then wrapped through his psyche like a wisp of smoke. She'd made it back okay.

Of course she had.

He'd protected her, as he should.

The door creaked open a sliver and a shadow passed behind it. "Who… Griff!" Amy opened it fully. "What happened to you? Oh my god, your face is bleeding. A lot."

"I, uh, can I sit down?" Griff pressed his hand over the wound. He tried not to smile but his heart felt like it did a flip at seeing her. She was safe. His beautiful mate was okay. "Oh, and here's your sketchbook. You must have forgotten it." He pushed the book forward.

"Come on in." Amy tugged him by the arm and took the sketchbook. "Thanks. Let me see that injury."

"Thank you." He stumbled inside, one eye covered

with his hand over the cut on his cheek. Dizzy, and he was getting a headache.

"What on earth happened?" She pulled out a chair at the kitchen table. "Sit." She tossed the sketchbook onto the living room couch.

He sat in the chair and leaned on the table. "I was, umm, gathering firewood. Closer to your place than mine. Tripped and fell. Must have landed on a stick. Easy to do."

"That is a nasty cut. Almost like a long, deep scratch." She moved his hand to examine the wound. Her hands shook as she touched his cheek. "Stay here and I'll get something to clean you up with." She headed for the bathroom.

"Thank you." He shivered at her touch and the dregs of any anger he felt at her ignoring his warning faded. She was okay and that was all that mattered.

His bear would start healing the wound quickly, but for now, the cut hurt like crazy. The fight with the lion had tired him out, and now that the adrenaline had left his body, he was getting sleepy again. He needed to rest so he could heal.

He hoped she believed his story. No way he could explain what really happened. Not now.

Maybe not ever.

She was stressed from the encounter at the creek. He sensed her fear, though she hid it well. She was alive and okay and that was the most important thing.

Sure, there were humans who knew about the Deep Creek Bears. Quite a few humans in Oakwood knew. The bears were very careful with who they told, because if the news got out to the public that a band of shifters existed—much less lived in the area—the whole dynamic of Deep Creek would change.

Elijah said the government would probably swoop in and try to round everyone up for testing. Same with the lions. The shifters tried to keep their secrets, secret. If he and Amy ever mated things would be different, but that was a moot point. Right now he needed to keep her safe, and that was the extent of her need to know.

Amy reappeared from the bathroom with a wet rag. “Let me see it.”

He moved his arm away and squinted. How would she react?

“That’s a pretty big cut.” She frowned. “What did you land on, a machete?”

“Hardee-har. I’m not whining that much, am I?” He shook his head. “Just a stick.”

“It’s long, but I don’t think it’s deep enough to need stitches.” She pressed the warm rag against his cheek and rested her other hand on his shoulder. “It needs treatment.”

“Ouch.” He pulled back but she reached for him. Warm tingles spread through his body, even though his face stung. She was so close he could pull her to him with little effort, wrap his arms around her and tug her close. His bear growled, making it clear that it wasn’t going to wait for his human to decide that being with her was the right idea.

He closed his eyes and focused on pushing the bear back into its cage.

“Aww, I’m sorry you’re hurting.” She touched his chin and tipped his face up. “You’re lucky, you know. You could’ve poked out your eye.” She dabbed at the cut. "Then we'd be dealing with another problem. Still, this is a pretty horrible wound."

He breathed her in. *God, she smells good. Mate.*

Her leg brushed against his, sending jolts up his thigh, and his cock stirred. *Not now, dammit!*

She nudged the wound with the edge of the cloth, oblivious to the effect she had on him.

So what? He could protect her. He was strong.

She touched the wound with the washcloth edge.

"Ouch!" Pain killed the sexy-times mood and he leaned away from her again.

"Hold still. There's dirt in the cut and I need to clean it well or you're going to get a nasty infection. It'll feel better once I put some medicine on it."

She peered closer at the wound, her hand on his shoulder, and he closed his eyes as her sweet breath warmed his face.

Mate. His heart thundered. He needed her. Bone deep, soul deep, he *needed* her. He didn't want to wait. He'd never felt a pull so fierce. Nothing like this. Something wrapped around his soul and squeezed as it bound him and Amy together.

Now he understood the way his friends changed when they found their mates. The way they acted like stupid cubs, all lovesick and dumbstruck.

Dammit. Why now?

He could imagine Elijah just grinning. Teasing him on the phone had not been very nice, but he owed Elijah some payback.

The lions would take her away from him if they got the chance.

The thought of loving Amy then losing her pretty much crushed any desire to pursue any kind of relationship. He'd put her in danger by being near her. Elijah would be sad to hear that. He opened his eyes and peered into hers.

As long as lions walked in Deep Creek, he couldn't have Amy.

My beautiful, perfect Amy.

"What's wrong?" Amy raised her eyebrows. "Sorry it hurts, but I need to make sure it's clean before I put a bandage on it." She smiled. "Suck it up, tough guy."

"I'm okay." He said it with his mouth but not his heart. He was most definitely not okay. *I won't be okay till she's mine.* And she couldn't be his. Not really. Not unless a miracle happened and the lions left. A war would only cause heartache for both sides.

Couldn't he have both?

Why not?

Maybe he could. His bear growled agreement.

She stopped and caught his gaze and for a moment, time stopped. He pulled her closer, his bear intent on feeling her lips on his.

Just a kiss.

He closed his eyes…

"Hold this on your cheek. I'll be right back." She tossed him a clean kitchen towel as she leapt out of the way. "I need to get the first aid kit out of the bathroom."

"Okay." He held the towel to his face as he watched her scurry down the hall, her blond hair almost reaching her backside. His heart thudded. He'd almost kissed her. She knew it, too.

If he didn't stop thinking about her like that, he'd lose control. The pull was so damn strong but he would never force Amy to do anything she wasn't comfortable with.

He wasn't that kind of bear.

No human male had claimed her yet. Good thing, otherwise Griff would have to rip his head off. His bear growled inside him. Okay, rip his head off and his limbs, too. Maybe she did have a boyfriend back where she came from. The thought sent ice through his veins.

"Here it is." She came out of the bathroom with a small box. "There aren't any huge bandages, but I think I can fix you up."

I bet you can. "Do you have a boyfriend?"

"What?" Her eyes widened.

"I'm just wondering. Are you dating anyone?"

She put her hands on her hips. "Did that stick to the face knock you out? I don't see how my relationship status has anything to do with your injury. Do you?"

"Well, no," Griff mumbled. "I've been meaning to ask. Ever since the night you asked me the same question. All's fair, right? I know you said you had an ex, but what about after him?"

She leaned back, her mouth twisted into a semi-smirk. "No boyfriends and no plans to have one. How's that?"

Griff flushed, his heart skipping a beat at the news. No boyfriend was great. No plans to have one? He could handle that. "Well… I guess it's good."

"Okay." She laughed a little, her voice a bit shaky. "I think you need to take it easy, cowboy. You have an injury."

"Yes, ma'am."

"Put the towel down." She examined his cheek. "The bleeding's stopped."

She didn't know that he'd heal quickly, and by tomorrow, the cut would be barely a scratch. Still, he'd let her treat him and then she could take all the credit for his healing. She'd like that, and shit, it felt good to have her touching him, even in the nurse capacity.

"Look up so I can reach." She applied antibiotic cream then placed a gauze pad over the wound, holding it into place with two fingers.

Griff tried not to stare at the rise and fall of her breasts, which were positioned right in front of his face. He squeezed his thighs together. *Breasts near my face.* His breath quickened. *Stop thinking about it. Stop.* The situation was about to become embarrassing for them both.

"Sit up." She held the gauze with one hand and the tape in another. "I don't have enough hands to do this. Can you hold the gauze?"

He put his fingers up to hold the cloth in place so she could tape it. He checked out her thin nose and high cheekbones and perfect, full lips a few shades darker than her skin tone. Lovely.

His stare caught hers and she looked away. She ripped off pieces of tape and applied them to the gauze and pressed them to his skin.

He winced every time she touched the flaming wound. Healing or not, it hurt like hell. He wanted to ask her about the near-kiss but she didn't seem to be in the mood at all. Maybe he should try again. His bear was intent on getting a kiss soon.

"You won't believe what I saw in the woods today," she said. "I can hardly believe it myself."

"What?" He watched her face for any sign that she had figured things out.

Her hands shook and her lower lip trembled. He blinked. Part of the reason she was scared was him. He hated that he'd caused her to be afraid.

"A mountain lion." She pressed down the last piece of tape and stepped back. "And a bear. There, that should do it."

"Really?" He swallowed hard. Did she know? *Not possible.* "Where?"

"I was sketching down near the creek. I am guessing that's where you found my sketchbook, so you must've come along after the excitement." She closed the box and set it on the counter. "First, there was a huge mountain lion—scared the hell out of me. It was drinking water out of the stream, then it looked at me like I was lunch, and it started growling and crouching like it was going to leap over the stream. Then, out of nowhere, a giant brown bear rushed out and started fighting with the lion. The lion swiped the bear across the face…"

"And then? What did you do?" Griff balled his hands into fists. He'd forgotten how upset he was at Amy for venturing out into the woods. Right now he had to protect his identity, for her sake as much as his. The less she knew about shifters, the safer she'd be.

"I ran." She brushed her hair from her face. "I can't believe they were so near and not afraid of a human. Thankfully neither of them chased me. I'd be dead."

"Yes, you would." Griff paused. "You know, I need to file an incident report about what you saw so that we can spread the information that a lion and bear were spotted here."

"Tell me where to sign. I don't want anyone else running into them. You didn't see them?"

He shook his head.

"I could smell them. They were that close."

"I told you the woods were dangerous and that you shouldn't be out there alone," Griff said, trying to tamp down a growl. "You saw two dangerous creatures in one afternoon. I'm not really surprised."

"I'm okay now." Amy took a deep breath and Griff could hear the hitch when she inhaled. She was shaken up. "It was daytime and I wasn't even far from the cabin, so that surprised me. I thought those things came out at night."

"We've had reports of them out twenty-four seven."

"I would rather have not run into a bear and lion, but I did and I got out alive. Call it lucky or call it fate, but I will take it."

"I need to bring you one of the park safety booklets, and maybe some bear spray."

He breathed in her scent and it permeated him to the core. He was responsible for her; she simply didn't know it yet. "This is my property, so we'll file the report together, though I didn't see the bear or lion, just paw prints by the stream."

"What were you doing out there wandering around? Spying? Why weren't you looking for firewood near your own cabin?"

If you only knew. He huffed and fiddled with the bandage. "I've cleared most of the dead wood around my place, so I needed to look elsewhere. Thanks for patching me up."

She leaned against the counter. "What were you doing out there in the woods by yourself? Isn't that *dangerous*? What if you came across a giant brown bear? What would you do then?"

"I'm a trained park ranger. It's what I do. I range."

"No gun? No uniform, either."

"I'm off duty."

"Fine." She flipped her hair over her shoulders. "I'm glad you're okay." She studied him a minute, her eyes large. Accessible. "Want me to drive you home? You probably shouldn't be walking with that nasty cut. I'll bet it's giving you one big headache."

"It was." He leaned forward. God, his mate was gorgeous. *Made for me.* "I'm feeling better now." Under the bandage, the cut had started its rapid healing, and he longed to scratch it. "I can walk, but I'd like to sit a few more minutes and maybe get a glass of water."

"You got it." She filled a glass from the tap and set it in front of him. "Better hurry before it gets dark outside and the really scary creatures come out. Dragons and trolls and stuff." She winked at him.

His bear paced.

"Very funny." He drained the glass in gulps, trying to cool the heat his mate had ignited in him.

"You didn't seem surprised that I said I saw a bear and a lion. I'll tell you, it scared the hell out of me. I've never been that close to a wild animal, much less two." Amy refilled his glass at the sink, her back to him. "Why is that?"

He shrugged, even though she couldn't see him. He studied her figure from behind, the way her curves angled in just the right places. His bear would love to push her up against the sink and hold her in place there. He licked his dry lips. "I told you there were dangerous animals. My ranger buddies and I found a lot of lion tracks out in the forest this winter. Deep Creek has always had bears, but they don't usually cause a problem."

"I see." She shut off the water and set the full glass in front of him. "It just seemed odd to see the two fighting. Is that a normal thing?"

"It isn't unusual." He took a sip of his drink. "More territorial than anything, I think. This forest belongs to the bears, and the lions encroach, and it causes trouble." He set the glass down.

"What makes it the bears' land, anyway?" She crossed her arms and leaned back. "I mean, why isn't it the bunnies' land? Or the squirrels' land? You're talking like the animals are people. Do the animals draw up a pact and partition off the land or what? Seems kind of odd, the way you refer to the forest as bears' land."

"Yeah, I guess it does sound kinda odd."

She motioned him. "Come on, let's sit in the living room and talk for a few minutes until you're comfortable with walking home. Or, I'm happy to drive you."

Griff stood, then held the table to steady his movements. If he didn't know better, he'd say that Evers had poison in his claws. That, or the slice was worse than it looked. "I've heard the locals call it the bears' land," he said, and walked toward the living room. "I guess I picked it up from them."

"The forest belongs to all of us." Amy moved her sketchbook to the coffee table and sat on the couch. "It's too beautiful for one animal to own it all. Even if that animal is human."

He smiled. "You know, you're right." He sat beside

her on the couch, his legs wobbly. “The forest here is some of the most beautiful in the country.”

“It is. I’ve never felt so at home.” She crossed her legs on the sofa and propped on an elbow. “I can see why your family chose to live here.”

Griff studied his hands. “My parents loved the Deep Creek area. I kinda feel like I honor their memory by staying here. Really, where else would I go?” He surprised himself with his frankness. He rarely spoke so openly with people outside the den, yet around Amy, he talked about whatever ran through his mind.

Amy leaned her head back and ran her hands through her hair. “I’m sorry for your loss. It’s tragic.”

Griff traced the line of her silhouette with his eyes. Her forehead, nose, lips, chin, then neck. He’d kiss every inch of her. His bear would devour her in all the right ways.

Now that Elijah knew, it was a matter of when, not if.

“Thank you. It’s been a long time.” He picked at the bandage, trying to scratch the cut. “Tell me more about your family.”

She chewed her lower lip like she was trying to decide whether to tell him the truth or make something up.

“Well? Any serial killers or killer clowns or anyone else exciting?” He hoped his joking would make up for the intrusive question.

She looked away. Still no words.

“I’m sorry. I’ve been rude.” He wanted to reach out to her and comfort her with a touch to the shoulder, but she might take it the wrong way. She’d made it clear she didn't want a boyfriend and his bear was waiting on his mate.

"No, no, that isn't it." She looked up at him and fat tears glistened in her eyes. One rolled down her cheek. "You want the truth? It isn't pretty."

"In my experience, it rarely is." He scooted closer to her then held his head again, his bear fighting to not wipe away her tear. "Of course I want the truth."

All the teasing and joy left her face. "My parents are alive. They just don't want me. Never have. My mother lives somewhere in California with the man she married after my father left. She's had a couple more kids but none want anything to do with me.

"As for my father, well, he was a traveling salesman and he met a lot of people while traveling, if you catch my meaning. The last I heard from him was four years ago when he asked to borrow some money because he'd lost what he had in a bet on some kind of livestock racing."

His heart ached for the hurt she'd experienced. If he could take it away, he would. *Touch her.* He had to make the connection so she could feel his love. He couldn't let her suffer.

He put his hand over hers on her leg. Her hand was tiny under his, compact and warm, like it was the night he'd covered it on the water faucet handle. "I'm really sorry," he said. "I never should've brought up family. They are the people we get stuck with from birth, not the people we choose."

"That's true." She sighed. "I don't know any of my grandparents or extended family. My mom was basically the closest thing I had to a typical family, and even she wasn't ordinary. Obviously. I don't know what's worse, having family you care about murdered or family that doesn't care, alive."

"Yeah. I don't, either. Makes it hard to have a relationship, that's for sure." He squeezed her hand. "I do understand. It's tough growing up without family. I don't have any cousins or grandparents that I know of."

"Having no family sucks."

"Being alone isn't all that great, either."

"No." She shook her head. "It isn't. Sometimes it's all you can do to keep from getting hurt again. If you're alone, no one can hurt you or the ones you care about."

"Very true." He shook his head. She was voicing exactly what he'd always felt. But somehow, coming from her mouth, it sounded wrong. Almost selfish. He wanted to tell her that things would be better if shared with a beloved.

"You live alone. You must agree."

"Maybe I just haven't found the person I'm supposed to be with." He swallowed a lump in his throat. His head pounded, his face throbbed and he was exhausted, but there wasn't anywhere else on earth he'd rather be than sitting with Amy on the couch in his family cabin.

She tensed under his grip. "Do you believe in that stuff?"

"What stuff?"

She looked down and her hair cascaded forward. "Soul mates."

"I do believe in soul mates. I don't believe that it's always possible to be with them when you find them. How about you?"

She kept her head down. “I used to. Now, I’m not sure. I’ve been hurt too many times.”

“By the wrong people. If you’d found the right person, you wouldn’t have gotten hurt.”

Her shoulders sagged.

“Maybe. I don’t know, Griff. All this talk is pretty heavy stuff for an afternoon, don’t you think? You’re injured so I can’t help but wonder if you hit your head when you fell.”

“I don’t have a head injury. I’m okay.” He laughed and immediately regretted it. His head pounded harder and he held it. “So what do you want to talk about?”

“You sure you’re okay?” He noted the concern in her voice.

“Yeah, though I may need some ibuprofen for this headache. And some sleep.”

“I’ll get you some medicine, but no sleeping till I’m sure you don’t have a concussion.”

“I don’t. I promise I’m okay.”

“I’ll get your medicine. Be right back.”

She got up off the couch and headed to the kitchen. He closed his eyes and held his head. If the stupid headache would go away, he could talk to her without sounding too much like an idiot. Or maybe he should just go home.

“Here you go.”

He opened his eyes and took the glass of water from her. She dropped two pills into his other hand.

“Thank you.” He popped the pills in his mouth and drank the water.

“No problem. Now we need to talk for about half an hour so I can make sure you don’t have a concussion.”

"What shall we talk about?" He leaned back and put his arm over his eyes to shield the light.

"Tell me more about the forest around the cabin."

"So do you believe me now?" He lifted his head and looked at her, realizing he wore the biggest grin his injury would allow. "After I told you at least twenty times."

"It wasn't that I didn't believe that there were wild animals." She stared at him with wide eyes. "I truly never expected to see a bear and a lion fighting. One of them might be dead. I didn't know what to do, so I picked up a stick."

"A stick won't do much against a bear and mountain lion."

"I've heard that making a loud noise and throwing things can make bears and lions run away, but I was too scared to make noise."

Griff leaned close. "Yes, that's a problem. Never run from a bear or lion. They will chase you down as prey. Never turn your back."

"It's a little scary."

"It's much easier to simply avoid the forest." His head still throbbed and he longed to lie down. Preferably with Amy naked at his side.

She nodded then looked up at him. "I know, but I want to go out there to draw and paint."

"I have an idea." He rubbed his face, careful not to touch the bandage she'd put on him so carefully. "Maybe it will work."

"What? Are you going to tell me that there's a bear-and-lion-free area in the woods that is perfect for painting?" She reached up and pushed his hair out of his eyes. No hesitation, like she'd done it a million times.

He smiled, a warmth growing inside him and spreading throughout his body. "I wish. No, what I was going to suggest is a picnic with me. Soon. I need to look at my work calendar, but how about you let me take you on a picnic." A picnic couldn't hurt. The Sen Pal would be unlikely to see them.

She sat back, mouth partly open. "Are you serious? A picnic?"

"Yes, what's wrong with a picnic?" He leaned toward her. "I can even pack it."

"Nothing's wrong." She looked away, blinking slowly. "I haven't ever been on a picnic."

"Then say yes. I know of a beautiful spot, kinda off the beaten path, but not too far from the road."

She smiled and looked up at him. "What makes you think that spot is safe? I'll admit, I'm nervous about running into another large animal—bear or lion."

He looked away and held his smile back. Maybe there was a chance to have his mate and keep her, too. "I think there's always a risk of running into a big bear."

ELEVEN

GRIFF POKED HIS head into the cave. Murmurs echoed through the half light like the buzz of a hive of bees. He was late for the meeting and the other bears were all already here.

Dammit.

He didn't want to use the sleepy excuse again, though that was exactly what happened. He had lain down to rest and crashed hard. Must've shut off his alarm without even realizing it. When he woke, he dressed and headed for the cave as quickly as he could.

He crept into the small entrance room and moved into the next larger room, where all the torches had been removed except one that had been lit and placed in a sconce. He shivered. Even with clothes on, the cave was chilly.

He heard Elijah's voice. They'd started the full-moon meeting. He slipped into the next room, ducked his head and slid into the nearest chair.

"Glad you could join us, Griff." Elijah paused while everyone looked to Griff.

So much for stealthy bear.

"Sorry," he said. No excuses.

Elijah continued, speaking to the entire group of bears in the room. There must have been fifty. Griff didn't realize there were so many close by. And probably not all were in attendance.

"After researching the maps, we found one peculiar thing. All the footprints and the times lions were sighted—it all leads back to you, Griff."

"Me?"

The crowd muttered.

"That's right." Elijah took a large gulp of the soda sitting near the podium. "Most of the lion tracks are Evers, but I can't be one hundred percent sure. Whether he's team leader or just vindictive loner, remains to be seen."

"No one tried to stop him because there aren't other prints with his. He's truly been given free rein." The golden glow of the lantern lit Preston's face from below. "Why is that? It's very unusual behavior for a lion. We've never seen them hunt in formations of less than two."

"I think he's just after me." Griff stood. "My guess is that he has gone rogue from Maximillian at this point."

"I think it's time to find out."

"The sooner the better."

"I don't know how we're going to find out for sure unless he tells us." Griff paced to the front of the room. "I'm sure Elijah told you of the attack at the creek near my family cabin."

The crowd murmured acknowledgement.

"What's this about a mate?" Elijah leaned forward in his seat. "You aren't leaving here until you tell me."

Griff should've known Elijah would want to know all the details. He wasn't a bear to wait around for things to work out before he was in the loop.

"Her name is Amy." He paused his pacing. "She's

renting my family cabin for two months. That's all I need to share right now."

Elijah harrumphed. "Two months? That's barely enough time to get to know each other." He leaned on his elbow.

"It's fine, sir." Griff stood in front of him. "She won't keep me from my duties, though now I know the strong pull of the mating bond. I will protect her and the clan."

Elijah's head shot up. "Amy is human?"

Griff tried to contain his smile. "She is."

The laugh that echoed through the cave would've made anyone think Elijah was crazy. Griff knew the meaning.

He'd accepted Amy.

"SON!" MAX STOMPED through the recreation center, sending lions scurrying. "You let him go?"

Marco cringed. When his father was angry, there was no getting through to him. Riding it out like a wave was all a person could do. Sometimes the wave was a half pipe and sometimes it was a tsunami. This one, hard to tell yet.

Mason wrung his hands behind his father. "You know Evers. What could I really do?"

"He's right, Dad—" Marco began.

"Silence!" Max bellowed. His white hair fuzzed out around his golden face like a dying star.

Mason and Marco were quiet and the rest of the lions headed for the door, getting out of the recreation center as fast as they could.

Max turned on the boys, his face now the color of a radish. "I can't believe you just *let* him go. You really believe he went out there to think? Have I not raised you to be any smarter than that?"

Marco swallowed but didn't speak. Max did not want answers at this point. Max wanted complete acquiescence.

"Dammit, dammit, dammit." Max stomped. "He could get killed, you know. The bears are crazy. They won't take into account that Evers has issues. They'll just kill him. Then where will I be? One less son."

"I'm sorry—" Mason started.

"Be sorry if Evers dies. Both of you. Because right now, you've put me in a position. We aren't ready to fight the lions. If I send you in after him, I could lose you, too."

"He wants to do this alone." Mason stuck his hands in his pockets. "I think we should let him."

Max whirled on Mason, his white hair flying out around his head. "We don't live in a bubble, boy. Whatever Evers starts, we're going to have to finish. If Evers kills Griff Martin, we're forced into a war we aren't ready for. Mark my words, it will be a war unlike any we've seen. More loss than we can even imagine. Too many weapons involved now."

Marco nodded. "I know you're right. We couldn't stop him. This battle is his."

"He alone should fight it." Mason stood beside Marco.

"I want you two to go find him. Track him down and try to get him to come home. I don't care how long it takes. Otherwise, this may be the beginning of the end of the lions of Deep Creek."

TWELVE

"It's so beautiful up here, and the trees are dark and lush." The forest passed by the Jeep window as they wound their way into the park. "Thank you for bringing me." Griff had his gun in the open compartment between them, and she glanced at it occasionally to see if it moved.

Being afraid of guns was something she'd never thought she'd confront. Griff told her he usually carried it when in uniform, but she was a bit uncomfortable actually seeing it.

Just for protection.

"Thank you for coming." Griff placed his hand on her knee.

She stiffened then relaxed when she realized that he wasn't moving his hand. He was resting it there because he wanted to feel her, be close. Nothing creepy. Ever the gentleman, that was Griff. His fingers, warm and strong, held her tightly, but not too tightly. With authority but not in a domineering way.

"I'm ready to be there. Soak up some rays and eat a bite." They'd been traveling since about 11:00 a.m. and it was well past noon now. Her stomach growled.

"Me, too." Griff smiled big and patted her knee. "Glad you're hungry because I packed some mean sandwiches."

"Mean?" She pushed her sunglasses up on her nose. "What does that mean, 'mean'?"

He laughed. "Mean means a big sandwich. Lots of meat. These are traditional big boy sandwiches."

"I'm sure they are delicious. By the way, I brought my sketchbook and pencils. Hope I have time to use them a bit after we eat." She looked out at the woods, the trees taller and older in this part of the forest. They hadn't traveled higher in elevation, but were deeper into the park where old growth still thrived. "It's so amazing. And green."

"I wanted to apologize again about not being able to make it Friday night."

"Oh, it's okay. I was pretty tired anyway." She'd had mixed feelings when he'd called to cancel because of a work meeting, but once she went to bed, she was glad she hadn't pushed it and tried to go out that night. Relaxing was proving to be a very tiring activity.

"Special ranger meeting. Not on the calendar but mandatory attendance. In other words, if you want to keep your job, you'd better be there." He gripped the steering wheel with both hands as they wound around the curvy road.

"Everything okay?" She leaned back and looked out at the tree canopy. Amazing how much the leaves had developed in a week. Another week and they'd be ready for the summer sunshine.

"Yeah, mostly." He slowed to take a curve.

"Your face sure healed quickly."

"I do heal pretty fast. Good genes."

"Ahh. I see." *More like good jeans.* She fiddled with the seat belt. "What did you discuss at the ranger meeting?"

Griff blew out a breath. "More reports of lions in the forest, and that's unusual. We're tracking sightings to help us try to figure out where the group is located."

"I thought mountain lions were solo creatures except for mating." She didn't want to give away that she'd been looking up the animals Griff talked about. Studying all the details and also ways to avoid and divert an attack.

Just in case.

She didn't want to leave her life in anyone else's hands unless she had to.

He sighed and gripped the wheel tighter. "Typically, they are. These lions aren't behaving the way we're used to. We're seeing evidence of pride behavior. You don't need to worry. We're setting up more security. We can handle it." He squeezed her knee and flashed her a full-on smile that reached all the way to his hazel eyes.

She loved the way his dimples showed up when he was super happy. Like hidden gems, they could only be found when everything was going well. Wait… *loved*? That was a pretty strong word, even for just a body part. She turned away.

"Okay." She watched the vista going by out her window. His tension worried her, but she tried to push it aside. Today was going to be a fun day. She looked for animals as they drove. In some parts of the woods the trees were so dense you couldn't see even a few feet into the forest. "What about bears?"

He pulled his hand from her knee and used both hands to steer.

"What about them?" Griff glanced at her then

looked back to the road, his knuckles whitening on the steering wheel.

"Aren't you having bear trouble, too?"

"Oh." He shrugged and adjusted his rearview mirror. "It wasn't brought up."

Hmm. She rode in silence. What he'd said made no sense. Both lions and bears were large and scary and the park rangers should've made plans to protect people from both.

From what she'd looked up, bears didn't typically approach people to eat them. They wanted their candy bars. Unless you came up on a mama bear, then you'd better give her and the cubs a wide berth because she would attack if she thought her babies were in danger.

Like any good mama would.

"Everything okay over there?" Griff raised his voice. "You've gotten quiet."

"I'm fine." She clasped her hands in her lap and watched the scenery.

Tall, granite rock faces rose on one side, where the mountain had been cut away so that a safe road could be built. The other side dropped off at least a thousand feet. Thankfully, guardrails lined the open side, though they didn't really look very protective.

"Let's try to go to the bar next week, is that okay?" Griff's voice was low and smooth. "Make up for this week."

Amy turned to look at Griff. "I'm pretty sure that works for me but I need to check my dance card."

"Do people still use dance cards?" He raised his eyebrows and she stuck out her tongue. He smiled as he turned to watch the road.

"Well, let me know." He turned and quickly stuck

his tongue back out at her then focused on the road. "I don't want to exceed the guest limit."

"Of course not." She put on her best fake high society persona. "That would be sooo tacky."

They both laughed and Amy's insides warmed. Felt so good to be sharing feelings with a man instead of hiding them from him. If only she didn't have to go back to the city.

"Almost there." Griff turned the right blinker on. "One of my favorite spots. Maybe my very favorite spot."

"Yay! I'm starving."

"We have to hike a little ways in, remember?" He pulled into a parking spot in the almost empty lot.

Amy wondered if the summer crowd filled the park with hikers and bikers and kids and campers. Or if the park was quiet even then. Right now, it was magical in its solitude.

Her stomach growled so loud she rubbed it, her face flushing.

"I don't remember that. You're trying to starve me to death, aren't you?" She tied her hair behind her head.

Griff hopped out of the Jeep. Then he leaned inside and spoke in a low, authoritative tone. "Do you make it a point to go on picnics with people you don't know, Ms. Francis?"

She giggled and got out of the Jeep. A picnic with Griff was a perfect way to spend the day. She pulled out her pack of art supplies and shut the door.

"Only in the mountains."

They walked a ways in silence. Amy took in the beauty of the path—the variety of stones along the way and the small crops of gray and pink mushrooms growing in the damp undersides of dead logs. Leaves of every size covered the ground, along with pinecones and pine needles. Velvety ferns sprouted from the nest of compost and once in a while, she spotted a chipmunk racing by.

Griff carried the basket, swinging it as he walked. The gun was inside. Amy tried not to think about it. She was sure it was loaded, but it was nothing to worry about. He was trained to use it and he'd only brought it along in case they ran into a large animal and needed help.

She sighed.

"Everything okay?" He reached for her hand.

She squeezed his hand and interlocked her fingers in his. That felt better. "I'm fine. Relaxing."

"That's the point." He stepped over a small tree trunk that had fallen over the path and held her hand up while she followed. Low-cut hiking boots had been the right choice.

"Thanks for bringing me out here."

"My pleasure. I feel a lot better if I'm in the forest with you. It's not that I don't think you can take care of yourself. But with the recent problems with the lions—"

"And bears…"

"And bears." He stopped and faced her. "I don't want anything to happen to you. That's all."

"Thank you."

He leaned in and kissed her on the forehead then grinned sheepishly. "Sorry, I can't help myself. You're so darned beautiful."

"Thank you. You aren't too bad-looking yourself."

She winked at him, hoping her joking would play off the awkwardness of the moment. It was nice to have someone compliment her for a change. Darren made a point of trying to make her feel horrible about herself and she'd only realized that after he was gone. Even if Griff was exaggerating, it was sweet to hear.

A large bird swooped through the trees and let out a long screech. Amy startled and Griff pulled her close with one arm.

"Just a hawk." He set the picnic basket down and rubbed her back. "Probably announcing we're in his territory. Nothing to worry about."

She relaxed into Griff's hug. "Sorry. I guess I'm more on edge than I realized."

He pushed her hair back and traced around her face with his fingertip. "Guess we should get moving. Where we're going, you won't be able to help but relax." He grabbed the basket.

"Let's go then."

She followed a step behind him as the trail meandered deeper into the forest. The more she paid attention, the more animals she saw. Rabbits and other small creatures scurried along the ground and squirrels chattered from the trees. She even saw an opossum waddling alongside a large downed tree. So much nature to draw after they stopped to eat lunch.

"Can I ask you a question?" Griff didn't turn to look at her.

"Of course." She pulled her pack up higher on her back and walked a little faster. "Can you slow down a bit?"

"Oh, sorry. I'm used to patrolling." He eased his

pace. "I've been thinking about what you told me at the diner. About your ex."

Ice zipped through her veins. Not a topic she wanted to discuss. Especially when she was trying to relax. "What about him?"

He kicked a small rock from the path. "You said he was controlling, but I got the sense there was more. That maybe he was...abusive. Was he?"

She stepped over a small branch that lay across the trail. Griff was extremely perceptive. She wasn't sure how much to tell him. She gripped the backpack straps.

"Emotionally, yes. Physically, a time or two. Why?"

She saw him tense but he still didn't look at her.

He stopped and she about bumped into him.

He turned and looked her in the eye, rage blooming across his features. "I want you to know that I don't approve of a man treating a woman like that. Ever." He stared out into the woods for a moment and when he looked back, there was a sheen of tears in his eyes. "The fact that my behavior reminded you of him makes me feel awful. I promise you, I will never treat you that way. I may be a little overprotective, but I will always respect you."

"I know," she murmured. "I've learned that about you. You are nothing like Darren. He was an angry man with a terrible temper. That isn't you."

"It's not. Thank you for believing that." He walked, staring at the ground. "Do you think you'd ever consider another relationship? Or has this Darren guy ruined all men?"

"I don't know," she whispered. "I just don't know."

AN HOUR LATER, sweat coating her body, she stopped in the middle of the forest. Trees all around her, she couldn't have found her way out if she had the whole day.

She'd been thinking a lot about Griff's statement and what it could've meant. Did he want a relationship? She wasn't really sure, but his willingness to talk about feelings was a refreshing change from most of the other men she'd ever dated.

She tugged her backpack up onto her shoulders. "This is not fun."

"We're only five minutes away. You can do it." Griff switched hands, swinging the wicker picnic basket. "Then, we can rest."

"And eat." She rubbed her stomach. "Lead on."

Next time, she'd get a better idea of his destination because they clearly had different interpretations of "close by" and "short walk." The woods were dense, and if they were attacked by a wild animal, no one would find the bodies.

Though the trees were tightly packed, a dirt path meandered through the area like a squiggly line drawn with a brown crayon, though it obviously hadn't been used in a while. Downed leaves covered the entire forest floor and piled over the path in places. A chill passed through the woods and Amy scanned for the source. No wind, nothing. Maybe just the world taking a nap. She shivered.

"Few tourists come out here."

"It's no wonder," she grumbled.

"Come on." He motioned her ahead to the edge of the stand of trees.

"Are we there?"

"And, stop." He stood in front of her and she stopped.

"What?" The pack wasn't light. "Why are we stopping if we're so close to being there?"

"I'll show you." Griff took her pack and slung it onto his shoulder. "Close your eyes and don't open them until I tell you. Don't worry, I'll lead you the last bit. I won't let you fall."

Too tired to argue, she closed her eyes and held out her hand. Griff's large hand closed over hers and the warmth immediately traveled up her arm to her heart. She tried not to peek as he led her a few steps around the crooked path, rubbing her hand with his thumb as they went.

Then he stopped.

"Keep 'em closed." He let go of her hand and moved behind her. He placed his hands on her shoulders and whispered, "Okay, you can look now."

Amy opened her eyes just as a blast of fresh air breezed by, taking her hair from its tie and tossing it around her face. She pushed the strands behind her ears.

Her mouth fell open. "Incredible!"

They stood in a small open meadow filled with tall grass topped with tiny yellow flowers. Down the mountainside below, the world looked like it had been chopped off and they were floating on an island of green. Spread as far as she could see, the other mountains lined up for the beauty pageant. Hundreds of peaks, some with domes, others with craggy tops or rockslides down one side, they staggered and stacked beside each other in a pattern only nature could provide. Some even had snow at the very top.

"What a view." Her breath came in short gasps, and she forgot how tired she was.

"I'm glad you like it. Back here—" he motioned "—is where we'll eat. We still have the view."

"Great." She almost hugged him then stopped herself. "With this view, why is no one else up here?"

"No access roads. You have to hike in and honestly, I don't think people realize what they're missing. It's a well protected secret, though some know of it, of course."

"I hear water." She turned to see where Griff had placed the picnic basket. Down the rock face, rivulets of water streamed into a larger creek at the bottom. A small waterfall splashed its way down on one side and large boulders piled around the scene like picnic tables.

"Like it?"

She clapped her hands together. "I love it."

"There are caves here, too. Today, we'll eat outside." He climbed up on the larger rock and scooted the basket closer. "Come on." He held out his hand. "Let's hurry. There's so much I want to share with you and I feel like we're on a timer."

"Glad I wore jeans." Amy reached for him and his hand clasped around hers.

With little effort he hoisted her up onto the rock and nearly into his lap. She dusted off her hands and stood to take in the mountain view.

"I wish I could enjoy this every day." She shielded her eyes from the sun.

He wrapped his arms around her from behind and suddenly she was in his embrace. She didn't fight it but leaned back against him. The wind lifted her hair and tossed it about and he pulled her close then turned her to face him.

He ran a fingertip down her cheek, sending chills racing to her core.

"You can enjoy this every day," he whispered. "All you have to do is choose to."

"I'm only here two months."

He brushed her hair back and she shuddered at his gentle touch. No one had ever been so tender with her. She couldn't stay in the mountains. She didn't have the money to stay longer than two months, or a job. Or even a place to stay if she did. Staying was wishful thinking on both their parts.

"What about today?" He pushed her hair away from her face and looked into her eyes. "Can you give me today?"

"I fully intend to spend today with you." She blinked, her heart thudding. Maybe she could stay. But so many things would have to fall into place. And staying was such a big step, one she hadn't considered before. "You owe me lunch, and I'm starving."

He laughed and she grinned, proud of herself for getting the last laugh for once. Usually it was Griff that made the funny comment. She stared up into the sunlit sky.

The day couldn't get any better.

He pulled her face toward his.

Then his lips met hers.

Warm and tender, she didn't have the chance to complain, but she didn't want to, either. She wanted more of him. More kisses, more everything.

She kissed him fully, wrapping her arms around

his neck and pressing her body against his. He pulled her tight, his hands splayed against her back.

The evidence of his own arousal pressed toward her and she ached to feel him. Every hesitation she'd had fell away.

Yes, she could give him today. Would give him today. She and this sexy man out alone in the wilderness? Heck, she'd be insane not to at least try to get some action.

She'd worry about her plans to leave the mountains another day.

His tongue looped and slid along hers and she thrust hers toward him. His fingers in her hair, he pulled her head to him and stepped back on the rock, knocking the picnic basket sideways a little. Amy tried to push the basket away with her foot. Better be a blanket in there because having sex on a bare rock was going to be scratchy.

He tugged her closer and her body met his. She ran her hands up his firm abdomen to his shoulders, then lifted on tiptoes to kiss him more fiercely.

With a groan, he locked her in a tight embrace, his fingers playing along the top of her jeans' waistband, just under the edge of her shirt.

Shivers raced up her back at his touch and she melted into him.

A loud squall sounded that echoed across the open field and she and Griff both looked. Fear slithered up her spine.

He stepped away and scanned the area, and she held on to his arm.

"What was that?" She tried to stay close to him

without leaning on him. "Or who was that? It almost sounded like a woman screaming."

Griff focused his look on the area of the woods where they'd come from.

Amy shook her head. Another hiker in the area? Now she needed a blanket, earplugs and maybe a privacy screen. The not-so-advertised location was getting awfully busy.

The scream echoed across the meadow and off the rock.

She didn't see another person anywhere.

Then the squeal morphed into a low growl that rumbled her insides. Then two growls.

Griff gripped Amy's arms and yanked her toward him.

Two large black mountain lions walked into the meadow, about forty feet away, the tops of their backs visible over the flowers and their tails high. Regal in the afternoon sun, they sauntered like they owned the land.

"We should go." Griff slipped his hand into the picnic basket and pulled out his gun.

"I don't want to be around them." She put her hand on his arm, aware that hers had gone cold from fear. "I'm scared."

Griff held the gun out in front of him. "You're safe. Don't worry."

"What if they attack?" She kept backing away. The last time she'd heard that, it wasn't true. It also wasn't Griff.

"Here's hoping they're smart enough not to."

She watched the two big cats slink near them then

stop and watch. Now only twenty-five feet away, their golden eyes bored into her. Stately. Beautiful.

Dangerous.

Griff hollered at the lions and they stood still, then looked at each other as if they were discussing something.

Almost like they were human.

Amy picked up a rock and flung it at the duo. As soon as the rock bounced on the ground near them, they took off running across the meadow and into the forest.

As beautiful as the mountain lions were, Amy shook from fear. Two lions.

"Good job." Griff grabbed the picnic basket, all business. "I don't think they'll be back. But we should go."

"I'm not risking it." Amy rubbed her arms. Griff was upset. She could tell by the way he'd grabbed the basket so hard.

Griff nodded and helped her off the rock, all the while scanning the area. "I need to report seeing these lions."

"Okay."

He held on to her hand and ran his thumb along the backside. "Let's go. Maybe we'll meet a friendly bear on the way out, for the picnic win."

She smiled. Good thing he felt safe. It did help her. He was trained and he had a gun. Everything was going to be fine.

Still, the air seemed colder, the scene starker—as if something had broken paradise. Amy walked beside Griff without saying a word.

What now?
I kissed the landlord.
And I liked it.

THIRTEEN

THE OAKEN BARREL was tucked between the Laundromat and the corner grocery, its entrance positioned two steps up from street level. A rickety handrail led up the steps to the large wooden door. Amy had arrived a bit early to check the place out and she peered up and down the street before heading into the bar.

No sign of Griff yet. She'd talked to him a few times on the phone in the past couple of days but he'd been pretty busy setting up extra security because of the lions in the Deep Creek Park. She steeled herself before entering the bar. No sign of anyone, really, which was completely different from the Friday night Atlanta scene. People lined up outside bars to get in there. Here, it looked like she'd be able to go straight in whenever she was ready. No velvet rope in Oakwood.

She'd worn her hair down and straight and didn't dress up. Intentionally. Jeans, a pale blue button-up shirt and flats. Nothing fancy. She hadn't seen Griff since the picnic earlier in the week, and he'd acted odd on the way home after they spotted the lions. Like he was preoccupied with something. Their telephone conversations had been friendly but not too deep. Mostly more conversations about their pasts and their jobs. She'd learned a lot about being a ranger and she'd told him about ADvert and how she wasn't planning to go back into that kind of work again.

She fiddled with one of the buttons on the front of her shirt. She could wait on him to get there to go on in. Or not. After all, he could already be waiting for her inside. He hadn't really said where to meet. She checked her phone to see if she had a text from him. Nothing. She wasn't about to text him and ask, either. That might appear needy. He knew she would be here, and he'd told her he'd let her know if he couldn't make it.

Now she was second-guessing herself. How far was she going to let things go with Griff? She hadn't rented the cabin to be social—quite the opposite. *It's supposed to be me time.* She'd told him she would come, and a tiny part of her was looking forward to seeing him. More than a tiny part, but she had a hard time admitting that to herself.

She'd spent a lot of time thinking about the kiss and replaying it in her mind and wondering what might have happened if the lions hadn't shown up.

She already had the plan figured out. She'd stay a little while and if Griff was acting weird, she'd head home—the painting she'd been working on wouldn't finish itself. She hadn't told him she'd spend most of Friday evening at the bar. She'd agreed to come, have a beer, and meet a few people. That was it. She climbed the steps and grabbed the handle of the heavy oak door.

Wonder if he's here yet.

She pulled the door open.

A funky music vibe hit her as soon as she stepped into the darkened room, and she spotted a handful of patrons sitting on stools or standing around the room. An empty dance floor was positioned in the center of the bar, its lights flashing and thumping in time with the music.

The bar appeared to be non-smoking. Still, the room air was stale and heavy with odors. Old beer and even older perfume. The dim glow of neon lit the place to a manageable level and two large fans spun slowly overhead.

Where is everyone? No Griff in sight.

Tables spread around the periphery of the room. The bar itself, sitting against the far wall, was a massive construct of dark wood and mirrors, and a raised lounge with pool tables and darts lay off the left side of the room. The Oaken Barrel was pretty much like any other bar she'd seen in the US.

Dark, noisy, and more than a little lonely feeling.

She turned to leave, but a firm hand grasped her shoulder. She turned to see a bright smile illuminating a pale, effeminate and striking face, somewhat angular in its attractiveness. Not Griff.

"Hello there, beautiful," the man said. "I've not seen you here before."

Why would such a handsome man be talking to her? Even with such a lame line. She looked around to see if another woman was nearby that he might be talking to, but no one was even close to them.

Maybe he was a bouncer. *Kinda thin.* Then again, Oakwood was small. Would they need a bouncer at a bar? Probably not.

She looked back to him. Eyes so light in the dimness, they had to be blue, and short hair that appeared to be recently trimmed. She stammered, "First time I've been here."

He took her by the elbow and led her to the bar.

"Then I need to welcome you properly." He winked. "Come on. Let me buy you a drink."

Amy looked around for Griff. She wasn't in the habit of accepting drinks from strangers. Not even model types like this man. No question about it, he was handsome and he gave off a strong vibe of power. Something about him screamed strength, even though he was lean. "I—"

"Make my night and let me buy you your first drink at the Oaken Barrel." His firm grip increased on her elbow, and he guided her forward. "Come on, I won't bite."

It's not that big of a deal. She nodded. He was being a little pushy, but maybe that was because he couldn't hear her well in the dark bar. "Okay. I guess that's all right."

She'd watch to make sure he didn't slip anything into her drink, but the last thing she wanted to do was piss off someone in the small town. This guy might be the mayor or something. He was handsome and she was in public, and she wanted a drink.

They maneuvered around the empty dance floor to the bar. He never let go of her elbow and she let him lead her.

Griff would arrive soon, anyway. *Yes*, she admitted. She was looking forward to seeing him again. Here she was, at a bar, a good-looking guy was buying her a drink, and all she could think about was Griff. How had he gotten under her skin in only a few weeks?

He'd get under anyone's skin, she consoled herself. *He's a good guy.* Knowing he'd lost his parents as a child made her hurt for his loss, but she'd never been one to go for pity cases. No, whatever it was that intrigued her about him was real. It was just the worst timing in the world. Her time at the cabin was going to come to an end quickly and she'd learned back in college that long-distance relationships never worked.

A ballad played over the bar speakers, and the man pulled out a bar stool for her. "Sit with me a minute," he said. He waited for her to sit, then pulled up a stool beside her. A gentleman. "I'm Evers. What's your name, beautiful?"

She smiled a seventy-nine percenter. *He probably calls every girl beautiful.* "My name's Amy."

"Nice to meet you." He motioned for the bartender, his gesture as fluid as a ballet dancer. "What do you want to drink, Amy?" His eyes peered at her with an almost feral intensity, like he was scrutinizing her every gesture, maybe even her thoughts. It was unnerving. If they'd been alone somewhere, she'd really be flipping out.

Live a little. Stop being so anxious. "I'll have a rum and soda. Thank you."

"You heard the lady. Rum and soda. I'll have your best craft beer. Mountainfest if you have it." Evers directed the bartender. "And a glass of ice water."

The bartender, a youngish guy of maybe twenty-two, set napkins in front of them. "You got it. Right back."

Evers turned to her and flashed his smile again. "So what brings you to Oakwood? Not a lot here besides the national forest, and no offense, but you don't look like the mountain climbing type."

Music began thumping again, but the bar area was quieter. She looked around. Not many people. She'd have to question Griff about his statement that a lot of people hung out at the Barrel on Friday nights. From what she saw, that didn't appear to be the case.

She turned and studied Evers, his piercing eyes as hard and shiny as polished rocks. He met her stare. His genteel conversation didn't really jibe with his stern look.

Something was off about him, but she couldn't quite put her finger on it.

He raised his eyebrows. "So why are you here in this sleepy little town? That voice tells me you're from the South—or at least south of here. Why would you be up here in this part of the country? Vacation?"

"I'm from Atlanta but I…came here to think. Get away from the fast lane for a while." She fidgeted with her napkin. "No, I'm not planning to climb any mountains." She bit back the laugh that bubbled up in her nervousness.

Where was Griff? This was getting more and more awkward.

A gaggle of chatty girls burst into the bar, and Amy turned to see the distraction. They moved in a group of hair and sequins and lots of makeup. Amy shook her head. She'd never been like that.

"Believe it or not, this place will be full of people by eleven," Evers said, swiveling on his stool. "I don't think there's anything else to do or anywhere else to be on a Friday night. Not around here. Not unless you wanted to hang out in the forest."

"No forest for me." So Griff had been telling the truth about the bar after all. Where was he? He was late. This guy, Evers, was getting creepier by the moment.

The bartender set the drinks in front of them, then poured the ice water. "I'll put it on your tab."

"Perfect." Evers took a gulp of his beer and scanned the room, his gaze stopping on the group of girls dancing together.

Amy watched him stare at the girls. Was he in the bar hoping for a hookup? Those girls seemed too young to be out flaunting themselves.

He turned to her. "How long are you staying in town? A week? Two?"

Alarm bells sounded in her brain. She shouldn't be telling a complete stranger her plans. That was not smart. She sipped her drink to buy time to think. He seemed nice enough, but you couldn't really ever tell, could you?

"I'm not sure," she lied. "Depends on how quickly I recover my sanity. I lost my job, and now I'm trying to figure out what direction I want to go in. You know, what I want to do with my life. Next steps and all that."

"I'm sorry to hear about the job. I hope Oakwood proves to be relaxing for you and that you can figure out what you want to do with your life." He smiled, his teeth gleaming. His hair shone. Hell, everything about the man sparkled, like he was some big-screen vampire. "Some people come here and never leave, you know. Not me, though. I'm just visiting."

Amy couldn't help but stare at his perfectly white teeth. His sharp pointy teeth. She shook her head to clear the image. Having such an imagination was sometimes a curse, but the vibe Evers was giving off wasn't completely a rational one. Still, being with him kept her from being alone.

She looked around for Griff again. The bar was

filling up fast, but she didn't see him anywhere. He'd stand a head taller than almost everyone in the room, so she was pretty sure he hadn't arrived.

"Waiting on someone?" Evers took another swig of beer. "You keep looking around like you're searching for somebody."

She ducked her head as the flush crept up her neck. Busted. She should go ahead and tell him the truth. After all, he'd find out when Griff arrived. "Yeah, my landlord was going to meet me here to introduce me to some of Oakwood's residents. He's a park ranger. Maybe you know him? Griff Martin?"

Evers could've broken the beer bottle with the squeeze he gave it. "I know of him," he said. "So he'll be here tonight. Interesting."

He knows *of* Griff? What? Amy took another sip of her drink. *What the heck does that mean? Awkward, much?*

She peeked at Evers. He skimmed the room with an intensity that made her uncomfortable. He was looking for someone. She dared not follow his gaze. Something about him felt wrong.

Her gut feeling was getting worse by the moment.

He felt wild. Not the free-range wild, but sinister like a wild and feral animal. Like his pretty shell was hiding a rancid psyche. She was used to creeps in bars, but they weren't usually so handsome. She sipped her drink.

If things went bad, she didn't need Griff to rescue her.

The music changed to a techno-pop ballad and grew a bit louder, but still not too loud to talk over.

Evers stood. "Let's dance."

"I don't—"

"One song." He tugged her to standing. "I'm sure your landlord won't mind."

She really didn't want to dance with the man, but he wasn't giving her much of a way out. If she said no, she'd definitely look rude. Maybe Griff would hurry up and get to the bar and cut in. Otherwise, the dance was going to be a long one.

"One." She turned her drink up and finished it, then set the empty glass on the bar. "But that's it."

He took her hand. Leading her to the dance floor, he caressed her palm, his fingers bony and coarse and cold. She shivered. When they reached the floor, other dancers moved to make room for them. Amy saw the look on some of the girls' faces. They'd all rather be dancing with Evers. For once, Amy had the beau of the ball holding her in his arms, and he danced like a prince.

She'd rather be dancing with her landlord. Her park ranger.

She was really interested in what the deal was with Evers and Griff. Evers had tensed at the mention of Griff's name; though slight, she'd seen it.

The bar lights lowered even more and the song warbled over the cheap sound system. Now the air was thick with body odor and alcohol and other thick smells. Amy was a little dizzy from the drink but okay to dance.

Then the song changed to a slow ballad.

Evers pulled her close, his hands low around her waist, dangerously close to her ass. Glad for her decision to wear jeans instead of a miniskirt, Amy wiggled to move away from his hands but instead ended up pressing into him as he slid one hand into her back pocket.

Great, he probably thought she did it on purpose.

"That feels nice," he hissed in her ear. "That's more like it. No more cold fish—I knew you were a hot-blooded girl." He pulled her even more tightly to him, running one hand up her back to her bra strap and sliding a thumb underneath.

"Stop that," she whispered. "Now." Her heart raced. Either the man had two pairs of tube socks rolled up in his jeans or...

"Fine, have it your way." He slid the hand down her back and into her other jeans pocket. He yanked her to him.

The alcohol's warmth snaked through her veins, and she closed her eyes as he swayed and moved against her.

I think you know what I want. It's what you want, too. Don't deny it.

She heard the words in his voice, but he hadn't said anything.

Yes, I can project my thoughts into your mind at will. Only what I want you to hear.

Her tipsy mind played tricks on her. She lifted her head and looked at him. The room spun, and she realized she'd had way too much to drink. She knew better than to down drinks quickly and now she needed to extricate herself from this mess.

You look like you could use some fun.

Now she knew something was going on. Something crazy. She tried to push away from him but he held her more tightly.

"Oh, no you don't."

"Let me go." She raised her voice. "Now." He held her so close, she had no doubt he heard her over the music. If he didn't let go, she'd have to employ some of the tactics she'd learned at the gym. Personal safety moves she'd hoped she'd never need.

He pulled his hands from her pockets and grabbed her arm. "You don't want me to let you go. You want this." He put his other hand behind her neck and forced her face toward his, then kissed her. His lips, bitter-tasting and firm, were unyielding.

She fought, pressing her lips together and trying to shove him away, but he held her in place. No one noticed what was going on or tried to stop him.

Anger bloomed in her and she drew on it for strength. He had no right to kiss her or try to force her to do anything. Even though her head spun, she knew he was way over all the lines.

She stomped on Evers's foot and when he tried to back away, she kneed him in the groin. Hard. He yelped in pain and went down on his knees.

Amy was ready to kick him in the face if he came at her again, but suddenly, Evers flew free of her, landing on the dance floor with a *thump.* Griff loomed over him, his hands curled into fists and his face contorted in a ferocious scowl.

FOURTEEN

EVERS.

Rage. Can't shift. People.

He stood over Evers, shaking, wanting to beat the shit out of him and drag him outside, but he had to keep his cool, no matter how angry he was.

One, two, three… He breathed out tension.

The asshole was all mountain lion—he'd known as soon as he touched him. He'd slashed Griff's face at the creek. The other lions that were at the picnic? Marco and Mason, the only solid black mountain lions in the pride—heirs to Maximillian. Probably looking for Evers or helping him scout.

Now Evers had forced Amy to kiss him.

Griff's pulse raced. He no longer cared to explain anything to Evers. He didn't care if the lion knew the truth about the rainy day his parents died or what he'd done to try and save his father. He had just put his hands on Griff's mate. Things had gotten even more personal than they were.

"What the fuck?" Evers jumped to his feet. *You know who I am.*

"Yes." He clasped and unclasped his hands, his fingers begging to be around the fucker's neck.

"So you do remember me." *You will remember my name until you die.* He growled. *Sen Pal, but you know that, too. You knew in the woods. Guess I didn't hit you hard enough to knock sense into you. I would've killed you then but you didn't follow me into the woods when I ran.*

"Leave Amy alone. Never come near her again. You do not force a woman to kiss you or dance with you or even breathe near you, you lowlife asshole." *I will kill you the next time I see you. Or I might kill you tonight, anyway.*

Griff clenched his teeth and used every bit of willpower he had not to snap Evers's neck in front of everyone.

Amy stood, wide-eyed, and hand over her mouth. She backed away as the dance floor cleared. The music continued to play, but no one danced. Instead, they formed a lopsided circle so they could watch the men fight.

Mine.

Half drunk or merely excited, the humans had the look of hunters in their eyes. They appeared to hope for a death match. Sometimes they were so primitive. Griff shook his head. He couldn't fight Evers here.

He had to protect his den, and his job as park ranger. Even if all he wanted to do was kill the sleazy little bastard, he couldn't.

"She's not yours." Evers put his fists up. "She wanted to dance with me. Have a drink. We weren't doing anything she didn't want to do. Ask her if you don't believe me."

"You will leave her alone!" Griff roared and lunged toward Evers, tackling him to the ground. *Fuck.* So much for self-control around humans. Yeah, Elijah was going to be mad, but he held a lot of control over the rangers and if he decided this was the end of Griff's job, then so be it.

People scattered, backing away from the two men. Amy was somewhere, but he didn't see her. He saw red.

His bear reared up and fought for control with his human, trying to come out, but Griff held on. He wanted to slash Evers into symmetrical ribbons of flesh and leave him flayed open on the floor as a warning to anyone who would touch his mate. He couldn't do that. Not if he wanted to have a chance at keeping his job. He also had a duty to keep the shifter secrets.

His bear paced through the mantras.

No secrets to keep.

No bears of Deep Creek.

No Cave of Whispers.

He wrestled Evers, trying to pin him to the floor, but the lion was stronger than his scrawny body appeared. Griff opened his mouth and let out a snarl of frustration. If only they were in the woods, he'd rip his throat out.

Evers squirmed out from under Griff and pulled free. The men stood, facing each other, both panting. Griff breathed his bear into retreat. *Not yet. The chance will come. Not here.*

Patience.

"Things are going to change." *Patient or not.* Evers wiped his arm across his busted lip and then spit on the floor. "There's nothing you can do." *We're coming. Not just for your girl.*

"Bring it." Griff motioned the crowd back. "I'm ready. Step one foot closer and I'll arrest you." Oh, what he wouldn't give to shift now and really take care of Evers.

Not now. Soon. Max isn't going to wait much longer for his revenge. You bears don't stand a chance. Evers dashed out the door with Griff trailing behind him. Griff ran as fast as he could, but the slender man was faster and Griff fell behind bit by bit.

He followed until Evers shed his clothing, slipped into his mountain lion form mid-run, and bounded down the street and out of sight. If he hadn't been worried about Amy, Griff would've shifted into his bear and followed the lion to really beat his ass.

Then kill him.

He needed to find Amy. She was probably even more confused than before. First, he needed to let the bears know that Evers was in town.

He pulled out his phone to call Elijah. The Sen Pal was in Oakwood. Not just in the forest—actually in the town. At least, Evers was, and that was enough to worry about. The black mountain lions he'd seen at the picnic, Marco and Mason, were the pride leader's sons. Were they part of a plan, or was Evers on his own?

Things were getting serious.

He'd just finished a quick chat with Elijah when Amy walked out of the bar. Though her hair was a bit rumpled, she looked okay. Maybe a bit shell-shocked, but physically okay.

"I went to wash my face then realized you probably needed more tending than I did." She stood close. "Are you okay? Who was that man, Evers? I got the feeling he knows you."

"I'm okay." He put his hand on her shoulder and she didn't push it away. "Are you? Did he hurt you?"

"No, I'm okay." She shook her head and her hair swayed like a curtain. "Plus, I got the chance to practice my self-defense moves, and I'm happy to say I didn't hesitate when I needed them."

Evers could have forced her to leave with him. He could've put something in her drink. It was scary dealing with people with no integrity. Thank goodness Amy had a brain in that beautiful head.

"You did great. Evers is not a good guy. I'm sorry you ran into him."

"You fought pretty well yourself. I guess they teach you how to do that in ranger school."

"Something like that." Griff ran his hand over her hair, smoothing the sides. "I'm sorry this is how the evening turned out. He's a really bad man. Someone who's wanted revenge against me for a very long time. He'll do anything to get to me, including hurting the people I care about."

Amy nodded and pushed her hair behind her ears. "Yeah, he tried to force me to kiss him—"

Griff pulled her close, holding her head against his chest. "Don't think about him. I'm going to take care of him and make sure he doesn't get another chance."

"I'm mad at myself." Amy tensed in his arms. "I shouldn't have accepted a drink. I know better."

"You know that doesn't mean you gave him any kind of permission to assault you." Griff held her at arm's length. "Buying you a drink didn't give him any right to kiss you or touch you in any way. You weren't obligated to him because he bought it."

"Oh, I know that. I've had similar things happen before, in Atlanta. That's why I took the self-defense class with some ladies from the office. There are men like this everywhere. Usually I handle them fine. Tonight, quite honestly, I'm thankful you were around to help me out."

"Come on. I'll take you home." Griff held out his hand to Amy. "You're welcome. I hope I didn't overstep my bounds by...getting upset with him."

She shook her head *no.* Her hair lay around her shoulders in a tangle. "So what does he want revenge for? What could make him so angry that he'd act like that?"

Griff rubbed his face. He should tell her the truth. At least most of it, leaving out the shifter stuff, of course. "It's a long story, but the short version is, he blames me for his parents dying in a car accident when we were teens."

A lone vehicle moved down the road and Griff stared at the driver, making sure it wasn't Evers. It wasn't. Just the old guy that owned the clock shop.

"Why?" Amy's eyes were full of questions. "How could you be at fault for a car accident? Were you driving?"

"No, I was too young to drive. He blames me because I came upon the wreck in the forest after it happened. I was there when his father died. His mother was already dead. Looked like they'd taken a curve too fast or something and ran off the road into a tree."

She put her hand on his shoulder and a permeating warmth bloomed at her touch and into his skin. "It's not your fault they died. You know that."

"I do know. He thinks I'm to blame. I couldn't save them. I tried. He's out for blood." Griff stopped and looked into her eyes. He couldn't let her out of his sight again. "Come on, let me drive you home."

Amy took a step back. "I can drive."

"You can barely stand. You must be quite a lightweight with alcohol. You need to let me drive you home."

"I'd be okay."

"I can give you a ticket."

She scowled at him. "Yeah, I guess you could."

"There's no shame in having a designated driver. Plus, I can check and make sure Evers didn't go to the cabin."

Amy smiled, but her bottom lip quivered. "I *was* dealing with him. Sort of. I had the situation under control."

"Did you now?" Griff moved closer. *Protect her. Ease her mind.* Her scent, sweet as honey, rolled over him stronger than all the bar smells. How could he explain that it was his duty to protect her, without scaring her off?

Without saying he was her mate?

It was a duty he very much enjoyed. Things had changed. The Sen Pal were here, and they knew about Amy. Griff had to change his plan. She was no longer safe in her anonymity, and he needed to tell her everything. There was a chance Evers didn't know she was Griff's mate, but it wasn't going to take him long to figure it out.

"Yes, I did. I would have kneed him in the face, the next second. I'd already gotten a few licks in."

"That would take care of him," Griff said. "Sorry I took over your fight. I couldn't bear to see him touching you."

"His kind is nothing I haven't seen a million times

in Atlanta." She smiled, but still trembled. "I've always handled it on my own. Even the creepy kissers."

Griff's heart clenched. He didn't want to think about other men with Amy. She was his. His mate. And Evers knew about her, too. The cat was out of the bag, and the lion knew it.

"Let's go. I'm driving." He winked. He didn't want her to think he was being controlling, but no way was she driving in her current state. In his current state. He needed to be near her.

Amy's eyes sparkled from the reflections of the streetlamps. "Fine. You win. Drive me home. But only if you'll come in for a cup of coffee when we get there. I barely got to see you tonight, and you promised me an evening together."

Griff swallowed hard. She'd asked him in for coffee. Everyone knew that was a metaphor for...something. She clearly wanted to see more of him tonight. "I can do that." His bear danced.

"Before or after you give me a ticket?" She fake punched him in the chest.

"Depends."

She leaned into him. "What will you do if I resist arrest?" The berry scent of her shampoo wafted up and he wrapped his arms around her.

"Try me," he growled.

"I love a challenge." She pushed against him. "Do you have handcuffs?"

His erection grew and he whispered in her ear. "Darling, I don't need handcuffs to hold you down."

She blinked, her pupils dilated. "Oh yeah?"

"You'll feel so good you'll hold still and beg for a

longer sentence." He kissed her, pulling at her bottom lip with his teeth.

She panted. "Let's go."

His bear rose up on hind legs and pawed at the air. *Mine*. "Ready for house arrest?"

FIFTEEN

AMY FLIPPED ON the coffeepot and the familiar gurgling and hissing filled the cabin, followed by the aroma of fresh drip coffee. What a night. The run-in with that creep, Evers, had set her on edge. Good thing Griff had arrived when he did. It wasn't that she couldn't take care of herself. She could. But it was nice to have someone else on her side for once. Someone big and strong.

Then, she'd gotten tipsy—something she tried not to do at strange bars. And she'd come on to Griff pretty hot and heavy and asked him back to the cabin and promptly fallen asleep in his Jeep on the drive back.

She glanced at Griff. He hadn't seemed to mind. He bent over the fireplace in the living room, building a small fire. She shivered at the sight. Spring in the mountains had proven cooler than she'd expected. Building a fire was new territory for her. Her apartment in Atlanta had a gas fireplace. Flick a switch and *boom*, insta-fire.

She'd trade the insta-fire for Griff, any day.

Though the spring days in the mountains hinted at warmth, the nights were chilly. Add in fog and the eternal dampness that seemed to permeate everything in the evenings and early mornings, and the cold rivaled that of early winter.

A warm fire in the fireplace and a cup of coffee? The perfect solution. Add in Griff? It really couldn't be any better.

He took a rolled newspaper and lit the kindling. Little twigs snapped and popped as the flames engulfed them and spread to larger twigs. Soon, the cabin would be more than warm enough.

"How do you take your coffee?" She took advantage of Griff's back being to her and raked her gaze over his ass. Twice. His fine, fine ass. Nicely rounded but not too big. Perfect in blue jeans. Her face flushed. Normally, she wasn't so brazen, but tonight she was setting records. He was right in front of her and no one was watching.

Nothing wrong with looking.

His obliviousness to his own attractiveness multiplied his appeal. Add in her mediocre sex life up to now, and she didn't stand a chance of visual celibacy. Then add the strikeout at the picnic, and she was ready for another shot.

Why even pretend? After that kiss, she was up for anything, and she'd told him as much. Her fear of being unwanted and damaged had been erased by a few weeks in his company and some beer.

"Black with a touch of honey." He turned and smiled. "If you don't have honey, I'll take a half teaspoon of sugar."

"No honey, but I've got some sugar." She pulled the canister from the cabinet.

"That'll do nicely."

She peeked at Griff while he continued to stoke the now roaring fire. The heat fanned across the small space in waves. The cabin was already getting toasty.

"That should burn for a while," Griff said. "I'm going to go wash my hands. Be right back."

She nodded and he headed for the bathroom. Her hands shook as she stirred his coffee. First, the kiss at the picnic had confused her because in all their phone conversations since the picnic, Griff hadn't mentioned it. Then, the bar incident had shaken her more than she'd let on, so him wanting to take her home had been a welcome gesture. Inviting him in for coffee felt like the natural next step, and he'd offered to make a fire—how could she resist? He might think she was inviting him in for something else, which was true, but she wasn't sure she wanted *him* to think that.

Oh yes, she did.

I wanted him to come in. I want to be with him. Even if it's for one night. I do want him.

The realization sat like a boulder in her stomach. After Darren, she had been one hundred percent sure she didn't want a man in her life, yet here she was with a crush on Griff. Or maybe it was more. That made for a terribly inconvenient situation since she'd be leaving soon.

No-strings sex sounded like a great compromise. But it wasn't all she wanted, and admitting that to herself felt weird and right at the same time. It was like looking at the truth and feeling dumb for not seeing it sooner.

She sighed.

Why did she feel so comfortable with Griff anyway? She'd only known him a few weeks. Sometimes it took that long for her to find out a guy's name, much less invite him to her home for a late-night coffee and chat. She was playing with fire and she knew it, but something kept pushing her to be around him. That something was his fine ass. She smiled. Yeah, she wanted him.

Even if he was a little overprotective. His amount of overprotectiveness was adorable.

"Pink towels?" Griff snorted and joined her at the kitchen counter. "I'd have pegged you for a yellow-towel girl."

"I left those at home. I'm in my pink phase now." She handed him his coffee mug and took her own. "Pink is so…spring—don't you think? You know, florals and sunrises."

"Uh-huh."

"No, seriously. I change colors with the season. Summer is when I break out the yellow towels. Fall, orange. White for winter, of course."

He tried to stifle a smile, but the crinkles at the corners of his eyes showed his amusement.

"You look tired."

"Long day."

The warmth of the coffee soaked through the mug and into her hands. She watched him sip his coffee—his firm jawline moving fluidly as he swallowed. Griff was so rough and tumble on the outside, but such a sweetie underneath.

She gulped at the hot coffee then winced.

Too hot.

He set his mug down. "That's excellent coffee. Thank you." A faint shadow of scruff climbed up his neck and onto his cheeks, a far cry from the beard he'd had when they first met. An improvement, for sure. It must've taken him all winter to grow that beard. No matter, she was glad he'd shaved it.

"You're welcome. It's too hot for me to drink right now."

"I like it hot."

She watched the flames pop and wriggle in the fireplace. The cabin would be warm all night from the fire. Long after Griff left. A pang ached in her as she realized she didn't want him to leave.

Maybe he'd stay. If she could get up enough nerve to ask.

Griff pushed up his sleeves. "I'm happy you rented my cabin." He turned toward her, his hazel eyes dilating as he looked at her. "Really happy. If you hadn't, we wouldn't have met. I guess what I'm trying to say is that I'm really glad I met you, Amy Francis." His voice had trailed to barely above a whisper.

She forced herself not to look away, even though the intensity of his look scared her a little. It wasn't the look of a one-night stand. How she knew that, she wasn't sure, but she knew.

Her heart pulsed in her throat. She sensed, somewhere, somehow, that her coffee cup was taken from her hands and set down on the counter. His eyes never left her own gaze, but came closer. Griff's large hands cupped her face and he stroked her cheeks with his fingertips. So soft. She closed her eyes right as her breath caught.

Yes.

Her lips barely parted as his mouth touched hers. Shivers raced through her, and she pressed her mouth against his again.

Warm. Gentle.

"I'm so glad it was you," he whispered against her

cheek. "So glad you're mine...my tenant." He ran his tongue across the seam of her lips. Once, then again.

Tingles slid up her back and she shuddered as he pulled her closer.

Another kiss. *Yes.*

She leaned forward, and he settled her tight against him, his hands holding her hips to him. His tongue slid into her mouth, warm and wet and insistent. Her thoughts swirled with each stroke of his tongue.

Bliss.

Peace.

Happiness.

He must've felt it, too, because he leaned into the kiss and sought out every bit of her mouth with his tongue. She tried to keep up with his thrusts but it felt like his tongue was everywhere. He bit her lower lip gently, pulling it, then letting it go. Then he came in for another kiss, and this time he skipped her mouth and kissed her cheek, her chin, the soft spot beneath her ear.

She floated, eyes closed. More, she wanted more. Did she say it aloud? Was she still standing? Griff's hand moved to the small of her back, keeping her on her feet as he kissed her again, more deeply this time.

His tongue slowed, moving against hers in a languid rhythm. He moved her toward the couch and her feet felt like she was sliding through the air. She tugged him to her.

She pulled away, wiping her mouth with her sleeve. "I'm sorry," she stammered. "You know I have to move soon..." She ducked her head. Maybe it was best to come right out and ask him. That was so awkward. "I'm not sure what you expect, Griff."

His green eyes almost glowed in the firelight. "It's okay, Amy. I don't expect anything."

"But the kisses—"

"Are wonderful. Can't we relax and see what happens? I'm not going to hurt you."

"It's not that." She squinted, trying to read him. "I don't want to hurt *you.* The kisses are great, fantastic even. More than that..."

"You feel it, too, don't you?" His voice had lowered a full register, and the words vibrated through the air. He brushed her hair behind her shoulder. "You do. I can tell. You feel it."

"What?" Her heart pounded. "What are you talking about?" She was afraid to hear the answer, but somehow she knew he was right. They were meant to be together. Even if she fought it, it was there. She was completely kidding herself that she was only looking for one night with Griff.

And that scared the hell out of her.

"The attraction between us. The need to be close to each other. Not merely a desire, but a *need.* Maybe for a night, but probably for longer." He pushed her against the counter and kissed her again before she could respond. This time, the insistence in his kiss was fierce, demanding. He devoured her mouth and pressed his body against hers.

She leaned in, savoring the electricity of the moment. She did feel an attraction to Griff. She wanted him. All of him, and not just a kiss.

Not once, but over and over until she couldn't stand his touch, if that could ever happen. She wasn't really being fair to him if she was hopping on him on the rebound. She needed some time to think and unfortunately, her time at the cabin was limited.

"Enough," she panted. She slid away from him. "I can't do this right now. We need to talk. I want to make sure this is the right thing for us before we go further. Let's take our coffee to the living room."

Griff laughed. "We can talk all you want, darlin'. I'm in no rush to go home. When you're ready, there's more where that kiss came from."

"Do you have to leave? I don't have anyone renting after you. Not yet." Griff stoked the fire, leaning into the heat and savoring it. Finally, he'd come to terms with how things would play out. War or no war, Amy was his and he would have her and protect her. Evers knew about her, Elijah knew, and soon the whole shifter community would know. He'd have to eventually reveal the truth, but for now, he'd protect her best by not telling her anything.

Why risk scaring her away?

"I-I don't know." Amy squirmed on the couch. "I don't know what I'm going to do."

"I'm not pressuring." He flashed her a smile. "But I'll keep the cabin available until you know."

"There's more to it than that." She twisted a strand of her hair and tucked her feet under her. "I need a job. A focus. But thanks for the offer."

He was going to have to be gentle and make sure he didn't frighten her away or let his bear scare her. He'd listened to the stories she'd told him about her ex, and tried not to flip out. She'd had some rough times but now he was there for her.

The first kiss had wiped away any doubt that she

was his mate, sending shots of pleasure straight to his heart and sealing out any doubt, but he couldn't completely get a fix on her feelings. She was his and he wasn't going to let her go, even though she kept worrying about time limits. Maybe she worried about her ex still. She wasn't as forthcoming as he'd like but he would keep trying to get her to open up.

Right now, he needed to possess her—all of her.

Mine.

"I understand." He dropped a larger log on the fire. It should burn a while.

Amy's face and neck were flushed with desire and her hair was a mess from their embrace. With the golden glow of the firelight splashed across her, she'd never looked so beautiful.

She'd stopped the kissing for now, but they'd made a connection and she felt it just like he did. That was a start.

He poked at the logs, watching the flames lick the wood. He still needed to work out the details of how to protect her from the lions. Maybe he could take her to Elijah's to wait out the upcoming war.

He almost laughed. She'd never agree, even if she knew he was a bear, and he had no idea how to tell her without scaring the shit out of her.

How to lose a girlfriend in one sentence: *I am a shapeshifting giant bear.*

That would pretty much do it.

"I can't believe how fast the two-month lease is going..." Amy picked at her jeans, her flats long discarded. "I need some *me* time. As you can see, that isn't working out so well. No offense."

Griff nodded and slid onto the couch beside her. He

understood. Having a mate was going to be a different experience for a confirmed bachelor, yet it was something that felt as natural a transition as shifting did.

Until it happened, he didn't understand it. Now he did. He thought about Amy night and day and couldn't stand being apart from her. She was smart, sexy and independent. He loved all of it and couldn't quit thinking about her. He sipped the cold dregs of his coffee.

"I understand *me* time," he said. "I've had a lot of it, living alone up here in the forest as a park ranger. I'm by myself a lot. Probably too much *me* time."

Amy picked up her mug from the coffee table and sipped the coffee. "Do you like being alone?"

"I used to, yes." He set his coffee cup onto the side table. "Lately, I've been thinking about how lonely I've really become. Soul-deep loneliness. I started to realize it when you came into my life, and I don't think that is a coincidence. A man can't live alone forever."

"Oh?" She leaned back against the armrest and put her feet up. "I'd kind of gotten the impression that you didn't want a relationship because you'd lost your family."

Griff froze. He didn't realize he was so transparent. "That has been the case, Amy." He held his head in his hands. "I didn't protect my family and they were murdered because of it."

"You were a child."

"I know. But I should have done something to protect my sister. I should have tried."

She rubbed his leg. "That's a horrible situation and you're in no way to blame."

He looked at her. "Thank you for saying that. It's a hard issue for me."

She scooted closer and took his face in her hands then kissed him on the lips. "You're amazing, Griff. Any woman would be lucky to have you."

His bear roared. She scooted back and stared into the flames and he moved her feet into his lap.

"I think if I had someone—someone who wanted me as much as I wanted her—I think even winter would be a happier time. I'd have someone to talk to and watch movies with and even get out and snowshoe or cross-country ski with."

He rubbed the soles of her feet, working his way to her toes.

"Mmmm. That feels amazing." Amy sighed. "Yeah, my boyfriends have all been losers. Drawn to an artist, but with no fire in their own bellies. No one I could ever commit to spending a lifetime with."

So she'd had boyfriends, plural, not just dates. Griff scowled. The fire popped and sent a small shower of sparks onto the hearth.

"That tickles!" Amy pulled her feet away and tucked her legs under her. "My feet are too sensitive."

"Sorry." *Boyfriends. Grrr.* But he didn't want to be a boyfriend. He was her mate.

"Tell me what you like in a woman, Griff. What do you look for? Ideally." She peeked at him.

"Why do you ask?" He gave her his sternest look. "Interested in applying for the position?"

She responded with a pillow to his face.

"Oooof." He grabbed at the pillow, intent on whacking her back, but she held on.

"Oh, no you don't!" She laughed and hit him again, this time on the knees.

He swiped at the pillow, missing again. She jumped

up, holding it in front of her, taunting him. He reached for her, tackled her around the waist and pushed her down onto the couch. She giggled and he held her tighter.

"Let me go." She laughed, trying to hit him in the head with the pillow. "Now. You aren't playing fair."

"Anything's fair. I don't recall setting any rules." He snatched the pillow and threw it across the room. "No more pillows."

"But—"

"No more." He stretched out beside her, one arm around her waist, his body pressed against hers from chest to knees. "Just me and you now. Doesn't that feel better?"

She yawned. "Yeah. It does. I'm glad we got out of that bar. This is much more my style."

"Mine, too."

He listened to the crackling and popping of the fire. He laid his head on her soft chest and she ran her fingers through his hair. Her heart pounded and he closed his eyes to listen. If every moment with her could be so special, he'd convince her to be his mate in half a heartbeat.

"You didn't answer me," she whispered. Her fingers caressed his ear.

"What?" He snuggled closer, feeling the fire's warmth across his back. He was about as close to heaven as he ever expected on earth. Who knew that snuggling one's mate in front of a warm fire could feel so damn amazing? The events from earlier in the night faded fast. Elijah was speeding up preparations, Evers was nowhere near and Griff was spooning with his mate.

Life was good.

"What do you look for in a woman?" Her fingers stilled and he was sure he heard her heart skip a beat.

"I look for someone like you."

"No, seriously..."

"Seriously."

"I'll bet you say that to all the girls."

"There aren't any other girls. I've never really had time to include girls in my life. Besides, I prefer women." He ran his hand up the rear of her shirt, trailing his hand across the soft skin of her back.

"No one else, come on..." She squinted at him.

"Not in a long time. And never anyone important." He fiddled with her bra clasp.

His bear growled with impatience, pacing. More than lust, more than desire, the bear needed to claim its mate.

Needed Amy.

But Griff had to make sure Amy wanted him, too, and the thought scared the hell out of him. And he could not claim her until she knew everything.

"Oh, you're just saying that."

"I've never said it to anyone." He held her at arm's length, every cell in his body quivering in anticipation at the next words. "You are the woman for me, Amy Francis. My heart has known it since I first met you. Let me prove it to you. Besides, I think we've talked long enough."

THE KISSES CAME hard and fast. Griff planted them on her shoulder, her collarbone, her neck. Amy, dizzy with desire, lay back on the couch.

"That feels so good." She closed her eyes. If this never stopped, she'd be the happiest woman on earth.

"We're just getting started." He held himself over her and kissed her again, slowly.

His response was perfectly in time with hers and he slid his hand over her breasts, gently squeezing them, then tugging off her bra. She moaned. When his mouth met her nipple, she arched her body toward him, her mouth half-open. If she could capture this moment in time, she'd revisit it daily till the day she died. She'd never had such sensual sex.

He sat back and trailed a fingertip down her stomach, the featherlight touches leaving a row of goose bumps in their wake.

She opened her eyes, heavy-lidded. "Why did you stop kissing me?"

"Oh, I'm not done. Just taking a second to look at you. You're so beautiful."

She shook her head.

He took her chin and tipped it up. Leaning over her, he said, "You're exactly what I want in a woman. Beautiful inside and out."

"That's so sweet." She looked away.

He ran his fingers down to the waistband of her jeans and tugged. "Are you sure you want this? Sure you want me?" He peered down at her, his finger poised over the button.

She nodded, her eyes half-closed. Right now, there was nothing she wanted more. She'd worry about repercussions tomorrow. If she didn't die from pleasure while having sex.

Griff bent and kissed her belly button and she giggled. He undid her jeans and pulled them off with a flourish. She shivered and crossed her arms over her chest.

Lying on the couch in only her underwear, she looked down to make sure she had on her pretty panties. *Yep.* Red lace. *Granny panties could've been embarrassing.* How awesome would it be to have a lover who didn't judge you on what kind of panties you wore? Griff might be that guy, but for tonight, she was happy she had the red lace.

He pulled the quilt down off the back of the couch and covered her up to her neck then stood. "Hold on a second."

It's getting hotter by the moment. She held out her hands. "Come back."

He pulled his T-shirt off and tossed it on the chair, and she drank in the sight of him. His chest, broad at the top with a smattering of hair in the middle, looked like it belonged to a model from a menswear catalog. Not a gym rat and not a scarecrow, but a just right in-between.

He took his wallet out of his pocket and pulled out a packet and set it on the table. Then he removed the rest of his clothing as she watched. Good thing she didn't have a bucket of popcorn or she would've choked. Griff wasn't a man ashamed of his body. If anything, he didn't realize how attractive he was, but he wasn't shy.

The firelight painted him in hues of gold and orange and his back muscles gleamed in the glowing light. He was turned so she couldn't see his front completely, just occasional glimpses of hair on his stomach. In the half darkness, the situation almost felt like a dream.

A really awesome dream where he was slow dancing and stripping for her alone.

And he was.

She noticed a set of silver scars, parallel and curved, across his shoulder blade. Three lines, like furrows or eyelashes, but about four inches long. Maybe an animal scratch. The only mark on otherwise unblemished skin.

"Close your eyes, Amy. Relax. Let me feel you. You can trust me."

An overwhelming sense of warmth came over her and it wasn't from his touch. Yes, yes she could trust this man.

Completely.

She closed her eyes and almost immediately felt the quilt yanked away and his hand slid up her leg to her pussy. She let her knees fall open a little, though she shivered from his light touch.

"That's it," he whispered. "Keep your eyes closed."

He stroked the inside of her thighs, then rubbed with his thumb, and she pushed against his hand, hoping he'd move to her more sensitive areas. His touch sent her nerve endings into a frenzy of pleasure.

"There's no rush." His breath was hot against her bare legs.

He slid off her panties. She smiled.

"I said keep your eyes closed and just feel," he said. "No peeking. No thinking. No second-guessing."

"Okay. I'm trying." She lay back and concentrated on not moving, though her legs shook slightly under his touch.

"That feel okay?" He trailed a finger into her wetness.

She nodded, aware that her hips thrust forward of their own accord at his touch.

He pushed his fingers in, slowly, his other hand massaging her clit, and she tensed, clenching her hands.

"Are you okay?" He stopped moving. "Do you want me to stop?"

"I'm trying to relax. Nothing is wrong. Just go slow."

"You got it. Nothing I'd like better."

He stroked and rubbed with both hands, lightly then more firmly as she moved against his fingers.

She focused on his touch. He wasn't Darren. He wasn't going to take her emotions and stomp on them with no regard to her own feelings. Griff cared about her.

"You okay? Tell me what I can do."

"Feels so good."

Griff took his time and was making sure she enjoyed their lovemaking. He wasn't selfish.

"Please don't stop."

He rubbed and massaged until she squirmed and her thighs were wet with arousal. He moved against her, but was in no hurry to actually enter her.

She reached for him, trying to return the pleasure, but he batted her hand away.

"Time for that later." His chest was red with the flush of desire.

"Promise?" was all she could get out.

"Oh, I promise." He pushed his erection against her leg.

She moaned under his ministrations and her pleasure deepened.

When was he going to fuck her? She was sure she had asked him to at least three times but he hadn't answered. He finally tried slipping a finger inside her again, and this time she didn't tense. She gripped the couch cushions and moaned. She needed more and now.

"Please." Her voice sounded foreign to her, strained. "I can't wait any longer."

"I'm not going to make you wait." He gently pulled his hand away.

"What're you doing?" She lifted her head to see.

She heard the rip of foil. She hadn't been on the pill since Darren, so a condom was a wise idea.

"Oh." She laid her head back on the couch and waited.

"Ready?" He crouched over her in the darkness.

"I've been ready. For a while." She giggled, nervous energy dancing in her stomach. "I think that's obvious. I want to feel you inside me, Griff."

He lay on top of her, moving her legs apart as he did. She was so wet, he entered without any resistance. She met his thrusts immediately. He felt so right, so perfect.

With his weight on her she couldn't move much, but she rocked up toward him as much as she could, trying to feel him everywhere at once. He held himself off her and she pulled him back onto her. She wanted to feel the weight of him.

She peeked at him and he smiled. The heat of the fire plus their exertion caused them to sweat and their bodies to slip as they moved against each other. He pushed her hair out of her face and stared down at her as he moved inside her, each thrust sending shocks of desire through her. Soon, she couldn't tell where one thrust ended and the next began. He moved faster, and his smile turned to an intense gaze as he took her, though she could barely see him in the darkness. She tried to keep her eyes open as the pleasure of his thrusts took over, but they closed on their own and she focused on the rhythm of his movement.

When he bent and kissed her, warmth bloomed in her pussy and her climax hit her fast and hard. Somewhere, seemingly far in the distance, yet maybe from inside her, she heard Griff moan as he came.

Once wasn't going to be enough with Griff. Not physically and not emotionally. She'd never had such a fantastic lover. So caring and thoughtful. Her crush was becoming more and she wasn't even going to try and fight it.

Not tonight anyway.

SIXTEEN

What in the fucking hell?

Griff sat up, his limbs stiff and sore and his back like a twisted Slinky. *Where am I?* He stretched his arms above his head and looked around. He'd slipped on his T-shirt and sweatpants from the Jeep. He was on his couch.

Correction. The couch in his old cabin. The cabin Amy rented. He rubbed his eyes. Yep, he was in his old cabin.

His family's cabin.

Damn! He'd fallen asleep after sex. That was bad. He should've talked to Amy more. Made her feel as special as she was. Yeah, he was tired for weeks after hibernation, but how could he fall asleep with his mate in his arms?

His mate. Oh god, he'd made love to his mate.

It was more wonderful than he'd ever imagined. So much better than purely physical sex. With his mate, there was a bond that only the two of them could share. Sex between mates was better than regular sex.

Now he knew.

And he was going to have to tell Amy everything.

Elijah was going to laugh his ass off. Then, he was going to have to help Griff come up with a plan to protect her.

Oh gods, he was going to have to tell her about his bear.

They weren't bond-mated, he knew that. He hadn't performed the bite that sealed their souls together. He'd had sex before, but of course that wasn't with his mate. Still, he hadn't felt any magical stuff happening, other than the normal orgasm. No strands of energy meshing, as his mated friends had mentioned. Good thing, as he hadn't discussed it with Amy yet.

He hoped she would agree to be his mate. Forever.

He'd fallen asleep right after sex. Not his best romantic move. Hopefully, he was worried over nothing.

Where was Amy? She wasn't on the couch with him. *Dammit!*

He finally decided he wanted a mate, even in dangerous times and with Evers lurking about, and he might have seemed to minimize how he felt by falling asleep. He'd talk to her and clear it up immediately.

That meant they could have makeup sex.

Sort of.

He scanned the main room of the cabin, then stood and tugged his sagging sweatpants up on his waist. Well, he'd gotten dressed, so maybe he hadn't fallen asleep immediately. He scratched his head and yawned. No fire left—only ashes with a few orange coals winking from the fireplace. Coffee cups sat on the kitchen counter with a few other dirty dishes, and the kitchen chairs sat in disarray.

Maybe Amy was asleep in her bedroom. Not like the couch was roomy enough for both of them. Sex was one thing, a sound night's sleep quite another. He crept down the short hallway and stood outside her door, hand on the doorknob.

Dare he? *Hell, yeah.*

This was his cabin, his bed and his Goldilocks.

He pushed the door open slowly and peered inside. The room was dark, with only a sliver of light coming in from the crack in the curtains, so he crept to the bed. *Wonder if she wears clothes when she sleeps?* His dick hardened remembering her soft, bare pussy against his fingers. *Mmmm.* He couldn't wait to explore more. He ran his hand over the bed, the cool sheets soft under his hand and...no Amy.

Where the hell was she? He flicked on the overhead light. The bed had possibly been slept in, as it wasn't made, but she wasn't in it now. A silky peach-colored nightgown lay on the pillow, and he grabbed it and smelled it. Sweet, floral...and female.

Mine. The thought resonated deep in his bones.

If things had gone well, he could've been cuddled up to that silky nightgown covering his mate. Now, he had to find her. He'd only begun to show her how many ways he could love her.

Oh my gods.

I love her.

Hurry.

He rushed out to the hallway and knocked on the bathroom door. No answer, so he opened the door. No Amy.

Where the hell was she?

He headed for the kitchen, running scenarios in his mind and sending his stomach into fits. What if Evers had snuck in and kidnapped her? His bear growled and reared up inside, pawing at the air and ready to rip Evers to shreds. He'd kill him if he hurt Amy. What were the odds Evers had shown up and taken Amy while he slept?

Griff shook his head. He'd have heard the commotion and Amy would've called out for him. There were no signs of forced entry.

No.

He spied a piece of pink paper on the counter beside the coffee cups. She'd left a note. He snatched it up.

Griff,

Didn't want to wake you. Such a beautiful morning! I'm going to Rocky Knob to sketch. Don't worry, I'll stay at the overlook. I need some time to think about what happened last night. You're probably feeling the same way.

You go on home when you get this note and we can talk later, okay?

xo

Amy

Griff crumpled the paper then banged the counter with his fist.

She'd gone out alone into the mountains. Why didn't she listen? This was bad. If she ran into Evers, she might not escape this time. Now that Evers knew she was Griff's, he'd be out for blood.

Griff growled and ran his hand through his hair. He had to get to her before Evers. He needed backup. If the Sen Pal were out in the forest, who knew how many lions he'd face?

He dropped the paper onto the counter.

He pulled out his cell. Barely a charge. *Great.* He dialed.

"Powell? It's Griff." He struggled to hold it together. If Evers put one finger on Amy…

"Yeah, man, what's going on? Where've you been? Elijah was looking for you last night."

Griff knew Powell would alert every den member within fifty miles. "Busy. No time for small talk. I need your help. I'm sure Elijah filled you in on what happened with Evers, the Sen Pal Enforcer."

"Yeah, he called me."

"Today, Evers is after my mate. We have to go after them, now."

"Shit! Where?"

"She went up to Rocky Knob. Evers is probably tracking her. Can you grab some guys and meet me?"

"Of course. I'll let Elijah know, too. Do you think the Sen Pal are attacking?"

"I've not seen any signs that this is anything other than Evers." Griff gripped the phone. "Marco and Mason were prowling around, but they didn't bother me and Amy. I'm guessing they were hunting Evers. After thinking about all this, I think he's gone rogue. I'll bet Maximillian sent them to find him. There may be other lions out searching for him, too, so let everyone know. I don't think they are on offense yet, or the twins wouldn't have run."

"Okay. I'll get a few bears and meet you up there as quickly as I can."

"Hurry. She won't stand a chance if he catches her."

"We'll be there. You go. Be careful. He's a nasty lion."

"That asshole is dead meat." Griff clicked to end the call and stared at the time. One o'clock. No longer morning, and definitely after lunch. Amy was in trouble—he felt it.

He had to get to her.

He stripped off his clothing—he'd make better time as a bear. He headed out onto the porch and noticed the dark clouds over the mountains. Rain beat against the ground and puddles had already formed in the indentations in the yard. Spring weather changed quickly.

When Amy had left, the weather must've been good and she obviously hadn't checked the forecast. He closed the front door and stood on the porch looking out toward the peak called Rocky Knob.

The rain was going to make things much harder, especially if the clouds were low-hanging and covering the mountains with fog. His bear screamed for release.

Mate. Needs me.

Hold on, boy. We'll take the Jeep, then you can run.

AMY SCOWLED AT the mess around her car. Her emergency blinkers flashed in time with the rain beating against her windshield. She'd turned off the radio a few minutes ago so she could think. She was stuck and she wasn't sure what to do.

Why couldn't sketching be a simple, no-risk thing? Even Griff couldn't have predicted a rockslide. She was following his requests—she wasn't out in the woods alone. She was in her car sitting in the middle of the road. She sighed and leaned her head back on the headrest.

She'd decided to give her and Griff's relationship a real chance.

The sun was shining when she left. She'd gotten a few sketches done at the overlook, then was packing up to head home when the rain started. By the time she got to her car, everything was soaked. She'd pulled out of the overlook parking lot and onto the road and was headed home and that's when hell had broken loose.

At least that's what it felt like when part of the mountain slid down. At first, several boulders bounced down and landed on the road in front of her, blocking her way, then a loud rumbling started. It shook the car and she'd looked up in time to see the mud and rocks coming down the face of the mountain beside the road and straight for her car.

She'd thought she was going to die. She covered her head and ducked down as the rocks pelted her roof and the mud oozed down around her tires. Thankfully, no large rocks hit the car and the slide ended with her stuck, but alive.

She gripped the steering wheel. The car wasn't going anywhere now.

The car was a clunker anyway. What were a few more dents and scratches? She'd laugh if she were back at the cabin warm and dry, but right now it wasn't very funny.

She'd figured if she sat in the car and waited, someone would happen by. It was a national forest, and tourists visited all the time. So far, no luck. She stared out the side window into the rainy landscape.

She'd had plenty of time to think about how her relationship with Griff had progressed. The way he touched her. Kissed her. The way they'd fit together so perfectly. The fact he would talk to her about his feelings and ask her about hers. He seemed too good to be true.

If he would have her, she'd be his girlfriend in a heartbeat.

She didn't want to get hurt or hurt him, and she'd only be in the mountains a little while longer. He knew that. She couldn't stay in the tiny town—what kind of job would she be able to do? Without money, she wouldn't have food or be able to pay rent.

No, it wasn't practical to stay in the area.

It had been almost an hour and no one had ventured up the mountain road to save her. Of course, one direction was blocked by the slide. Maybe there were other slides, too. Or maybe they'd even closed the park because of the weather.

She was going to have to get out of the mess herself. Then she'd have to listen to Griff complaining about her going out alone again. Who knew that just driving down the road could be hazardous? Normally, it wasn't. It was like the mountains were cursed or something. Like someone didn't want her here.

"Shit." She tapped her cell phone again. No signal and almost no charge left. She slipped the phone into her pocket. That was one thing she'd be glad to get back to when she returned to Atlanta. Consistent cell service.

That, and good sushi.

She tried to push open the driver's door, but it wouldn't budge. She peered out the window. A medium-sized rock blocked the bottom of the door. It had fallen in such a way that it wedged itself between the ground and the door. No way the door was opening. She crawled over and looked out the passenger-side window.

Mud had oozed down the mountainside like a slow-motion waterfall, and she wouldn't be surprised if it was most of the way up her tires. Who knew mudslides could get so bad, so fast? She knew the spring rains caused a lot of slides, but this was a significant pile of rocks and mud.

As if to punctuate her predicament, the rain picked up and beat on the car roof harder.

She laid her head against the seat. Griff had jinxed the mountains. He'd been the one to keep pointing out the dangers. Why hadn't she listened?

Because he's not always right. She frowned.

What he'd done to her last night certainly felt right. His touch, so gentle for such a large man, had awoken nerves in her she hadn't realized she had. The way he looked into her eyes—like she was the only woman on earth—had intensified her pleasure.

She sighed. Maybe she should give him a chance. Even if it was only for a couple weeks, as long as she knew that going in, and he knew it, too, what was the harm in a little fling? Sex relieved stress, right? And stress relief was one reason she had taken this vacation in the first place. But he didn't seem likely to agree to a temporary arrangement. She gripped the wheel.

Dammit, Amy. She laid her head on the steering wheel. Now was not the time to think about Griff Martin and sex. She had a bigger problem.

Right now she needed to get back to the cabin.

Whether she'd be spending the night in Griff's arms didn't matter now. She'd waited in the car long enough—she didn't want to be stuck on the side of the mountain at night. Not with lions and bears roaming the woods. Who knew what else? With more rain pelting the ground, the mudslide could worsen and cause more rocks to fall. She didn't want to be in the car if that happened.

She scooted back to the passenger side and unlatched the door. When she tried the handle it didn't move at first, then slowly, there… The door creaked open, and the sound of the pouring rain filled the car. The smell of wet dirt quickly permeated the air and she wrinkled her nose. The mud right outside the car looked to be at least eight inches deep, coming up nearly to the side of the door opening. If she stepped out, it'd come well over her ankles.

"Yuck." She tugged the door closed and backed into the driver's seat. What could she do? Not many choices and all but one would include her getting wet. She wasn't staying in the car. Maybe if she climbed onto the car roof, she could see a way to get out without tromping through so much mud. She'd get soaking wet, but wet was better than wet and muddy. She paused. Not really much of a choice. She didn't want to sit in the car any longer, waiting on someone to come rescue her.

She rolled down the driver's window and pulled herself out. The roof was slippery and she struggled to climb on top of the car. She'd worn sneakers—at least they gave her a bit of traction. The dented roof bowed under her weight yet felt stable. She peered around, but with the heavy rain and foggy mist, visibility was terrible.

Rain pelted her as she slid in the muddy clumps that had landed on top of the car. She pushed her wet hair out of her face and sat, her jeans soaked and dirty. On one side of the car, the mountain rose above the road, a chunk of the incline missing where it had fallen away and down onto the roadway and Amy's car.

The spring thaw had likely made the loose dirt unstable, and the rain had helped push everything downhill. Bits of snow and ice thawed in the mud, and a huge boulder blocked the road down the mountain.

"Good thing that rock didn't hit the car." She wiped the rain out of her eyes. Not a creature in sight.

"Yes, you are one lucky lady."

She whipped her head around. Standing on the opposite side of the road was Evers. Dressed in blue jeans and a black shirt, he looked the bad guy part, only rain-soaked. *Damn imagination.*

Her heart thudded and her mouth went dry. *Shit.* This was bad. Why couldn't it have been Griff who found her? Why was Evers on the side of the mountain, standing in the rain and smiling at her like the cat who ate the canary? What were the odds?

"What are you doing up here?" She wiped her hands on her jeans. "In the rain? Not a great day to be out."

"Same as you, I suppose. Sightseeing. Look at the sight I found!" He stuck his hands in his pockets and grinned. "I hoped I'd run into you again, Amy. I didn't think it would be so soon, but I'm happy to see you. How about you? Are you happy to see me?"

"Where's your car?" She backed to the edge of the roof. Something about this was wrong. Very wrong.

He shrugged. "Don't have one with me." *Don't need one. You know that.*

Lightning flashed followed by a long roll of thunder that echoed off the cliffs. The rain, already assaulting and cold, seemed to get even colder in the wake of Evers's words. Amy shivered, soaked. Her T-shirt stuck to her and she rubbed her arms.

She didn't take her gaze off Evers. She didn't trust him one bit. Some guys joked around about forcing their way. Some meant it. She didn't doubt Evers's intent for one minute.

Griff, where are you?

"Are you going to call the sheriff for me?" she asked. Her teeth chattered. "And a tow truck? I need help."

"Nope." He toed his boot at the ground. *Griff isn't coming. But I'm here.*

She pondered his words. Was he really speaking in her mind or was that her imagination, too? Was she making up his conversation? Her heart hammered and she shook, her teeth chattering. The cold was getting to her, or maybe it was her fear, or maybe both. "Who then? I can't get my car out of this mess."

"I can handle this, beautiful." He took a step toward the car then backed away from the mud, shaking his boot. In the pouring rain, he almost looked like an apparition. A dark one. "Do you doubt my ability to help you? You know I want to help you."

"But..." Why wouldn't he call the police? Or a tow truck?

"If you'll remember, we didn't get a chance to finish what we started last night." He paused. "Now, we can. Without interruption. No one else is here to bother us or stop us. A little rain never hurt anyone."

Fear rose in her throat and she scrambled on the car hood, almost sliding off onto the muddy ground. "No. Get away from me."

"I don't think you're in a position to have much say in the matter."

She pulled out her phone again. *Please work.* No signal. She stuck it into her pocket. What did she have in the car that she could use as a weapon? *Nothing.* Dammit, she had a tire iron in the trunk, but the keys were in the ignition.

Your phone won't work out here. "I'm coming for you, beautiful." Evers paced the edge of the mud, stooping to pick up a branch, then poking it into the mud to gauge depth. "Soon, you'll be coming for me. If you catch my drift." He laughed. "I know you want me. You're just too prim and proper to admit it. I've known a lot of girls like you. A whole lot of girls."

"I'll never be with you! Never!" Fear intertwined with rage and she was suddenly warm. She knew what she had to do. She had to get to the tire iron, and quickly.

"Griff doesn't like anyone touching his girl, does he?" Evers circled the rockslide area. "I didn't know he had a girl, but now that I do, well, I can't tell you how happy that makes me." He yelled the last part, as the low rumble of thunder shook the air. "Not that he knows what's happening here, after I paid him a visit."

She ignored him and slid off the car into the mud. She'd run all the way down the mountain if she had to. So what if she got muddy? That no longer mattered. She'd get away from this creep. The mud came up over her ankles, and was cold and wet and heavy on her feet. She lifted her foot. Yes, she could move. She reached inside the car and grabbed her keys, then hurried to the trunk.

Evers headed for her, stepping around some of the

rocks that had bounced far out onto the road. *I'm coming, Amy.* He'd still have to go through the mud to reach her. She fumbled with the wet keys then popped the trunk. Where was that stupid tire iron? She'd seen it when she packed the car in Atlanta.

She dug around, pushing aside a bottle of antifreeze and a couple dirty rags. The trunk was pretty much empty, but the tool had to be in the compartment somewhere. Lightning lit the inside of the trunk then a clap of thunder followed. The storm was close.

Where was the damn tire iron? Evers grinned. She dug in again; this time she found it, under the rags. She grabbed the cold length of metal and pulled it out, then leaned against the car and held up the tool, her hands shaking. Unsure of how menacing she looked, she'd not hesitate to use the weapon if Evers pushed her. She'd told Griff she could take care of herself, and she'd meant it.

I am woman; hear me roar.

The whole situation would be funny if it weren't so real. She'd rather be schooled in guns or something but she'd have to rely on her self-defense classes. Weird how she'd never felt she needed one in the city, but then she was out in the woods and suddenly her life was in danger almost every day. Who would've thought that was possible?

"Oh, no you don't." Evers slogged through the mud toward her. "You won't hit me, beautiful." *You'd better not hit me, bitch. You'd better not even try.*

"Watch me." She brandished the tire iron over her head. "Don't come any closer."

Before she had the chance to swing, Evers was on her, pulling the weapon out of her mud-slicked hands and knocking them both to the ground. The mud filled her mouth and she spat and struggled to get Evers off her.

He lay on top of her, heavy for his compact size, and so strong. She couldn't move. She felt his breath on her face, mixed with the rain. *You like that, don't you?*

"You won't be needing this." He held the tire iron up and tossed it away.

It clanged against a rock when it landed. Tears filled her eyes and she hammered Evers with her fists.

"Leave me alone!"

"You're coming with me. Stop fighting it." *You can't win.*

He yanked her upright, holding her wrists, and dragged her away from the car. She slipped, scraping her knees on the rocks in the mud.

"You're hurting me." She winced and he pulled harder.

"That's what you'll get and more, if you don't cooperate. Now stand up and come on." He grabbed the tire iron off the ground. "Don't make me use this."

Thunder boomed in the distance and the rain slammed against the ground in sheets. She couldn't help the tears that fell. At least Evers wouldn't get the satisfaction of knowing the difference between her tears and the rain.

"Griff isn't coming to get you, I'm sure of that." Evers yanked her. "Or should I say, I *made* sure of that."

No. He wasn't going to win. She struggled to escape, and slipped out of his muddy hands. *Go!* She made it to the grass, but sharp pain behind her knees had her rolling on the ground. My god, he'd actually hit her with the tire iron. *Griff, help me!* Tears flowed freely now and she stared up at the rainy sky, pain radiating from her calves.

Evers stood over her, tire iron in hand. "The next blow will be to your pretty head if you don't cooperate, got it?"

She nodded, curling into a fetal position. Muddy tears stung her eyes. If only she'd listened to Griff. She could still be at the cabin in his arms. Maybe in her bed. Why did she always screw things up?

Evers raised the tire iron. "Get up. You're coming with me now, or I'll use this again."

A series of loud growls filled the air, and Evers turned. A grimace crossed his face and he dropped the tire iron. He began peeling off his wet clothing.

"Oh no," she whimpered. "No..."

Naked, his back to her, he roared. His body contorted and bulged like something else was inside it, trying to get out.

What the hell?

She sat up, her legs aching from the blow. She held her head, dizzy from pain.

Where Evers had been just a moment ago stood a golden mountain lion, mouth open and panting. Behind him, several large brown bears paced.

She screamed.

GRIFF SNORTED AS Amy's scream pierced his bear heart. He would fucking kill the lion for hurting her. He motioned to the other bears with his nose. They circled in on the mountain lion, trying to cut off any path of escape. They'd left their vehicles in the road and shifted as soon as they came upon the rockslide.

Evers. His gut had been right. Evers had gone after Amy.

He could smell her pain.

Her fear.

His mate was injured. His bear roared and white-hot anger gushed through him as he gnashed his teeth. The rain slid off his fur and dripped onto the ground. He nodded to his friends. There would be no leniency.

Get him.

Griff wanted to run to Amy, make sure she was okay, but first they had to deal with Evers. Plus, she didn't know the whole situation and he didn't know how she'd respond to being charged by a huge brown bear, no matter how gently he tried to approach her. This wasn't how he'd hoped to tell her the news that he was a shifter.

Things were going to change and he'd tell her as soon as she was safe.

He let out another growl and the other four bears replied with grunts. Evers didn't have a chance. No other lions were in sight, and Griff figured that Evers was alone. He didn't scent Marco and Mason, or any other lion, but the rain could be interfering.

Griff loped toward the lion, enjoying the click of his thick claws on the wet ground. He'd slice Evers to bits. Watch him bleed out. Enjoy making him suffer.

Out of the corner of his eye, he saw the others flank the cat so he couldn't escape. They knew to let Griff be the one to take out the lion.

He growled again, this time from deep in his gut. No one hurt his mate. No one.

For a brief moment, he locked gazes with Amy. Covered in mud, she held her hand over her open mouth. Fear contorted her face, and her tears mixed with rain. A flash of what might be recognition crossed her gaze. Was that possible? Maybe, since she was his mate, but impossible to tell right now. Stranger things had happened.

The lion hissed and leapt onto the roof of Amy's car, his tail swishing as he paced, and his claws scratching against the metal roof. Griff dashed to the car and reared up on hind legs, pawing at the air with his claws. He wanted to see fear in Evers. As a bear, he was at least three times Evers's size. The lion responded with a snarl and a crouch.

Griff wasn't afraid. He didn't feel the rocks underfoot or the rain or the mud. He wasn't cold. All he felt was rage. Rage that Evers had dared touch his mate.

Was the whole Sen Pal pride in the forest and on their way to help Evers?

Damn, I hope not.

Five bears, no matter how big, would be no match for a pride of lions. Griff scanned the area and took a whiff of the rainy air. Still no other lions in sight or scent. Only Evers stood before him, and his fear smelled like rotten wine. Pungent and ripe. Griff slammed his paw down onto the car, rattling it. Evers leapt to the boulder jutting from the side of the road and tried to scramble up the muddy embankment where the slide had come from.

The bears closed in behind Griff in a wide arc. He heard their panting. They wanted justice, too. They knew what the lions were capable of. Some of them had mates of their own, and they would do the same thing if someone threatened.

He paused and looked back to Amy. She stood, eyes wide. Then she ran toward the embankment.

Dammit! Why was she running the same direction as Evers? Had she not seen him? Realization flowed over him. She was running from the bears.

She needed to get back down. If the Sen Pal were in the woods, they'd scent her before she got very far and they'd be on her in minutes. He growled his displeasure. If only he could yell at her, he would. He couldn't shift now. He had business to take care of.

The mountain lion roared and then scampered to a small ledge on the embankment. Pebbles and small clumps of muddy grass tumbled down in his wake. The rain came in sheets now, and a clap of thunder echoed off the mountainside. Lightning lit the scene in a blue flash. Suddenly, the earth below Griff's feet trembled.

Oh shit! Another slide!

The other bears moved as quickly as Griff did, but Evers was halfway up the rocky face and Amy was near the embankment. Griff watched as the mud and rocks began to fall down from the mountain above. The whole mountainside appeared to shake.

He backed away to avoid the brunt of the slide. How would he get to Amy? She was limping and going in the wrong direction. Away from him. She didn't know the bears were friendly. She was scared and choosing one lion over five bears. The bears paced. They didn't know what to do.

He looked back to the ledge. Evers had shifted to human form.

Dammit.

The rocks fell faster and more frequently now, bouncing down the side of the mountain. Amy was on the ground, arms covering her head, and Evers was making his way toward her, half sliding through the mud, his naked body already half-covered.

No! Amy!

He couldn't allow Evers to take her. Griff ran around the side of the car and tried to find a place to climb the slope. His friends were at his heels, but none of them could get close enough to help. Rocks rolled, landing on the car and all around it and the muddy clumps of earth followed.

The ledge above Evers and Amy gave way and started tumbling down the embankment right as Evers pulled her away and into the forest. Griff couldn't follow with the rocks pounding down on them. A second later, half the hillside came tumbling down in a massive slide, burying Amy's car up to the door handles in rock and mud.

Griff's heart thumped. Evers had taken Amy into the forest.

Oh, gods!

SEVENTEEN

"LET'S GO." EVERS pulled Amy's arm.

Amy tried to move but her legs ached from the whack across her calves. *Bastard.* If she could reach his hair she'd give him a yank, or better yet, a punch in the naked nuts. He held her arm tight and tugged her along.

A few pebbles showered onto her back and she leaned on him for stability. He hurried them farther away. The rockslide had barely missed them, and now Evers was taking her deeper into the woods. She might not ever come out. She was afraid to disobey him. Where was Griff? *I need you, Griff. Where are you?*

"Griff isn't coming for you."

"How do you know?" She winced as she took a step. "He'll come looking for me. I know he will."

"Because I killed him. Broke into the cabin and shot him in the head while he slept. Then I came for you."

"No!" *No.* That wasn't possible. She'd felt Griff's presence at the car, somehow. He wasn't dead. "You're lying."

He tightened his grip. "Let's move."

"What are you going to do with me?" Fear tried to take over and she fought it with every breath. If she was afraid, she might lose any chance that came for her to escape.

"You'll find out soon enough. Now hurry up before the bears catch us." He shoved her forward. "Unless you want to be eaten by bears?"

What was it with all the bears? More wild animals around than in the zoo and they all seemed to gather around her. What had happened to Evers back there? Had he turned into a...lion? That wasn't possible. People didn't turn into animals. She was hallucinating.

The only thing she knew was true was that there was a lion and a bunch of bears and no Griff. And Evers was naked. *Ugh.*

"Where are we going?" she asked. "My legs hurt. I can't walk far."

"Don't worry about it." Evers limped a bit. "You shouldn't have tried to run, beautiful. Just keep moving." He groaned as he tried to walk, almost falling.

"What happened to your foot?"

He shoved her forward again. "A rock. It's fine. Don't act like you care because I know you don't."

"Fine." She limped through the tall grass and wet leaves in the deep forest. Here, the rain was quieter. More like background noise. Her head spun. Her right leg was definitely swelling. She dragged it as they walked.

They'd walked for maybe fifteen minutes in silence when Amy's leg throbbed so painfully she collapsed onto the ground.

"Get up." Evers stood over her.

"I can't. My leg."

He kicked her leg. "That one?"

She doubled over, tears streaming down her face. "Oh my god," she cried. "Why are you so mean?"

"You're the one that didn't want anything to do with

me. Remember? I was going to do something for you, but you didn't want me."

"I didn't do anything to you."

Evers scowled and held his foot off the ground. "You're Griff's girl. Once I found that out, that's enough of a reason to hate you."

"What did Griff ever do to you? He's one of the nicest guys I've ever met. He wouldn't hurt me."

Evers shook his head. "He's got you fooled. He's a killer."

"Griff would never kill anyone." Amy rubbed her leg. "You're insane."

Evers sat on the ground beside her. He cringed as he positioned his foot. If only she could run, she might be able to escape. Her leg was hurting probably as much as his foot was, if not more. Too bad they couldn't have found some sort of shelter from the weather before collapsing.

"He killed my parents." Evers picked at a wet leaf. "A long time ago. I haven't forgotten. I made a promise that day that I'd hunt him down and take something he loved away if possible. Or just kill him if not." He shrugged. "So, guess what? You're it."

"No." She flinched. "He didn't kill your parents. He was out in the woods when the car wrecked. Your mother was already dead and your father was dying."

"He told you that?" Evers scowled.

"Yes. He wanted to tell you what happened that day, but you've never given him the chance."

Lightning lit up the forest. The rain had lessened, but still came down at a steady rate. Amy trembled in the chill. Springtime wasn't feeling much like spring.

Evers fisted his hands. "Griff lied to you and you

believe him. I don't know why everyone takes his word. He killed my parents. He'll pay for it. You'll pay for it, too."

"I thought you said you already killed him?" Amy smirked and tried not to look at him.

The punch came quickly and Amy felt her nose crack then blackness descended over her vision.

THE RAIN SLAMMED into his back and head with relentless precision, and Griff was certain it was trying to stop him from getting to Amy, but he didn't care. He ran. He'd find her.

His mate.

If the lion pride found her before he did—he couldn't think about that. His stomach clenched. It was bad enough she was with Evers, but if the rest of the Sen Pal was waiting on him to bring her to them, he might never see her again. He and his den-mates fanned out around the vestiges of the rockslide and into the forest. He knew this area well. No way Evers knew it as well as he did and that should work to his advantage.

Good thing, since nothing else seemed to be.

When he'd last seen them, Evers had Amy by the arm, dragging her. Both looked injured. Even if she got away, she wouldn't have a chance alone in the woods overnight. Getting lost in the forest was not only possible, but almost a certainty.

He sniffed the air. The rain made it difficult to pick up anything besides mud and water. In fact, he smelled no humans at all. No sign of her, no scent of Evers, either. The other bears growled their frustration at not finding her. Evers wasn't perfect. He had to have left some clues as they tromped through the forest. He was in human form, after all, and injured. No smells of rage or fear permeated the rainy day.

Griff ran. Straight into the heart of the forest, where the trees grew close together in a knot of darkness.

Where hiding was possible and dangers were definite.

They didn't have enough bears out looking for Amy. Elijah wasn't there. God help them if they found the lions now. If they chose now to attack, they'd find the bears so spread out, they might have a chance at defeating them. He'd called away a couple of the guardians of the Cave of Whispers. Elijah was going to be pissed if he found out or if things went wrong.

Things couldn't go wrong. They wouldn't. The rain picked up, slamming fat drops onto his head and making his headache worse. He growled and ran faster.

Griff headed down the remains of a winding trail into the deep woods. She'd headed this general direction, but tracking her wasn't easy. Lightning flashed. Once, twice, three times in rapid succession. The storm was overhead and boiling dark clouds filled the sky.

Yep. Thunder rolled almost immediately, vibrating the ground as the clouds collided. This was not the night to be out in, much less searching for someone in the woods.

The forest, deep green and laden with rainfall, closed in on him. More trees, more plants, more places to get lost. Large ferns sprouted from the ground like geysers and tree roots crossed the path in a jumble of knots and entanglements. All the animals had taken shelter and the place felt barren and lonely.

He knew his way. If he kept going straight, he'd come to the same stream that ran behind his cabin, though much farther west of it. A quarter mile in the opposite direction, and he'd be near his ranger cabin.

He never got lost, but Evers might. Amy would. No telling what the lions knew about the landscape? They'd certainly been all over the area during the winter.

Amy... He turned, listening for her over the rain. Where was she? She had to be close. She and Evers hadn't gotten much of a head start on them and they were running on two legs instead of four.

The thought of Evers's hand grasping Amy's arm so firmly pushed Griff on. Anger bubbled in his stomach beside the worry for her well-being. He wasn't only mad at Evers, he was mad at himself. He never should've gone to sleep at the cabin. Not without his arms tightly around his mate or a stern warning to her to stay put. And a locked door.

He should've never let this happen. Maybe he wasn't capable of keeping his mate safe.

He kept moving along the small path snaking through the growth. The trail had all but disappeared. Surely, in human form, Evers had come this way. It would be too difficult to climb the fallen trees and go through the underbrush of the wild forest. Amy had to be around this area somewhere. He stopped and scanned the small meadow ahead of him. Lightning flashed as he panned.

He saw her.

She lay on the ground, not moving, her arms splayed apart, her blond hair fanned around her head. Was she dead?

A large lump lodged in his throat and he swallowed against it.

He ran to her.

Her face was covered in blood and her nose was obviously broken. What the hell happened? He sensed she was breathing, but barely. Rage boiled up from his stomach and came out his mouth as a loud growl, his claws extending to full length as he rose up on his hind legs.

Where was Evers? He scanned the area, seeing only forest and a few downed trees.

A growl came from the underbrush. The sound seemed far away and near at the same time, as if it came from between the raindrops.

Where are you, Evers?

Find me.

I'll find you. I'll kill you.

The lion leapt out from the underbrush, his tawny coat bloodstained, his maw dripping foam. He growled, showing his teeth. *Not if I kill you first.*

Griff took a swipe at him, but the lion took a leap backward, then turned and crouched. He pounced, landing on Griff's shoulders, dragging his claws along his fur and tearing into the tender skin underneath.

Griff's shoulders burned where he'd been sliced and he reared up again to sling Evers off. The lion landed hard and slid a few feet in the wet leaves. He hissed as he got to his paws.

Meet me man to man. Evers punctuated his words with a growl. *We'll finish this on a more even playing field.*

You first. Perhaps Griff held an advantage in size being a bear, but Evers was much quicker. In human form, they'd be well matched. Neither would be able to run away, either—not that Griff would ever run from a fight. Especially when his mate's life was at stake.

Evers padded backward and shifted, his body morphing to naked human in just a few seconds. Griff followed, letting himself slip into human form, the burn of muscle and bone changing offset by trying to watch Evers for a sneak attack.

"That's better." Evers raised his fists. "I prefer to see your face when you die."

"I don't care how we fight." Griff clenched his fists and teeth, trying to contain the red rage that flooded his vision. "I'll win."

"You better do it quickly if you want to save your girlfriend. Looks like she needs some medical attention."

Griff punched, his blow glancing off Evers's cheek. Evers swung back but Griff ducked.

"I'll take her off your hands." Evers huffed as he moved forward in a feint. "I don't know what she sees in a bear like you."

Griff bent and tackled Evers, knocking the breath out of him as he struck.

"Ooof." Evers's back hit the ground. He tried to roll away but Griff held him down.

Griff lay on him, his hands on Evers's throat, his bare legs holding Evers's lower half down. He squeezed Evers's throat. Evers coughed and shook his head free, pulling at Griff's hair.

Griff's eyes watered. He rose up and kneed Evers between the legs as hard as he could. Evers cried out and doubled over on the ground. Griff didn't let him go, but pinned his arms.

Anger consumed Griff, fueling his need to destroy the man who'd hurt his mate. Somewhere, deep in his mind, he heard Elijah warning him to control his anger, but the voice was so faint. Evers was under him, weak and pathetic. He'd hurt Amy. Elijah had paid with an eye for scuffling with Evers. Evers was a bad man who would never change. It didn't matter how much they tried. The man was evil and deserved to die.

Evers tried to shove Griff off. "You killed my parents!"

"I did not! Your mother was already dead when I came upon the accident. I tried to save your father. Even though I knew he was a lion. I even carried him to the Cave of Whispers. Do you know how hard that was for a scrawny teenager? He was injured too badly to be helped." Griff pressed down on Evers's shoulders, his thumbs near his windpipe. He had Evers under him and he was not letting him go. "I'm sorry he died. I tried to save him. The bears buried your mother there, too. Out of respect."

"You killed them." Evers's face contorted as the air began to be forced from his throat. "I'm going to take your girlfriend to make up for it. And she won't die an easy death." The last sentence came out as a gurgle as Griff held his neck tightly.

Griff saw red again. He grabbed Evers by the hair and began slamming his head against a rock on the ground. Again and again. *Amy. You hurt Amy and you're not getting the chance to hurt her again. Ever.*

Evers relaxed as blood flowed from the back of his head. Griff kept pounding.

All the years he'd worried about Evers. The fear

he'd had after seeing what Evers did to Elijah. The rain washed it all away. Evers wasn't going to hurt anyone again.

Griff sat back on his heels and wiped his face. A weight that had sat on his soul for many years was gone. Yet he didn't feel any lighter.

"Oh my gods, Griff, did you kill him?" Powell ran up to him. "Oh my gods."

Griff stared up at Powell. He blinked the rain out of his eyes and looked around. "Where've you been?"

"We circled around the side way and grabbed our clothes. Figured you had things under control for the moment. Here's your stuff." He tossed Griff a bag. "Oh my gods. What have you done?"

Griff looked down. He felt the blood drain from his face. "I killed him."

"Oh, no." Powell bent to check Evers. "Yeah, he's dead all right."

"What happened?" Derek rushed up beside Powell. "Where's Amy?"

"Evers is dead." Griff turned and threw up.

Powell shook his head. "Griff, this is bad."

"There's Amy." Griff pointed. "Oh gods, I hope she's okay. What if she's not okay?" Tears streaked his face and his stomach cramped.

Powell was over her before Griff could get to her. He took her pulse and felt her neck. "She's alive. I think her nose is broken. We need to get her some help, quickly. Her pulse is weak, so she may have some internal injuries."

"Dammit." Derek tugged on his beard. "What the hell did he do to her? Get dressed, Griff. We need to help her."

Griff fought to stay on his feet, his legs weak. Tears poured now and his back burned like hell. He pulled his clothes and shoes from the bag and began putting them on. He had to get Amy to the hospital.

"Cell phones don't work. We've got to get to the road," Powell said. "We'll worry about Evers later. I have a feeling Elijah will have something to say about it."

"I don't care. Amy is safe now." Griff leaned to get Amy and winced at the white-hot pain that shot through his back.

"Looks like Griff needs medical attention, too." Powell turned Griff around. "He got you big time. That cut looks awful."

"Oh, it does look bad." Derek whistled.

"I'll be all right," Griff mumbled. His vision blurred and he stumbled a bit. "I don't think I can carry her to the road, though."

"Look." Powell pointed to Evers's body.

Griff and Derek turned to see. Evers had morphed to a lion again, majestic and beautiful, but certainly dead.

"At least you aren't going to have to explain a homicide in the park," Powell whispered. "He's just another mountain lion."

"His pride will be upset."

"Nothing we can do now. Like I said, Elijah will have a talk with you, I'm sure." Powell bent and picked up Amy. "Let's get her to the road so we can flag a car. Derek, you're going to have to help Griff. He's losing blood."

"No." Derek looked out over the mountains. "Not a car. We need to get her to the Cave of Whispers. We aren't far away and the lake can heal her and Griff both. That's where they belong."

Griff's mouth went dry. "No. We need a hospital." He didn't believe in the cave. He could never forgive himself if something happened to her. He'd already failed her and he wasn't going to fail her again by wasting time on some tall tale.

"Derek is right." Powell pulled Amy closer. "The cave will help. We'd be taking our chances on a car coming by if we went to the road. Might not see one for hours—and I can't carry her all the way into town. It may be a chance Amy doesn't have time to take."

"What if the water doesn't heal her?" Griff's stomach knotted. How could he trust his mate's life to a myth? What if it was all a fake? "I can't lose her. I've lost everything. I can't lose her now." Sobs racked his body and he doubled over to contain them.

"You've got to trust us." Derek put his hand on Griff's shoulder. "The water will heal her. You, too. Come on. I'll run back and grab your clothes from the Jeep then let's take her. We can be there in less than ten minutes, and as I see it, we really don't have a better choice."

"Let's do it." Powell took a couple steps. "We need to hurry. She's not stable. He hurt her badly."

"He won't hurt anyone else." Griff spit on the ground and took a last glance at the mountain lion's body lying in the wet grass and leaves. It looked so small and insignificant now. Nothing like the monster that had occupied it. Griff took a deep breath and winced as his back burned and throbbed. He'd trust his den-mates. They were right. Not many cars were in the park today in the heavy rain. Elijah believed in the power of the cave.

"Well?" Derek tugged at Griff's shirt. "What's it going to be?"

Griff looked from the mountain lion's body to Amy's broken body. He couldn't let her die.

He had to trust in something, and the cave might be his only chance to save her. Not saving his sister had caused a lifetime of sadness and regrets. If he'd only taken a chance then, she might be alive. Now, he had the opportunity to take a chance and save Amy. He had to step up, trust his den-mates, and have faith.

"Okay. I'm going to trust you guys on this. Let's get Amy to the cave. I don't want her to die."

EIGHTEEN

THE CAVE WAS cold and damp and Griff stumbled in the near-darkness. His heart thudded from the anxiety that boiled in his gut and his back burned from the long scratches Evers had sliced into him. Anxiety weighed him down. If he made the wrong decision, Amy could die. She *would* die.

"Hurry up, Griff." Powell's voice strained as he talked. He'd carried Amy the whole way, and as annoying as the bear could be, Griff owed him, big time. Den-mates were brothers of the best kind. The ones you chose.

"I'm trying." Griff moved into the next room of the cave and took down a lantern. "Get Amy to the lake. She's more important than I am. I'll get there."

Derek pulled another lantern from the wall and they lit them in silence.

"I'm taking her in to the shore." Powell grunted. "But you'll need to take her into the lake. She's your mate, and you need to go into the water, too."

The lantern flickered to life and Griff held it high, the beams casting long rectangles of yellow light across the wet cave walls. "I will." He followed Powell into the larger cavern where the lake filled most of the space.

Derek came behind, his lantern waving and bouncing patterns of light off the stony ceiling. "We shouldn't stay while Griff takes her in the water. This is their time. Their healing."

Powell nodded, Amy draped in his arms. "We'll wait outside, at the first sentry station. Come to us when you're done."

"Why?" Griff set the lantern on the ground. "I don't even know what to do!" He gagged. He'd thrown up several times on the trip to the cave and his head throbbed.

"It's simple." Derek set his lantern near Griff's. "You take her out into the water, and you wait. Clear your mind. Shoshannah might appear, or she might not. Either way, a few minutes in the water will heal you both, if that's what's meant to be. That is what Elijah says. I know you've heard him."

"Yeah, and be prepared," Powell said. "You're going to have some explaining to do. Amy isn't going to know where she is."

Amy moaned and twitched in Powell's arms then went limp.

"You better hurry." Derek's eyes grew wide. "That doesn't sound promising."

"Come find us when you're done."

"Okay." Griff held his arms out and Powell set Amy in them gently. She groaned but didn't move. He pulled her close. "What if it doesn't work? What do I do then? I can't lose my mate!"

"I don't know what to tell you." Powell's mouth set in a firm line. "Have faith. Go."

Griff nodded. *If I lose her, I have nothing.*

Powell and Derek took off without even looking back. Griff stared out at the black water of the lake. How deep was it? He knew it was cold. He wished he'd paid more attention to Elijah when he'd talked about healing people in the cave. Griff had never watched or been near. When he'd brought Evers's father, the sentries had taken him in. If she healed, Amy would wake up and be pretty upset she was drenched.

I'll deal with that.

He didn't even know how deep to go.

He took a breath. Only one way to find out. Stepping into the water, he winced. *Cold.* He took a few more steps, the only sounds in the cave his own splashes in the water. As the water came over his knees, then his hips, he realized it wasn't cold at all. In fact, it was as warm as a bath.

He sank, letting the water cover Amy, up to her neck. As the water touched his wounds, they sizzled. He didn't feel pain. The sensation was more of a tingling or light effervescence.

Amy stirred almost immediately, but she didn't open her eyes. She twisted in his arms, as if she was trying to get more of the water on her. Griff sank lower. His back fizzed and zinged. The pain stopped and was replaced with a permeating warmth.

He watched Amy's face for any sign of change.

None.

She had to get better. He couldn't live without her. He hadn't been living without her—he'd only been going through the motions.

Still no movement from Amy but his back felt completely new.

He closed his eyes.

Please let her be okay. Please, Shoshannah, or whoever is out there. Heal Amy.

Griff pulled Amy gently through the water, letting her hair fan around her like the petals of a beautiful flower. He watched her for any sign of life, but she lay still, her lips barely parted and her fractured face bruising. The split in her lower lip had begun to heal—at least it appeared to have started.

He leaned close to her face. She didn't stir.

Oh gods, what will I do without her?

He brushed a wet strand away from her face. If she could hear him, he couldn't tell.

Suddenly, Amy kicked and tried to sit up. Griff struggled to hold on to her, but she fought him to get away from his grip.

His heart sped. She was alive. *Thank the gods!*

He wiped her face with his wet hand and watched the magic of the water heal her broken nose, as the blood washed away.

She was going to be okay. And he would protect her for the rest of her life.

He smiled at her.

My mate.

Her eyes flickered open, wide, and she screamed.

He tried to hold on to her as she flailed.

"Amy, it's okay. It's me."

She paused. "Griff?"

"Yes." He pulled her close.

"I was with Evers…"

"Evers won't hurt you again."

She looked around in the dark cave, the light barely casting enough of a glow to see much other than the reflection across the top of the water.

"Where are we, and why are we in the water?"

Griff paused. How much should he tell her, now? Eventually, she'd need to know everything, but right now she was fragile. "Remember I told you there were caves in the mountains? You were bleeding," he finally said. "I brought you in the water to wipe off the blood. Plus you'd passed out. I hoped the warm water would wake you up. And it did."

She scowled.

"It's true!"

"Why didn't you just take me home?"

"It's a long way. I thought it best you wash off first. We can go home now." He moved toward the shore. "Come on, I'll take you."

"What aren't you telling me?"

"What do you mean?"

"I mean, I can tell there's something you aren't telling me. I remember Evers hitting me and that was out in the forest. So, I guess I did pass out. I also remember him turning into a mountain lion and that seems a little odd. There were bears, too. There are almost always bears around when I see mountain lions. Why is that, Griff? I didn't see *you* in the forest. Only bears."

"There are a lot of animals in the forest." He swallowed against the lump in his throat.

Amy tried to wrangle free. "You did. But you didn't tell me that they could turn into humans."

"Amy…"

"Where's Evers? What did you do with him?" She pushed out of his grip and backed away.

"Amy, please—"

"What did you do with him? Is he dead? Did you kill him?"

Griff looked down. He couldn't lie to her. "Yes. I killed him. He hurt you and he wouldn't stop hurting you until you were dead. I couldn't have that."

The look of shock on her face stabbed him in the heart. Of course she didn't understand shifter politics. She was human. He licked his lips. He'd said too much, too soon.

"I'm going to the cabin and getting the hell out of crazy town." She headed toward shore. "Do not follow me or I'll call the cops. In fact, I'm going to call them anyway. Report a homicide."

"Let me explain." Griff reached for her, but she rushed toward shore. "There's so much I need to tell you."

She turned, glaring. "No explanation needed. This area is full of crazy people and wild animals. I need to get out of here. You don't kill someone because you're mad at them. What the hell, Griff?"

"You don't understand." Griff moved toward her. "I love you. I want to spend my life with you."

"Don't take another step toward me." Her scream echoed off the cavern walls. "Do not follow me. I mean it!" She rushed out of the water and onto shore, dripping. She grabbed a lantern and headed into the room toward the cave exit.

At least she went the right way. It was a long way to the road and she could get lost. What should he do? She told him not to follow. Fuck that! He couldn't let his mate wander in the woods, lost.

He started toward the shore. At least the water had healed them. The realization washed over him. His back no longer hurt and Amy was obviously better.

For once, he was glad to be wrong.

Suddenly the cave shook, or was it just the ground. He stood still, feeling the vibrations beneath his feet. Earthquake?

Griff...

The voice came from behind him. He turned. Nothing.

Don't follow her.

He spun, looking for the origin of the voice. The lake was flat and calm. Serene, even.

Then, a small speck of blue light floated over the water, zipping and spinning like a dragonfly, yet soundless, until it was in front of him. It grew in size until it was at least twelve feet tall. Griff shielded his eyes.

You are angry.

He looked around for the source of the voice, but nothing was in the cave but the light. When he turned to the light, it had taken the form of a giant white bear with eyes of clear crystal, floating over the water.

"Shoshannah?" he whispered.

Yes.

"I have to get to my mate. She'll get lost in the woods." He stared at the bear, its beauty beyond anything he'd ever seen. Still, it held a power that scared him. He felt the history of his people and more in her presence.

The bear spoke, this time with its mouth. "I've instructed your den-mates to take her home. She will be safe until you return to her."

"She doesn't want me. She's going to leave."

"Not if you make amends. She senses you have upset the natural order. You must make things right. Then, you can talk to her and she will listen. Only then will you have a chance."

He waved his hands through the warm water. "I don't know what you're talking about." He did. He'd killed Evers in anger. Even though Evers had hurt his mate, he hadn't even given him a chance to make amends or change.

"You must bring his body to the lake."

Griff recoiled. "No! I don't want him alive again."

The great white bear reared up on its hind legs and blew out a puff of white smoke. Then she came down on all fours again. "The lake cannot give back life. It will transition him to the next dimension where he belongs. This is the order of things. In murder, he needs to be cleansed before he can move on. You also need to be cleansed for your actions or your heart will blacken like his. The only way is for you to bring him here."

Griff scowled. He needed to get to Amy. What if she left before he got to her?

"It's the only way to be absolved, Griff. Elijah would tell you the same. That, I promise you. Evers was never absolved and his heart continued to blacken until nothing was left but hatred and darkness. I know you don't want your heart to turn black."

"Of course not." Griff's mouth went dry. Elijah. He was going to be so angry when he found out what happened. Griff rubbed his head.

"Bears and lions once lived together and shared the Cave of Whispers." Shoshannah paced. "Only in recent times have they fought over ownership over something that wasn't theirs to fight over. Soon, they will fight again. Many lives will be lost in the upcoming battles."

"I don't want a war."

The white bear paced, puffs of white smoke curling over the water behind her. "It's coming. For now, you need to be right with yourself, Griff Martin. Then with your mate. Because once the war starts, there won't be time for reconciliations."

Griff took a breath. "Why have you never appeared to me before?"

"I appear when needed." If a bear could shrug, she did.

Griff nodded. "This is something I must do?"

"Look inside yourself. Tell me."

Griff closed his eyes. At first, he saw tendrils of white smoke, but as they parted, he saw Amy. She laughed. Then, he saw cubs. His cubs. Three, no, four! In his old cabin, running around at Amy's feet. But there was a dark presence lurking. It thumped and beat. It was his heart. Black. Uncleansed from the murder. The darkness surrounded his cubs and then Amy. Then they all vanished in a cloud of darkness.

He opened his eyes. "I will be back with Evers's body."

"You will find your path. Walk in the light and you will find peace."

Shoshannah faded until she was nothing but mist on the lake. By the time Griff reached the shore, even that had dissipated and the cave held nothing but water and darkness.

GRIFF RAN. THE rain hadn't stopped and his fur barely kept the dampness from his skin. More than a few times he'd slid in the mud and his lower body was caked in clumps of the sticky stuff. He didn't care. He had a mission.

Shoshannah was right. He had to absolve his crime. Killing Evers had felt right at the time, but it was wrong. Even though Evers had hurt Amy, Griff didn't have the right to take his life. Bear code was confusing sometimes but they weren't officially at war and personal attacks were quite different than all-out war. He should have talked to Elijah. Killing Evers hadn't been self-defense.

War was coming. Panic froze in his chest as he leapt over a large downed tree. Shoshannah said it was coming and Elijah had, too. How would he protect Amy? He put his head down and ran harder. First, he had to take care of Evers. Then, convince Amy to stay. Then he could worry about the upcoming war.

The thought scared the hell out of him.

Being a bear held a lot of worry and his head pounded in time with his heartbeat. He crossed a stream that had swelled in its banks from all the rain, and leapt up the muddy bank. Almost there.

The meadow where Evers lay had areas of flattened grass where they'd fought, and it didn't take Griff much time at all to find him. The lion lay on his side, tongue lolled out, eyes unseeing. So small.

He'd never be able to carry him back in human form so Griff carried him by the scruff. It was slow going, as Evers was long and lean and dragged the ground. The rain pelted his face and Griff wanted to be anywhere but where he was. The drudgery of carrying Evers back was hell.

Was this penance?

It surely felt like it.

He came to the stream and dragged the lion through it and up the embankment on the other side. Running wasn't possible and darkness fell over the forest. Though he could see better in bear form, the rain and now fog made visibility really low and Griff slowed his pace. He stopped to rest for a moment, panting and wishing he'd never agreed to bring Evers to the cave. No, he had to do it. For Amy, for his future cubs, for Elijah. Most of all, for himself.

He moved again, over downed trees and through the deep glades on the way to the cave. He remembered the day he'd found Evers's parents, and how he'd scented on them immediately. He'd known they were lions, but he hadn't cared. He tried to help them. No prejudice in him then—why had that all changed? Evers had lived his whole life angry because of something that wasn't true. Griff had acted on something stemming from the same thing.

The murder wasn't self-defense.

He was pissed, plain and simple. He could've kept Amy safe from Evers if he'd tried. The fact was, he wanted Evers dead at that moment, and that kind of anger was unacceptable. How could he even face his mate with blood on his hands? Tears streamed down his bear cheeks. He couldn't keep her safe and he couldn't control his anger. Maybe he wasn't even worthy of having a mate.

By the time he got to the cave, every muscle in his body ached. Barely a thought formed besides "get Evers to the lake." He'd never been so tired. Bone-deep, soul-deep, exhausted.

His feet didn't register walking through the first two rooms of the cave or dragging Evers to the shore of the lake. With no lantern, even his bear eyes could only see a shadow of the water. Still and dark, it spread before him in what appeared to be an endless pool of black.

What was he supposed to do next? He'd brought Evers. Where was Shoshannah?

He dropped the lion and drank from the lake, letting the water wash over his mouth and cleanse the bad taste away. He drank, gulped at the lake. When he'd had his fill, and Shoshannah didn't appear, he sat on his haunches to wait. Surely she'd come tell him what to do next. He waited, the silence deafening in his ears.

Hadn't she said something about taking Evers into the lake? He tried to remember.

"You must bring his body to the lake." The whisper came from nowhere and everywhere at once, inside him and outside.

He rose up and tugged Evers into the water and paddled into the lake with him, letting the warm, healing water release the tension from his muscles.

The water began bubbling around the lion and Griff backed away. A dim green light lit below the water and swirled like a mini maelstrom, the lion's body moving along with it. Griff paddled farther from the light and bubbling water.

A column of water shot into the air, green at first, then pure white. Evers's body disappeared and in its place, a wispy creature in the shape of a lion, made purely of smoke. The creature dashed through the air, jumping and spinning as if it had been released from captivity.

Griff stared, his mouth wide. Would the apparition attack him now?

Suddenly, a larger lion padded out into the air. Somehow, Griff knew it was Evers's father. He'd been buried in the Cave of Whispers after he couldn't be revived. Then, a lioness, small-boned and icy, appeared.

Evers's mother. She, too, had been buried in the catacombs. Father and mother nuzzled Evers and Griff felt love and peace throughout the cavern.

All was right again. Better than before. Evers, as dark as his heart was, had also been cleansed and he'd moved on to the beyond.

The smoke lions froze over the lake, and then shattered into a million crystals of white that dissipated almost immediately.

Once again, the cave was silent.

Evers was at peace.

Griff had done his duty.

Feeling rested and rejuvenated, Griff swam to shore. Whatever he was supposed to have done, he must have done it. Shoshannah was right; he did feel better now. He held no ill will against Evers anymore, and it was like a huge weight had been taken from his back.

He climbed out of the lake and shook the water from his fur. He'd no longer carry a darkness in his heart. He'd washed it away.

Now, he needed to go find his mate and convince her to stay with him.

NINETEEN

"I'M NOT STAYING." Amy stomped onto the cabin porch and fumbled to unlock the door with the key she kept hidden in the window box. "This place, these mountains, are messed up. Wild animals and even wilder people. Craziness."

"Please," Derek said. "You need to give Griff a chance to explain things. It will all make sense once he does."

Powell walked up beside her. "I promise, it will. We haven't lied to you, have we?"

"We helped you get home." Derek flanked her other side. "Please, wait on Griff to get here before you do anything rash."

Amy closed her eyes. How much more crazy could she take in one day? Evers had tried to hurt her—and Griff had taken her into a lake. She didn't remember anything in between. Either she was losing her mind, or these people were drugging her, or…something.

"Rash, like killing someone?" She rolled her eyes at Powell. "Or turning myself into a monkey or something?" She glanced at Derek. "What exactly do you expect me to do?"

She began to cry. Her head was pounding. Griff had killed a man. He'd admitted it. And in pretty much the same conversation, he'd told her he loved her. What kind of crazy was that?

"Everything will be okay." Powell put his hand on her shoulder and she tensed. "You need to hear Griff out. Please."

She wiped her tears away and shivered. Her clothes, still damp from being in the lake, were sticking to her in all the wrong places, and the blanket Powell had given her barely kept her warm. She wasn't going to let them see her cry. "Why? He killed someone. That isn't okay."

Derek spoke softly. "No, it isn't. But sometimes, there are reasons. Please, let us stay with you until Griff gets here. Then, let him explain. After that, if you want to go, I'm sure he will let you."

"Let me?" Amy turned the knob and pushed into the cabin. "I don't need him to let me do anything. I'll do what I want."

"Bad choice of words," Derek called from the porch. "May we come in?"

Amy thought about it. These men hadn't done anything wrong. They'd helped her find her way home. They'd been nice to her and maybe they'd answer some of her questions about seeing Evers turn into a lion.

Which wasn't possible. Had she hit her head? Not that she remembered.

"Fine. Come in." She left the door open and headed on in to the little cabin, flipping on the lamps and lights as she went. She dumped the blanket on the floor. "I'm not sure I'll be waiting to talk to Griff."

"He really cares about you." Derek sat down on the couch.

Powell closed the door. "He does. He's told us."

"Yeah, so he says."

He said he loved me. How can that be, after only knowing me a short time?

She went into the kitchen to wash her hands. The day had been so messed up. She didn't see any way to recover from it.

Griff Martin was a confusing man. Yes, she was attracted to him. Yes, she had even grown to care about him in the short time she'd known him. But love? She wasn't sure about that.

How could she have a relationship with a murderer? Why weren't Powell and Derek calling the police? Why wasn't she? She soaped up her hands and let the sink faucet run over them. Maybe she should talk to Griff one more time. Then pack her stuff and get out.

She obviously didn't belong in the mountains.

She dried her hands on the towel and set it on the counter. What she'd really like was a long hot bath and some time to think. She pushed her hair behind her ears.

How long would it take Griff to get to the cabin? It couldn't take much longer than it took her—he knew the way. Maybe he'd gone by his house first. She looked down at her damp clothes. If she didn't change, she was bound to get sick.

She headed into the living room. "I'm going to change clothes." She passed right by Derek and Powell. "I'll be back in a few minutes."

"We'll be right here." Derek leaned back on the couch.

"Mind if I make some coffee?" Powell asked.

"Help yourself." Amy continued down the hall and into her bedroom. She closed the bedroom door and leaned against it.

How had things gone so badly so quickly? Just last night, she'd been in Griff's arms, making love and talking about their lives. She even thought they might have a bit of a future together, if only for a couple months.

Hot tears filled her eyes again and she wiped at them. She hated when tears fell, but she couldn't help it. At least she was alone this time. She locked the door and kicked off her muddy shoes. She hadn't even noticed how muddy they were. The floors were probably filthy. She stripped off her socks, then her jeans and the rest of her clothes.

Too bad she didn't have time to take a shower. She didn't even want to look in the mirror to see what a mess her hair must be after being out in the rain and then in the lake. She pulled on clean clothes, with warm socks and sweatpants and a long-sleeved T-shirt.

"I should at least wash my face," she whispered.

She slipped out of her bedroom and into the bathroom. She pulled out a washcloth and turned on the sink faucet. She blinked at her reflection in the mirror. Where was the woman who worked at ADvert, handling dozens of accounts at once and bringing in multi-million-dollar deals to the agency at least twice a year? The face that stared back at her in the mirror looked nothing like the put-together woman that had arrived at the cabin, not that long ago.

She laughed. The irony. When she'd arrived, she thought she was worn down and needing a break. She thought the cabin was going to save her. Rejuvenate her. Yet, somehow, things had gotten worse. More complicated than ever. Instead of one man to worry about, she now had two. Darren was barely out of her life and now Griff took up a large part of it. She ran the washcloth under the warm water then wrung it out.

She washed her face, holding the cloth against her eyes. The heat and steam felt so amazing as it penetrated her skin. She turned off the water and dropped the cloth into the hamper. She'd face Griff and find out what the hell was going on. She deserved that.

One way or another, she'd get to the bottom of what was going on.

She headed back into the living room, more determined than before. She could handle Griff.

"Did you paint this?" Derek held up a landscape she'd mostly finished. "It's pretty nice. Love the trees. Oaks, mostly."

"Yeah, I started that last week. It's not finished." Amy took the painting from him and set it back on the easel. "Wish I had more time to paint."

"I know exactly where that view is." Powell sipped on a cup of coffee. "You captured it perfectly. Even the light hitting the rocks is exactly the way it is at mid-morning. You're really talented."

The sting of a blush crept up her cheeks and she turned away. "Thanks. It's really just a pre-painting. So I could get a feel for what the final painting would be."

"I hope you'll decide to stay." Derek walked to look out the window into the darkness. "Once you talk to Griff."

"Not likely." Amy crossed her arms. "There's something you can help me with, though."

"Anything." Derek turned toward her, stroking his beard, his eyes alight with amusement. "What do you need?"

She walked closer. "I want the truth."

"Of course."

"We always tell the truth," Powell said.

"Explain to me how Evers turned into a mountain lion. While you're at it, tell me why every time I see a mountain lion, there are bears nearby."

Derek and Powell looked at each other. Amy could have sworn that Derek's face drained of color.

"Well?" She tapped her foot. "He did change, didn't he? How is that possible?"

"I… I…" Derek stuttered.

"I think you need to talk to Griff about that, Amy." Powell's voice wavered and he didn't meet her gaze.

A knock sounded at the door.

"There he is." Derek rushed to the door.

"Thank the gods he made it." Powell joined Derek.

"Perfect timing." Derek grabbed the doorknob.

Amy turned in time to see Derek open the door. Griff stood on the porch, his broad shoulders filling out a red shirt, tucked into deep blue jeans. He was more than handsome. He had saved her. Now it was time to listen to what he had to say.

"We'll see you, Amy." Powell was out the door in a flash. He stuck his head back in. "Thanks for the coffee."

"Yeah," Derek said. "We'll let you and Griff have your talk in private. See you soon."

He disappeared out the door. Griff remained on the porch. "May I come in, Amy? We need to talk."

Amy's mouth went dry and her palms slicked with sweat. She cleared her throat. "Yes. We do need to talk."

TWENTY

GRIFF TURNED TO Powell and Derek. "Thank you for helping her get back, and for watching over her until I got here."

"Of course," Derek said. "We'll go to Elijah and tell him what happened."

"Thank you." Griff looked down. "Tell him also that I have done what Shoshannah asked of me, and that Evers is at peace now. I'll call him later. Right now, I have to take care of Amy."

"Will do." Powell headed down the porch steps.

Derek nodded then followed Powell off the porch and out into the yard.

Griff turned back to the doorway. He entered the cabin and closed the door behind him. His home, now home to his mate. Only he and his mate were not together. This was not going to be easy. He'd tell the truth and see what happened. That was all he could do.

"Thank you for letting me explain." He tried to take Amy in his arms but she backed away. He gulped. If he lost her, he'd have nothing to live for. Now that he had a taste of having a mate, he knew he needed her in his life.

She crossed her arms. "I want answers."

"Yes." He sighed. "You deserve them."

"Is Evers really dead? Did you kill him?" Her voice quavered.

"Yes." Griff looked away. "Unfortunately, he is." How was she going to take this news? The first time, she didn't take it well at all. Why did he think it would be any different now?

"What happened?"

Griff paced. "He tried to kill you. He dragged you off into the forest, do you remember that much?" He glanced up at her.

"Yes. We were trying to get away from the rock-slide." She paused, and wiped at a lone tear. "I don't remember… Oh my god… He threatened to rape me."

Griff fisted his hands, wanted to reach out and wipe her tears but realizing she needed her space right now. "Yes. And he would have, too, if we hadn't found him in time. He had beaten you pretty badly and you were lying in the grass…"

She scowled and held her head in her hands. "He hit me." She looked at Griff. "In the face." More tears fell. "It was awful."

Griff nodded, trying to bite back the anger that was trying to return. "You were seriously hurt. Internal injuries. Broken nose. When we first found you, we thought you were dead. You were lying in the wet grass in the meadow."

"I don't remember any of this. When who found me?" She wiped at the tears with her shirtsleeve. "I don't remember any of this. I'm losing my mind. Evers is dead. How do I know you are telling me the truth now?"

"Amy." Griff used his firm and hopefully truthful-sounding voice without raising the volume. "Let's go through this together. You aren't losing your mind. Today has been an awful day, but we survived."

"Why can't I remember it all?"

"You were out. From pain or injury, I don't know." Griff scratched his head and continued pacing. "As for who, it was me, Derek and Powell. Didn't they tell you they were there? A few other rangers were there, too."

"They wanted me to wait for you to tell me what happened. So all of them saw you kill Evers?"

Griff shook his head. "I found him first." The circles under her eyes and the mud in her hair reminded him of just how close he'd come to losing her. If only she'd let him hold her. He could take away some of the stress and pain she was feeling.

"What else do you want to know?" He had to take care of her.

"What happened next? I want to know everything up till the moment in the lake." She rubbed her nose.

"Can we sit down?" Griff pointed to the couch.

"Yeah. Wanna cup of coffee? Already have some brewed."

"That would be great. I'm exhausted." Griff sighed. "I'll help."

She poured the coffee in silence. Griff peeked at Amy while he stirred his sugar into his cup. His mate. The urge to take her in his arms overwhelmed him. She'd already rebuffed him. What if he'd screwed up everything? He set the spoon on the counter and reached for her hand.

She let his hand rest on hers for a moment and he savored the warmth. It gave him the strength he needed to continue. Then she pulled away. "Let's go talk. I need answers, Griff. Today was messed up and I don't know how I'm going to get past this."

"It was. I'm sorry. I screwed up. Let's go in the living room."

Well, it was a start. She hadn't pulled away immediately. That was promising, right? He needed to be patient. He knew she was strong but the events of the day were enough to rattle the strongest.

Hell, he was an emotional wreck.

They sat on the couch facing each other, Amy sipping her coffee. Griff looked around the little cabin, remembering the day he'd first met her. He'd thought it a bad idea to rent to her. He also remembered Charlotte running through the kitchen, her high-pitched squeals of laughter echoing through the small place.

Amy set her cup on the coffee table. "Well? Let's hear it." She sat up on the edge of the seat, like she was perched for a quick getaway. "What happened next?"

What he wouldn't give to shampoo the mud from her hair, then brush it till it dried. As much as he'd thought he didn't want a mate, he realized what he really didn't want was to lose his mate. Like he'd lost his parents and sister.

Loss was what he was afraid of. Right now, he had to fight for what he wanted.

"We followed Evers as he took you into the forest. We had to go around the rockslide, so it took us a little longer to get into the deep woods. By the time I found you, you were injured and passed out. Evers saw me and immediately attacked."

"And you fought back?"

"Of course. It was a hard fight. I was angry. He had hurt you, and he's wanted revenge against me since his parents died. He said cruel things, and I… I just lost it."

She leaned forward. “What do you mean?”

“I was so angry, I lost control. I fought hard. Harder than I’ve ever fought—I was so mad. I kept on fighting until he was dead.” Griff looked away. “I know it was wrong. At that moment, it was a lifetime of anger rolled into one moment, and topped with his violence toward you. I couldn’t take it. I snapped.”

“Oh, Griff, that’s horrible.” Amy put her hand over her mouth. “Did Powell and Derek try to stop you?”

“No, they showed up just after the fight. At that moment, our main concern was getting you help. I also had wounds. So at the time, we didn’t think about the repercussions of what had happened. I was afraid you were dying.”

“So you took me to a lake.” Amy smirked. “I don’t mean to be snarky, but I don’t think I had internal injuries. Otherwise I wouldn’t be sitting here drinking coffee.”

Griff inhaled. “There’s a lot more going on than you know.” He took a sip of his coffee. “I’m not really sure where to start.”

“The beginning?”

“Yeah. It’s a long story. Can I ask you to trust me?”

“What do you mean? Trust you about what? I wouldn’t even let you in here if I didn’t trust you somewhat.”

“I know. This is different.” Griff looked around the little cabin. Maybe someday this would be theirs, but tonight, he needed to talk to his mate in a more neutral space. Not one that reminded him of Evers or his own family. “Come with me to my cabin. I’ll fix us dinner. You can take a bath while I’m cooking, if you want. This is going to be a long conversation and I don't know about you, but I'm starving."

"So…trust you not to poison me?" Amy smiled.

Griff could tell she was nervous. Who could blame her? He was nervous, too. He was going to have to tell her about being a bear and that was going to make a difference in whether or not she accepted him.

"No, silly. Trust me by giving me some time to explain everything. I promise I'll tell you everything. The truth. All of it. I just need a bit of time to figure out where to begin and how to tell you the whole thing without it sounding like crazyland. After last night, surely you know I would never hurt you."

She nodded.

He touched her chin and lifted it so that he looked right into her eyes. "We're good together, Amy Francis. I've known since the day I met you that we're meant to be together and last night…well, that just confirmed everything. Please, let's go back to my place and I'll fix you dinner and tell you everything. I have something to show you, too."

Amy moved his hand from her face but continued to watch him. "I want to believe you. With all my heart, I want to. I do think we might have something special, but you've got a lot of explaining to do."

"I know."

"Let me get a change of clothes. I'll take you up on that offer of using your bathtub. And dinner, too. I expect you to tell me everything, or I'm packing my stuff and heading to Atlanta. Tonight."

"I understand. Thank you."

"Let me get my stuff. Wait here."

Griff watched her walk toward the bedroom. He

was going to get his chance to explain. He had to make it count. How was he going to explain shifters and cave spirits and magic healing waters to someone who had never heard of any of it? She might think he was insane. He'd have to do his best.

He'd have to show her his bear.

That thought scared him. What if she thought he was scary? Or ugly? What if she couldn't love a shifter? Doubt flooded his mind and the urge to flee gripped him.

Then, in his subconscious, he heard Elijah's voice. *Grandchildren.* He'd heard about his grandchildren in the Cave of Whispers. Maybe things would turn out okay, or maybe Shoshannah was playing a cruel trick on them both.

Amy came out of the bedroom with a small gym bag. "Let's go." She pulled the bag up on her shoulder. "The more I think about a bath, the more I like the idea. Wash off that lake water. Then, I'll be ready to talk."

Griff stood and motioned to the door. "After you."

TWENTY-ONE

AMY SOAKED IN the tub. She lay back, warm water up to her ears and bubbles popping faintly all around her. If she didn't move, she could pretend she was floating, meditating, far away from all her troubles.

Away from lions and murders and bears.

She couldn't. Too much had happened. She'd never have dreamed that coming to the mountains would cause such an upheaval. The things that had happened here made her time at ADvert seem like a shopping trip to the grocery store without her debit card. One good thing, she'd gotten Darren off her mind. He'd been replaced by someone even worse, and she could barely believe that was possible.

Evers.

She sat up, her heart racing. The faint scent of men's soap floated in the air. Evers scared her. He had targeted her. Was it like Griff said, revenge for his parents' death? Could that consume someone so much that they carried a grudge for so many years? He'd said he'd rape her. She shuddered in the cool air. She would've tried to defend herself but Evers was strong. She pushed her wet hair away from her face and lay back in the water again.

I don't know what to believe anymore.

Fear must've clouded what she thought she saw. What she'd seen Evers do on the mountainside couldn't be possible. People didn't change into animals. Maybe Evers had run when the mountain lion showed up.

No, I saw him change into a lion. And he changed back, too.

It made no sense. Sure, she'd seen movies where humans changed into bloodthirsty werewolves when the moon was full. Those were myths and Hollywood magic.

Right?

The water had cooled as she'd washed. She rinsed her hair with the plastic cup Griff had given her. Then there were the bears. Huge brown bears that weren't native to New York. Griff had said that he and his friends had rescued her from Evers, but she hadn't seen them. She massaged her temples.

Adrenaline pumped through her, icy hot in her veins.

If Evers was the lion, then were Griff and his friends…the bears?

She shook her head. Now she knew she was Alice and she'd fallen down the rabbit hole. No other explanation made sense other than they were all insane. Griff was going to provide the truth. She pulled the bathtub plug and the water began draining.

She'd ask Griff about the mountain lion. He was familiar with the animal life in the forest. Maybe he'd have an explanation, if he didn't think she was crazy as hell. Or he'd tell her that the people around here changed into animals and she was in some kind of fairy tale. Either way, the conversation was going to be interesting.

She grabbed a towel and stepped out of the tub.

Things were never simple. Last night, in Griff's arms, she'd been happy. Not merely satisfied. Not content.

Happy.

She wasn't planning their wedding, or even what would happen beyond her vacation. Things felt right. Then the mountain had fallen down on everything and now the whole world was a mess and she had no idea how to right it.

Now what?

She was at Griff's ranger cabin, naked, and alone with Griff out in the kitchen. He'd said he'd make them some food. Her stomach growled in agreement. Griff cooking; she laughed. That was a funny image, despite the trauma of the day.

Though living alone, she supposed he had to cook sometimes. Images of burnt grilled cheese played through her mind. Or maybe instant noodles. Or canned soup. Any of those would taste yummy after the day she'd had. The day they'd had.

She dried herself off and wrapped her hair in a clean towel. Griff had set out his robe for her to wear. She slipped it on. Green-checked flannel, it screamed lumberjack-chic. The sleeves hung well past her fingertips, and she rolled them up several times before cinching the belt at her waist. The robe dragged the ground by several inches.

Griff. Since she'd rented the cabin, he'd been in the wings to save her every time something went wrong. Things had been going wrong a lot lately. The spring, the bar, the mountain. This was supposed to be a relaxing vacation, but instead had turned into a series of crazy dangerous happenings. Was Griff the cause or the one saving the day?

She towel-dried her hair and looked at herself in the mirror. She looked like death. Large circles bloomed under her eyes, and a thin scratch slid across her forehead, angry red from the warm bath. She remembered getting it on her walk home with Powell and Derek.

She picked up Griff's comb and pulled it through her wet hair. Tugging at the tangles, she picked and pulled until her hair lay smooth about her shoulders. Her mind wandered back to how it felt to have him inside her. It felt right. Perfect, even. Would she get the chance again, or had the day's events ruined any opportunity for the two of them?

It all depended on what he had to say. What the truth was.

She steeled herself and strode out of the bathroom.

"How do you feel?" Griff called from the kitchen.

"Better."

"I'm glad. I figured a bath would help."

Getting the answers to all the questions would help more.

The ranger cabin was larger than Griff's rental. The living room opened up to the ceiling, two stories high, the walls made of reddish wood logs. The kitchen was at the far end of the room, separated by a breakfast bar, and the heavenly scents of cinnamon and bacon wafted toward her. She made her way over to Griff. Bacon made everything better, didn't it?

"Thanks for letting me use your bath."

"It's the least I could do." He plated scrambled eggs beside cinnamon toast and bacon. "You've had some day. And I have a lot of explaining to do."

"Everything isn't your fault."

"Most of it is." He placed the plates on the table,

already set with orange juice and silverware. "Let's eat." He pulled her chair out and waited for her to sit, then he sat opposite her. "We can talk afterward."

"Okay." She sat, not sure what to say. "Thank you."

Griff peeked at her, his smile not reaching his eyes. Worry lines in his forehead deepened. "You're welcome. I hope you like bacon."

"Doesn't everyone?" Amy rearranged her food on the plate. "Part of this was Evers's fault, not yours, you know."

"Eat. Then we can talk." Griff shoved a forkful of eggs into his mouth. "Not polite to talk with your mouth full," he garbled.

She smiled and tugged at a piece of her bacon. "He's the one that hurt me. Thank you for saving me."

Griff's face reddened and he took a sip of orange juice. "No need to thank me. It's my duty. My honor. Now, eat."

Amy ate her toast in silence. Evers was dead and Griff killed him. The thought both pleased and frightened her. If the police got involved they might think she was partly to blame. This was self-defense. Griff had gotten out of control, but it had started with Evers attacking. That had to be important.

"Toast taste okay?" Griff asked. His plate was almost clean.

"Yes, thank you." She picked at her eggs with her fork. "Griff, I want to tell you something, and I don't want you to think I'm crazy."

"What is it?" He took a long drink of his orange juice, his shoulders tensing at her words.

"When I was at the car. In the rain, I mean, maybe I imagined it, but I saw Evers turn into a mountain lion. He took off his clothes and then—well, his body actually changed. Into a lion. That's not possible, is it?" She watched him for a response.

Griff sighed and set his glass down. He licked his lips and didn't say a word.

"I'm serious. That's what I saw. I know it sounds crazy. People can't change into animals, right?"

Griff crossed his arms and nodded. "I need to tell you something, but I need you to promise me that you'll listen to everything before freaking out."

She set her fork beside her plate. This couldn't be good. "I won't freak out until you're done."

He wiped his mouth with his napkin. She met his gaze for a moment, then glanced away. No, this wasn't going to be okay at all.

"Maybe we should go into the living room. This is pretty important, and is going to take a few minutes to explain."

"Okay." Amy drank the last of her orange juice then stood, her knees weak.

Griff seemed so serious—more than usual, anyway. Whatever he was going to tell her was going to change her world, she was sure of that.

GRIFF RUBBED HIS head and leaned forward to prop his elbows on his knees. How to tell her? Amy sat across from him on the couch, waiting. She'd seen Evers shift. She wasn't freaking out over it, so maybe learning he was a bear wouldn't affect her too much.

Maybe.

He glanced around his sparse living room. It could benefit from having some life breathed into it. A female touch. There was plenty of room for a few cubs.

No, he and Amy would live in his family's cabin, at least while their family was small. He didn't need to daydream. She might run when he told her about his bear.

He might lose her forever.

The fire he'd built in the stone fireplace while she was in the shower crackled and jumped, casting yellow and orange reflections across the room.

If only he knew how she'd react to the news, he'd have more nerve. His heart thudded and he felt every beat in his temples.

"So tell me." Amy crossed her arms. "Did Evers turn into a mountain lion or not?"

She looked so tiny wrapped in his robe. One slit from his claws and the robe would be off her. He smiled.

"Is it funny?"

"No, no..." He shook his head. "I'm sorry. I'm trying to figure out where to begin."

"If you're going to tell me that Evers can change into a mountain lion, I'm not sure there is a place to begin. So just start."

He took a deep breath. She was his mate. He had to be honest, even if it scared her away. She deserved the truth and he probably should've told her sooner.

"Do you remember when you saw the bear and the mountain lion fighting at the stream behind the cabin?"

"Yes. I had gone down to the creek to sketch and the mountain lion showed up to drink. Then the giant bear came and the two started fighting. It scared me."

"Well, you know how I told you that I'd fallen on

a stick when I showed up at the cabin?" He stared at the fire. "That same day?"

"Yeah."

"That isn't exactly how it happened. I was scratched by a mountain lion."

He looked at her right as realization came over her.

"You!" she shrieked. "You are that bear!" She stood. "Oh my god. How is that possible?" She backed across the room. "What the fuck?"

"Amy, sit down and listen." He motioned her to sit. His heartbeat galloped and it took all his willpower not to grab her and hold her. "I promise, I won't hurt you. I need to explain... You said you'd listen to the whole story. Please, sit."

"Explain how a person turns into an animal? Like bears and lions? What about squirrels? Do you know people that turn into squirrels? I thought I was the crazy one."

"Sit." He patted the couch. If she wouldn't listen, then all hope was lost. "Please. Let me explain."

"I'm sitting over here." She sat on the easy chair. "Go on...explain. I want to hear this."

"Well," Griff began, "humans aren't aware of this—well, most humans—but there are animal shifters throughout the world. There used to be more, we evolved alongside humans, in fact, but our numbers have dwindled. We keep things secret because humans would trap us, study us and worse. So usually, we band together in remote areas and small towns where we're less likely to be found out."

"What kind of shifters?" She narrowed her eyes at him. "Werewolves?"

"Wolves, bears, lions…not werewolves like on television."

"I see. And you're a bear shifter?"

"Yes. So are Powell and Derek. They were with me along with a couple other bears at the slide. They came to help me rescue you." He scooted forward on the couch. "They helped me track Evers into the woods when he dragged you off. If it weren't for them, I might not have found you in time."

Amy rubbed her face then raked her fingers through her hair. "I saw it happen, but I was trying to convince myself it didn't. This is a lot to take in."

"I know it is. I swear it's the truth."

She leaned back in the chair and closed her eyes, rubbing her forehead with her fingers. The robe lay open a little and Griff felt guilty trying to peek.

"You should know," he finally said, "that the bears and lions have been fighting for generations. We are enemies."

She sat up, interest in her features. "Why? If there are so few shifters, why fight amongst yourselves?"

"That's a good question, but you know that there are other reasons for wars and fights. This battle is primarily territorial. The land around Deep Creek is very special. The cave I took you to is called the Cave of Whispers and inside it is a lake with healing powers. That is what saved your life. It also healed the scratches on my back."

Amy chewed her bottom lip. "So the lions want this cave? You know how absolutely insane this sounds, right? It sounds like an episode of *Scooby Doo*."

Griff nodded. He picked at a string on the hem of

his shirt. "But it's true. They'll stop at nothing to get it. War is coming. I fear that a lot of lives will be lost."

"That's too bad. Can't you work out a peace treaty or share the cave?"

"The lions have no interest in sharing, and to be honest, I don't think we trust them enough to even try to share the cave with them. There's something else about the cave. The 'whispers' in the name refers to a spirit that lives there. An ancestral shifter that serves the purpose of giving advice and glimpses of the future. An oracle of sorts. Her name is Shoshannah."

"Have you seen her?" Amy leaned forward. "I mean, is she real?"

Griff sighed. "Yeah, I saw her for the first time today. I've never believed in her, but she appeared to me today. Just after you left the cave."

"That's interesting timing."

"Yeah. She had me bring Evers to the lake so his soul could be released. When he died, when I killed him, he returned to mountain lion form. I went back and got his body and took it to the lake. He was reunited with his parents. It was...beautiful."

"Wow." She held her head in her hands. "I feel like I'm in a movie. A bad one."

"I know." Griff got up and grabbed a log off the pile and shoved it on top of the fire. "It all sounds crazy." He took the poker and moved the log into position then added another log and put the poker back.

"I still don't understand why you can't share the healing lake with the lions. It's not like the power will run out, will it?"

"No, but the lake only fully heals the shifter group that is in control. So right now, that's bears. Shoshannah takes the form of a giant white bear. If the lions had control over the cave, she'd be a lion, and lions would be healed in the waters, not bears. We'd only get a little relief."

"So complicated." Amy tucked her feet under her. "I can see how that would cause bad blood between the two groups. The cave would be a huge asset to have control over."

"Exactly. The lions never play fair. They cheat, lie, steal and do anything they can to try to win. We have to keep them from regaining the cave."

"The lions sound a lot like some of the people I worked with at ADvert."

"That's unfortunate."

"It's over." Amy smiled. "I'm not sure I believe all this, but I'm trying to process it. Of course I would've never believed in shape-shifting humans if I hadn't seen it."

"I can understand. If I were in your shoes, I would have a hard time believing it, too. So, there's more."

"Go on."

"Well, there's a bear law. Kind of a code of ethics among our clan. If someone messes with our mate, we're allowed to hit back hard. That is one reason I went after Evers like I did. Sure, we had the history, but it wasn't until he hurt you that I went ballistic. Still, I took it too far and killed him in anger, but Shoshannah said that was lifted from my heart by my bringing him to the cave. If I hadn't taken him there, his death would have rotted my heart, because I killed him in anger."

"Are you saying…?" Amy didn't move. Her facial features were completely blank, as if frozen.

"Yes." He steeled himself for rejection. He had to tell her. "You're my mate." Thank goodness he wasn't projecting his thoughts.

She blinked, but didn't move. Griff waited for her to bolt out the door, but she remained seated.

Finally, she spoke. "What? What do you mean, I'm your mate? What does that mean?"

"It means we're meant to spend our lives together." Griff sighed. "We're meant for each other. Fated, if you will."

Amy shook her head then stared into the fire. Griff tried to be patient. Not to push. But he wanted her to understand that she was more to him than just a fated mate. He found joy in her laughter, her love of art, even her pink towels. He wanted to be with her all the time. Protect her. Love her. Make love to her. Have children and grow old with her.

Now it was up to her.

"I—I don't know. I certainly feel something for you. I might even call it love." She twisted the ends of her hair. "This is a lot to throw on someone at once. To be honest, it all sounds a little crazy. What tells you that we are mates? Do you mean like soul mates?"

The fire popped and she jumped.

"Yes, it is a lot to take in at once. But you wanted all the truth and I am trying to lay it all out for you. Like I said before, I think you feel our bond, too. What about last night? What about when you were scared in the car during the rockslide? Didn't you feel my presence deep inside in those moments?" He leaned forward. Would she give him the chance to prove himself? Or had all the information been too much? "I've known since I met you. For obvious reasons, I couldn't spring it on you. You'd have been right back in Atlanta the next day."

"I do feel something, Griff." She moved to sit beside him on the couch. "I know I enjoy being around you. I think about you a lot. But this is a lot. Not to mention the whole bear thing. I am still finding that hard to believe."

"Being mates *is* a bear thing. That doesn't mean we have to rush into anything we aren't ready for. For me, knowing we are mates is the same as knowing who my parents are. It's something I just know. I'd imagine it's different for humans." He paused. "You asked for the truth and I am telling you everything."

"I guess that makes sense." She rubbed her palms on her legs. "I want to be near you, and I feel a lot better about Evers now that you've explained some of the bear stuff. I have mixed feelings about him being dead, though. I'm sad he was so unhappy that he had to hurt other people, though."

"Yes, some people are like that. I'm not sure he was ever happy after his parents died."

"So where do we go from here? I'm not going to be here much longer." She pushed her hair behind her ear. "I want to give us a chance. But I'm afraid of the war you're talking about and I'm afraid of how I would fit into this as a human."

"Do you have to leave?" Griff ached to hold her. His bear cried out.

"I don't have a job here, and I don't know if I could get one since Oakwood is so small. I don't have the money to stay a long time."

He waved her off. "That's no problem, we can figure it out. As for the war, I'll tell you what I know.

We aren't going to let them win without a fight. This is our land, and where our clan belongs. The Sen Pal mountain lion pride is brutal. They raze things that get in their way. They once attacked Henredon at night, leaving several dead humans in their wake. All because they wanted fresh grain."

"Wow. That's barbaric."

"They take what they want and they think the rules don't apply to them. It's my duty to protect the citizens of Oakwood, plus all the people that come to the forest."

"'Cause you're a ranger."

"That, and I care about the people in town. I feel responsible for their safety—at least as far as making sure their homes and the forest are safe for them."

"So Evers was a member of this mountain lion pack?"

"Yes. We think he was an Enforcer, though he was acting like a rogue. He didn't seem to be doing anything that hinted at organized information gathering or even intel on positions of our sentries." He stroked her hair. God, she smelled divine.

"But he's dead." She sat up. "Does that mean…"

He nodded. "Yes. More are coming. They will try to get to anyone who is close to a bear. Like you. They will come for you if you are still here. If you stay, you'll need my protection."

He felt her tense in his arms. God, he hated to scare her, but telling her to stay out of the woods hadn't helped a bit. She kept getting into trouble every time he turned around. "That is why I told you to stay out of the woods. I was worried for your life."

"Yeah. I see that now. So what are we going to do?"

"You're going to stay with me."

She sat up and looked at him. "What?"

"It's the only place where I know you'll be safe." He ran his fingers along her cheek. I have a spare bedroom if you need it. I'm not expecting anything. I just want you to be safe."

She put her head back on his chest. "I don't know. I need to think. So much has happened."

"Yes. How about you stay tonight? Tomorrow, we'll figure things out. I'll have time to talk to my denmates and we'll see what they found out about what the Sen Pal are up to right now."

"Sounds like a plan." She yawned. "Thank you for asking me to stay. I'll take you up on the offer for tonight, and then we can talk tomorrow about the rest of the plan."

"Hey, none of that." He lifted her face. "No sleeping. Not yet." He pressed his lips to hers and tingles shot through him. *Ahhhh. Mate of mine.*

"I need one more thing, Griff."

"Anything."

"I wanna see you as a bear."

"Tomorrow?" He wanted kisses, dammit. What if his bear scared her and she changed her mind about staying?

"No, now. Please. For any of this to make sense, I need to know it's all true. I feel in my heart that it's true, but I need to see it."

His mouth went dry. Was he ready for this? Showing a human his bear and them not knowing he was a shifter was one thing, but her knowing? That added a level of worry. "Okay, give me three minutes, then look out the door. I'll be in the yard."

"Why not here?"

Griff rubbed his hands together. "I don't want to freak you out."

She raised an eyebrow. "Okay…why?"

"It's not pretty. In fact, I feel ugly when my body contorts. I can't control it once it starts. Maybe one day I'll be comfortable shifting in your presence, but not this time, okay?" His heart hammered. Would she accept that answer? It was the truth. "Plus, my bear is big."

"Sure. I understand."

"Three minutes."

He walked out onto the porch and then into the yard. The night sky, sprinkled with a zillion stars, domed over the cabin, and the dark woods surrounded the clearing. He moved quickly, shedding his clothes and focusing on his bear. The frigid air enveloped him and he raised his arms to the sky as he felt the change coming.

He growled, pawing at the air as his body morphed and changed. Shifting didn't hurt, but the sensation was like no other he'd ever felt. Stretching and pulling, every part of his body morphed.

Bigger. Stronger. He sliced at the air with his claws.

His bear breath came in small puffs in the cold night air, and he peered at the cabin. Silhouetted against the window stood Amy.

TWENTY-TWO

AMY PRESSED HER hand to the glass. The bear that strode in front of the cabin was huge and dark, its eyes glistening in the night. It was the same bear she'd seen at the creek. The one that fought with the mountain lion. The same bear that had been at the rock-slide with the other bears. The one trying to keep the mountain lion from getting to her.

Griff is a bear.

She moved to the front door and went out onto the porch. She barely registered the cold air, intent on going to Griff.

He sat, his large bear body settling into the grass, then he lay down on his side.

Wobbly from fear, Amy forced herself to walk to him. Griff wouldn't hurt her. He'd said they were mates.

As she approached, the bear turned to look at her. She saw nothing but kindness in its eyes. She knelt in front of him and stroked his forehead, the fur softer than she had expected.

The bear yawned.

Amy sat down and he moved his head into her lap. He was warm. She rubbed his ears and stroked his forehead. The bear closed his eyes.

She could get used to this. If Griff was a bear, then

so what? Stranger things had happened, and Griff always treated her well.

Suddenly, the bear leapt up and stood over her. She pushed down a twinge of panic and looked up to meet his gaze. He winked, then took off running, heading toward the underbrush.

Amy stood up, chilled, and brushed the dirt off Griff's robe. He'd be back. She headed into the cabin.

AMY STRETCHED OUT on the feather duvet Griff had spread in front of the fire. She still wore his robe, but her hair had dried, and tiredness weighted her movements. *He really is a bear.* Oddly, the thought didn't terrify her, especially since she'd been able to sit with him a minute.

"I'll toss your clothes in the dryer in a little while," Griff said. "When the washer is done. You'll have clean clothes tomorrow. Tonight you don't need them."

"Thank you." Amy blushed at the thought of Griff handling her underwear. The clothes she'd worn to the cave were muddy and had needed to be washed. "I did bring more." She pointed to her bag.

He smiled. "Well, you won't be needing those, either."

"Says you, the giant bear. I'd imagine you don't get cold with your built-in fur coat."

"Not usually."

"Yeah."

Griff settled on the duvet beside her. "I didn't scare you? When I shifted?"

"No. Not really. Not after all I've seen today. It's been one long series of crazy events."

"I'm glad. I was worried."

"In an odd way, it feels right." *He wants me to stay here with him.* She didn't know which was scarier—staying with Griff or being alone in the cabin with mountain lions hunting her. Him being a bear wasn't even on the radar as far as things to worry over. If anything, his protective nature was charming. Maybe she really was crazy, but she was falling in love with a bear.

One who already called her mate.

"It's warm." Griff pulled his shirt over his head and tossed it to the floor. "Aren't you hot in that robe?"

I am now. "You trying to tell me something?" She stared at Griff's chest—muscled and thick—like someone who did a lot of heavy lifting and manual labor. A patch of hair grew up high, and a heavy trail of hair snaked from his belly button into the top of his jeans. It'd been somewhat dark when they'd had sex before, but in the firelight, there was no mistaking his build. She wouldn't get lost on that trail.

Griff smiled and she turned away, her face heating.

"Don't be shy," he said. "It's all for you."

Amy turned to him. The whole evening had been leading up to this. Her and Griff. Why was she balking now? Maybe the whole day had really been a dream—shifters and mudslides and bears and now Griff. *No.* She deserved this happy ending to a very rough day. She wanted him right now, and right now was all that mattered.

She ran her fingers over his abdomen, his skin soft and pliable. His flesh quivered, but she continued stroking, stopping at his waistband.

"Go ahead." He lay back to give her access.

She tracked over the top of his jeans and down the

zipper, tracing the prominent bulge contained there. She wasn't sure whose breath intake was stronger, hers or his.

He took her hand and placed it flat over his cock. She felt it surge as it hardened more. When she didn't move, he pressed her hand firmly against him and lifted his hips, pushing into her hand. "Feels so good."

She nodded. Brave now, she bent to kiss his bulge. The groan that escaped him made her bolder, and she slipped the zipper down. He grunted, then slid his jeans and boxers off.

Amy sat back on her heels. His thick cock stuck out from a dense patch of coarse hair. She moved closer, kissing his upper thighs gently as she made her way to his cock. She gave the head a quick flick of her tongue.

He moaned. "Oh gods, yes."

She wrapped her fingers around his girth and slipped the head into her mouth, swirling her tongue over the sensitive underside. He held her head and tried to pump into her mouth. She slid up and down, letting him hit the back of her throat while she gently squeezed his balls.

His thrusts became stronger and she worked harder to take him all in.

He pulled back. "Stop," he said, breath ragged. "My turn."

She scooted away.

"Oh no, you don't." His gaze had darkened with arousal and he licked his lips. "My turn," he repeated.

She giggled and tried to move, but he grabbed her by the ankles. He held her with one hand as the other ran up under the robe and over her bare pussy. She flinched as pleasure zinged through her.

“Oh.”

“Be still.” He rose over her, untying the robe in one motion. “Off.”

She sat up and slipped the robe off her shoulders. By the time it had dropped to the duvet, he had her flat on her back and his face between her legs.

“Impatient?” She panted.

“No, just wanting what’s mine.”

She giggled as his mouth hit a ticklish spot on her knees.

Little moans escaped unbidden as Griff nibbled his way up her thighs. She tried to close her legs but he held her open. Vulnerable. When his wet mouth closed over her clit, she came apart, her legs falling open and her head back, inhibition forgotten.

“Mmm.” He looked up at her and licked her then his lips. “So fucking good.” He licked her clit then tongued it hard. “Mine.”

She wanted to agree with him, but she couldn’t find her voice. He slipped one finger inside, then two, and began pumping them in and out, hitting all the right spots. She pulled his head closer and he rewarded her with hard licks and nips.

She wasn’t sure she felt the orgasm building as everything felt so amazing, but when it slammed into her, she arched her back and cried out as he finger fucked her into her oblivion.

GRIFF TRIED TO hold back the urge to claim Amy. Her orgasm had about been his undoing. He counted his breaths, trying to give her time to recover. And to pace himself. His dick ached so bad.

“Oh my god, that was fantastic.” She sprawled

across the duvet, legs and pussy shimmering with wetness in the firelight. Open and ready for him.

"We're not done." He stood. "I'm going to put a log on the fire, then I've got some wood just for you."

Amy snickered. "Really? Did you really say that?"

"Hey, no sarcasm," Griff said. "Only orgasm."

She rolled her eyes and he stepped over her, aware of the show he was putting on for her as his dick bobbed over her.

He chucked two large logs on the fire. "That should last a while. At least as long as I do."

Amy propped up onto her elbows, and he dropped to the floor beside her, putting one leg across hers.

"Condom?" she asked.

"Don't need one. Now that you know I'm a bear, I'll tell you I can't get human diseases."

"I'm clean. I prefer feeling the real thing. I'm on the pill."

Griff smiled and he was sure his dick was smiling, too. Nothing like a bare dick. As nature intended. "Good." He leaned in and kissed her. She felt so small under him. He caressed one breast then the other. He'd have plenty of playtime with them later. Right now, he needed to be inside his mate. The drive to claim her had intensified and become more important than his own pleasure.

He looked down at her beneath him. Her eyes had glazed over, and her lips were swollen. *Beautiful.* He'd never tire of her.

Mate. Mine.

"Amy?" he whispered.

"Yeah?" She looked up at him with wide eyes and acceptance.

"I'd like to claim you as my mate. That means forever." His voice strained on the last sentence. If she said no, how would he cope with the rejection?

"I thought you already had."

His heart pounded. "No, this will bond our souls together. But you have to agree." He leaned on his elbow.

"Of course." She wrapped her arms around his neck and kissed him. "I'm yours, Griff. I was meant for you."

"Are you sure?" He took a sharp intake of breath to control the dizziness that suddenly came over him. "I have to bite you."

"Bite me?" Her eyes widened.

"Not hard. You'll barely feel it, forgive the pun."

She giggled. "Bite me, then."

"I love you, Amy Francis."

"I love you, too, you big bear. And I want to be yours forever."

He positioned himself over her, wanting the moment to last forever. It took every ounce of willpower he had to be gentle and not rush. He didn't want to scare her with the force of his passion. *Breathe.* She lifted up to meet his advance, and he closed his eyes and pushed in.

This time, he would claim her.

Fucking your mate was supposed to be the greatest pleasure on earth, and now Griff believed it. He'd never felt so alive, so in touch with the here and now. He glided in and out, trying to time his thrusts with Amy's groans. Her pussy held him tight, and he lowered his lips to her shoulder. *So warm. So good.* When her moans changed from intermittent to near constant, he pushed deeper and harder. Tension built in his balls, and he thought he would burst from the pressure.

He slid in and out of her again, slowly building to a deeper thrust. Inside, he saw blue trails of mist winding through his consciousness and toward Amy. He opened his eyes. The mist danced over them like an aurora, surrounding both of them.

"What is it?" she whispered, never losing her pace. "It's beautiful."

"The bonding." He thrust faster. "It's begun."

The mist circled both of them, wrapping them in cords of light. Tingles of electricity shot through him as the cords bound them together and Griff grunted as he grew closer to release. Amy was so soft under him, so perfect. So wet.

She tensed.

She cried out and he came hard, nipping at her shoulder and claiming her as his, always, and the blue cords tightened then released and swirled above them in a mini tornado then flew straight up through the roof.

Griff laid his head on Amy.

She sighed. "That was amazing."

"*You* are amazing."

They were mated and Griff couldn't have been happier.

HE WATCHED HER SLEEP, her eyelashes fluttering as she dreamed. Hopefully, she dreamed about him and their future. The fire had burned down to barely a flicker, and the sky outside was on the cusp of dawn, rosy as a fresh camellia blossom. He'd not been able to sleep a bit, not even after another marathon sex session.

His heart filled with love for his mate, even more than before. Sure, they had things to work out, like where she'd live. How many cubs they'd have, though he suspected it was too soon for that conversation. The fact that they were bonded was enough for him for today, though Elijah would want to know more.

What was to come in the next weeks or months?

The Sen Pal were still out there. They'd stop at nothing to reclaim the Cave of Whispers. The fight for control of the forest would be long and bloody, but he'd make sure his mate was safe through it all. He stroked her hair.

"Mmmm," she whispered. "Griff?"

"I'm here." He bent and kissed her cheek. He could stare at her forever.

She didn't open her eyes. "I had a dream." She smiled.

He chuckled. "I hope it was about me."

"Yes. We had a cub. A daughter. We named her Charlotte. That's possible, isn't it? And safe?"

"I'd really like that, Amy." Tears formed in his eyes. "And it's as safe as a human birth. Lots of bears have human mates."

"And we lived in your cabin." She opened her eyes, slow-blinked, then closed them again. "The one I'm living in, not the ranger cabin."

"I've told you how special it is to me." He was in love, for sure. "I'd like lots of cubs."

"I think you can count on it. Especially if you keep up these love-making sessions." She curled up.

"Anytime. Wake me up if you're in the mood for more."

"Isn't it dangerous to wake a sleeping bear?"

"Not this one. Especially not when it's for sex."

He swatted away the pillow she lobbed at him then lay down beside her and pulled her into his arms. She snuggled into his chest and within minutes, snored softly.

He was so glad she'd come to the mountains.

She was worth waking up for.

* * * * *

To purchase and read more books by Kerry Adrienne please visit Kerry's website http://kerryadrienne.com/books/.

Coming soon from Carina Press and Kerry Adrienne

Read on for a sneak preview of what happens next in the SHIFTER WARS *series, with an excerpt from PURSUING THE BEAR.*

BRIA LANE TAPPED in the last stake to her small tent then gave a tug on the line to make sure it held. It wouldn't bear up to a strong gust of wind, but in the forest of Deep Creek National Park, she wasn't expecting any hurricanes. She put the small hammer back into its zippered pouch with her other wilderness tools.

I don't remember it being so hot here in the summer.

"A small breeze would be nice." She wiped her forehead with the hem of her tank top, careful to not disturb the holstered gun at her waist. Summer's oppressive heat had taken hold and wasn't going to let go anytime soon. Good thing she'd put her hair in a ponytail, otherwise she'd be melting.

This ivory tower professor has to get used to the heat.

She sat back on her heels and scanned the forest. Trees that had grown since her great-grandparents had first vacationed in Deep Creek towered overhead, mingling with shorter and younger trees and the occasional downed and insect-eaten trunk.

She grabbed her canteen and gulped the water. She'd be out soon and then she'd have to purify water until she picked up and headed to where her small RV was parked back at the campground. She'd already spotted a stream with swift-moving water, so that was a start, and she had her purification kit. She'd only be out in the woods for two days and nights this first trip, so she had plenty of supplies.

Insects hummed, making the forest sound like static. *Good thing for repellent.* She stood and hung her canteen on a low branch then began unloading the rest of her backpack. Inside were her bear-proof nets, her rations, extra bullets, camera, some extra clothing, GPS, a toothbrush, her notebook and not much else. Hiking everything in and back out necessitated frugal packing.

The sun was high in the sky already and she figured she'd hiked in about two miles since she left at sun-up from the RV campground at the edge of the park. She'd confirm on the GPS later. Right now, she needed to get her stuff ready so she could get to work.

The bears weren't going to find themselves.

Excitement bloomed in her heart. *I'm here. After all the dreaming, and all the years of school, I'm here. I'm finally going to prove that what I saw wasn't a fantasy.*

She pulled the camera out of the front pocket of her pack and hung it around her neck.

Just in case.

A crunching noise sounded through the forest and she turned to see where it was coming from. It sounded like a large animal, and she put her hand on her gun. A tall man crested the hill between trees in the more dense part of the forest. Wearing a trim-fitting white T-shirt, jeans and carrying a daypack, he made his way toward her at a steady pace.

Her mouth went dry and she unclasped the gun. Feeling its cold metal against her hand, she slid it out of the holster and held it close.

She'd protect herself. She'd trained. *Stand tall. Often a gun is a deterrent.* Her instructor's words echoed in her mind.

The man grew closer and the first thing she noticed was his beard. Trimmed neatly, yet long, she couldn't help but warm. Nothing like a good-looking bearded man, and this stranger was of the tall, dark and handsome variety. His black hair was pulled back and his cheekbones were high and chiseled. The T-shirt he wore was dirty, like he'd been digging in the forest.

"Afternoon." His voice carried over the landscape like slow-moving lava. Smooth, glassy and hot.

"Hello." She gripped the gun tighter.

He stopped outside the perimeter of her little camp and smiled. "What are you doing out here in the woods by yourself?"

"Camping." She bit her tongue not to retort sharply. *Be firm. Don't be antagonistic.* "You?"

"Oh, looking for dead wood that I can repurpose into furniture. Logs, branches, even tree trunks if I can come back and cut them up." He pulled his pack up on his shoulder and held his hand out. "Derek Poole. Resident Deep Creek craftsman. Well, I don't actually live in the forest, but nearby."

She held back. Camping this far out into the wilderness, you simply didn't run into people. She nodded but kept the gun trained on him. "Bria Lane."

He paused, taking his bottom lip into his mouth and sucking on it, then pulled his hand away. "Well, Bria, did you know it's illegal to camp without a permit in this park? Do you have one?"

Really? Who the hell is he? "No, I don't have a permit." She scowled. "But low-impact camping is fine."

He shook his head. “No, actually it isn’t. I’m also a ranger here in Deep Creek, though I’m off duty right now. You need to camp in designated spots, and you need a permit.” He looked around, his icy-blue eyes as cool as his demeanor. “This isn’t a designated spot. But I’m not going to ticket you. Not this time.”

Her shoulders relaxed. “Thank you.”

He pulled out his wallet and flashed his badge. “You’ll need to get a permit at the ranger station at either park entrance next time. And make sure you get a map of designated camping sites.”

“I will.”

Hands on hips, he stood and stared, his eyes piercing through her. He looked like he knew something she didn’t. He pushed a stray lock of hair from his face and tucked it behind his ear. “You can put the gun away. I assume you have a carry permit?”

“I do.” She scowled. “I’ve even taken extra classes.”

“Good. Put the gun away. I won’t hurt you.”

The words sounded in her head. *Did he say that?*

She shook her head. “I can’t trust someone I just met.”

“Fair enough. Since we’re both out here in the woods, we should at least be friendly. How about I help you hang your bear netting?” He pointed to the heap on the ground. “I’ve done it plenty of times.” He set his pack down.

“I guess that’s okay. Sure.” She watched him pick up the pile of net. “I’m able to do it, though.”

“I’m sure you can.” He leaned over to pick up the netting from the ground and she stared at his ass.

Figured that the good-looking ones were the ones doing odd things like gathering wood and being crafty.

Still, he seemed harmless. And he was a park ranger, so she needed to be on his good side. She put her gun back in the holster and snapped the strap.

"Where's all the wood you've collected?" She peered at the small pack on the ground. "That doesn't look like it would hold big enough pieces."

He turned. "I'm particular about what I pick up." His gaze raked over her and lingered a moment, then he closed his eyes. When he opened them, the hungry look had faded a bit and his eyebrows drew together in confusion.

She swallowed hard. *What is that supposed to mean?* She tugged her sweaty tank top down.

He didn't speak but went to work putting up the bear netting at a speed she'd never have matched. And now she didn't have to try to reach too high in the trees to secure it.

"Done." He wiped his hands on his jeans. Even more of his hair had come loose and he pushed it away. "Be sure you're careful out here alone. You really should be using the buddy system."

"Like you are?" She raised her eyebrows.

"Point taken." He winked. "In all seriousness, though, we've had some mountain lion encroachments lately. They've even killed one tourist."

"Oh, that's terrible." She removed the camera from around her neck and set it by the tent. "I didn't realize there were many lions around here."

"Yeah, you don't want to mess with lions. And reports are that there are a lot of them in Deep Creek this year. They're just as likely to kill you as to look at you."

"Wow. Thanks." She sighed and looked around

the woods. No animals. “I’ll be okay. Besides, I’m an Ursinologist.”

“What?” Derek freed his hair and it fell in long waves around his shoulders. He shook it loose and finger combed it before securing it with the elastic band again.

“Huh?” Bria closed her mouth as her heart thumped. *Damn.*

“What an Ursus…umm…whatever you said? I’ve always worked with my hands—I never was a college guy.” Derek kicked at the ground then looked up. “But I do what I love. That’s what counts.”

She swatted at a gnat. “Most people don’t know what an Ursinologist is. It’s someone who studies bears.”

“Bears, huh?” He shook his head and laughed.

“What’s so funny?” She crossed her arms. “It’s a valid profession. And I’m doing what I love, too.”

He stepped so close to her she had to look up to meet his gaze, and held his hands up in mock surrender. “Nothing wrong with it, Bria. I think it’s a fine profession. Here you are in the woods with me, so I guess we aren’t that far apart, career-wise.”

Derek was in her space and even though they weren’t touching, she felt his presence touching hers. One step closer and she could pull that hair band out and hop into his arms, straddling him as she kissed him. *Ugh. Stop.* She cleared her throat and took a step back. “I thought you were laughing at me.”

“No. I didn’t know there was a name for someone who studies bears.” He scanned the forest. “I guess you’re in the right place. Bears all around here. Probably closer than you think.”

"I hope so." She relaxed a bit. "Have you seen any this season here in the park?"

"Every day." He chewed his lip. "I'm out in the woods a lot."

Her eyes widened. *He'd seen bears.* Her pulse thumped in her neck and she leaned forward. "Where? Can you show me, or at least give me some pointers where to look?"

"My best advice is to keep your eyes open. You never know when a bear will appear right in front of you."

Available November 2016
wherever Carina Press ebooks are sold.
www.CarinaPress.com

ACKNOWLEDGMENTS

MANY THANKS TO my always awesome and forever amazing agent, Marisa Corvisiero. She works so hard for all her clients. Thanks also to my editor, Libby. I've known for a long time that she's one of the best in the business and I was so happy to be assigned as one of her charges at Carina Press.

ABOUT THE AUTHOR

KERRY GREW UP in the mountains of North Carolina and now lives in Raleigh, NC, with her husband, three daughters, seven cats, a bunny and some other small animals, including a panther chameleon. Her husband says no more animals until they get rid of some children, so she buys shoes instead.

In addition to writing, Kerry loves music and traveling to concerts in her Mini Cooper convertible named Sheldon. She is also a costumer, artist and loves to play guitar, badly.